Enemy of the Highlander

ᵕᔡ

Kate Robbins

Tirgearr Publishing

Published by Tirgearr Publishing
Ireland
www.tirgearrpublishing.com

ISBN 978-1-910234-15-0

A CIP catalogue record for this book is
available from the British Library.

10 9 8 7 6 5 4 3 2 1

DEDICATION

For Michelle O, who gets every word of this story, and helps make them count.

And to my street team: Nicole, Debbie, Kimi, Barb, Adriana, Ann, Fern, and Melba. You are all amazing and I am so lucky to have you. MWAH!

ACKNOWLEDGEMENTS

Thank you once again to my beta readers for their fabulous insight, and especially their passion in helping me work out the wrinkles: Vicki, Vanessa, Nicole, Barb, Nancy B, Michelle O, Kellie, Kimi, Fern, Lesleyanne, and Karen E!

Thank you especially to Vicki and Michelle O for listening to my endless ramblings and questions.

Thanks to Kemberlee of Tirgearr Publishing for her guidance and encouragement, and for always finding the right thing to say to make me laugh.

Thank you again to Vanessa and Ian for their photographic expertise and patience!

And thank you to Lynnette and Tracy for their design fabulousness and their help on my cards and banner! You all rock!!

Thanks to the awesome writers in the RWAC loop and to my Scribe Wenches for your support. You're always there to help and provide advice.

Thanks to my Guardian sisters, Ceci, Sue-Ellen, Suzan, Tarah, Lily, and Kathryn, for all your amazingness. You are the bomb, ladies!!!

Thanks to Dave, Nicholas, and Daniel for your incredible support on this crazy ride.

If I've missed anyone, please accept my sincerest apologies. I hope you all enjoy reading Enemy of the Highlander as much as I enjoyed writing it. This book marks the third and middle of the Highland Chiefs series. I had to consider all that had come before in the previous two books and all that will still happen in the next two. Can't wait to dig in!

I hope I've captured the magic and mystique of the north of Scotland as it exists in my memories and dreams. Come away to the Highlands and see for yourself.

PROLOGUE

Strathnaver, Scotland

He had her this time, and her furrowed brow and deep frown proved it. Ronan Sutherland shuffled the pouches and set them in front of his younger sister, Muren. Though there was three years between them, she had bested him at this game many times. Today, he would prove he was superior.

"No fair, Ronan. You changed the strings on the pouches."

"All is fair in games of chance, Muren. Do you know which contains the shell and which contains the stones?"

Her bottom lip quivered. She did not know. Somehow, that show of defeat in her quelled his victory. She was only four, after all. And he had changed the strings as she suspected, but as his father always said upon his rare visits, all is fair in times of war.

Muren reached her hand out and hovered it over the middle pouch. Ronan worked hard to keep from grinning. The shell was on her right. He watched and waited as she grappled with her decision. Her hand never wavered from above the centre pouch as she worked out the solution in her mind.

"I know which it is."

"Do you? They why do you not choose?"

She looked up and met his gaze, grinning. And then to his surprise, moved her hand and laid it on the correct pouch. How did she know? Ronan shook his head. She must have some sort of magic in her, was all he could figure.

Just as he was about to challenge her again, the extra stones for their other games bounced on the floor. They both regarded the

1

strange sight of the small pebbles hopping up and down.

The door to their chamber burst open just then, and their mother raced in. "Ronan, take your sister out the back way and go to the chapel. Now!"

"Mama, what is it?"

She pulled them both up by the armpits and pushed them toward the back door. "There is no time to explain. You must go to the chapel and tell Father Andrews I asked him to keep you safe. Go, Ronan, and do not make a sound."

Ronan grabbed his sister's hand and raced out of the cottage. He had taken his time walking down the steps so Muren would not fall. He also wanted to see what had scared his mother so. It scared him too, though he could not put a face to it, and made him squeeze his sister's hand a little too tight. She yelped.

"Hush. Mama told us to be quiet."

"You are hurting me, Ronan."

He eased up on her hand as they found the path to the chapel. Once through some low-lying brush and away from the cottage, he dared to look back. He wished he had not.

Dozens of giant horses, with the largest men Ronan had ever seen, were visible from the side of the cottage. He heard an angry man's voice yelling something he could not make out. The man must be inside with his mother.

Ronan released Muren's hand and ran back to the cottage. What could a boy of seven do against all those warriors? He did not know, but he was not about to let his mama face them alone.

When he reached the cottage, he crept around to the back. He crawled up on the old stone that rested underneath a window and peered inside. His mother's face was in her hands and she was weeping. A large man had his back to her with his hands on his hips. Ronan took in his appearance. Tall and powerful looking, he wore a bright green cloak, and his hair was dark and loose about his shoulders.

He then turned around. His papa! But why did his mother cry? Ronan climbed down from the rock and only then noticed Muren had followed him back.

"Stay out here, Muren. I will go inside to see what is happening."

"I want to come too. I want Mama."

"Shhhh. Stay out here or I will not play any more games with you."

Her bottom lip quivered again. Did she do it on purpose? Ronan took her by the hand and made her sit on the rock.

"I will be back for you in a moment."

"Ok, Ronan." Her voice was weak. He could tell she was scared too.

Ronan slowly opened the back door so as to make no noise. He then moved to the kitchen door and peered through a small opening between the boards. His father's big, meaty hands were on his mother's shoulders shaking her.

"Where is he?"

"I do not know," she said between sobs.

"How is it you do not know where our son is?"

"He is playing and probably will not be back for hours. Please, there must be another way."

"There is no other way. Artagan is dead and Ronan is my only other son. He must come with me and learn his place among the clan and as future Earl of Sutherland."

Ronan put his hand over his mouth. Go with his father? But he was happy here with his mother and Muren. He did not want to go anywhere.

"You cannot take him from me, Artair." Her voice was full of pleading. "He is my son too. I will never see him again."

"You do not get to address me in such an informal manner, whore." He grabbed a fist full of her hair and pulled so that she had no choice but to look into his face. "Now, tell me where he is or I will burn your home to the ground with you in it."

Ronan's mouth was suddenly dry. He threw the door open and raced toward his mama and papa. He jumped and landed on his father's shoulder and tugged at the arm holding her hair.

"You let her go!"

His father reached around and grasped Ronan by the scruff of his neck and pulled him clear with little effort. For a moment or two, he dangled from his father's grip, wondering what would happen next. He did not have long to wait.

"Put him down!" His mother screeched so loud it hurt Ronan's ears.

His father tucked him under his arm and proceeded to the door. All Ronan could see was his mother chasing after him and Muren coming in the back door.

"Ronan, Ronan! Where are you going? We have to finish our game."

Outside, his father walked with them to his horse and flung Ronan up so that he sat astride the beast. He then hopped up behind him and wrapped his big arms around him so tight he could hardly breathe.

"Mama, make him give Ronan back." Muren's cries were like individual daggers piercing Ronan's heart. He could not bear to watch his mother and sister weep.

"Where are you taking me?"

"You go home with me to take your rightful place as my heir."

"I do not want to go. I want to stay here with my family."

"You will go with me and you will do everything you are told, or I will come back here and take it out on them. Do you understand, lad?"

Ronan was certain he would lose the contents of his stomach at any moment and fought the urge. He swallowed but the lump lodged in his throat would not go away.

"I do not want you to hurt them."

"And I will have no reason to do so if you do what you are told. Do you understand?"

Ronan took one last look at his mother and sister. The decision was easy.

"Aye, Papa. I understand. I will go with you and I will listen."

"Good, now say farewell to your mother and sister. You will not see them again for a long time."

Ronan drew a deep breath and held his tears at bay. His mama and sister approached at his father's bidding.

"You may say your farewells now. If all goes well, I may return with him from time to time."

Ronan looked into his mother's eyes, wishing with all that he was worth that he could wipe the tears from them. He wanted to wrap his arms around her and he wanted hers around him.

"Be my big, strong lad, Ronan. Will you do that for me?"

"I will, Mama."

"Who will play with me now, Mama?"

"I will play with you, Muren."

"Be good and listen to Mama, Muren."

"I will, Ronan."

"Enough of this," his father said.

His father turned the horse and kicked its sides hard. They galloped away from Ronan's home and his family. He did not know what awaited him at his new home, but his belly was full of dread.

"Ronan Sutherland, you are now heir to the earldom and future chief of our clan. From this day, you must always remember who you are, first and foremost. No one person is ever more important than the needs of the clan."

"But what about Mama and Muren?" He was very near to tears now. He could not let them spill for fear his papa would hurt his family.

"You need to forget them. As far as you are concerned, from now on, they do not exist."

Ronan wished in that moment that he did not either.

CHAPTER ONE

Golspie, Scotland, 1432

A writ of bastardy.

For all his efforts and all he had put up with from his monster of a father, it had come to this. Ronan Sutherland stared hard at the unfolded parchment in his hand. Someone behind him coughed; another sniffed.

He should walk away, say to hell with Dunrobin Castle, the earl's title, all the evil he had seen within these walls, and be done with it. What kept him here was beyond his comprehension.

"My lord, 'tis been validated." Robert de Strathbrook, Bishop of Caithness fidgeted.

"By whom?" Ronan turned to see if the man would look him in the eye.

The bishop had been formidable in his day. Now instead, his robes dwarfed him, his cheeks hollowed by age. He would not have the stamina to travel to Edinburgh and engage the king's council.

"My priests took it upon themselves to conduct the act in my stead. Sutherland is one of the oldest earldoms in the country. It was not easy, but their diligence was properly paid, I assure you."

Ronan's guts burned.

"When?"

"The letter says the rightful earl will arrive in a sennight to claim the title. He said you should be out of the master chamber by then."

Ronan shook his head. "And I am to wait until he arrives before I learn of his identity?"

"Aye, lad." *Lad?* "He wants no one to speak of it until he arrives."

"So be it." Ronan turned to leave Dunrobin's great hall. A scurrying sound in the corner caught his attention and he paused. Be damned if he would tolerate eavesdropping while he still ruled.

Ronan crossed the hall in three strides and whipped the large tapestry aside. John Sutherland. He might have known. The man slithered in and out of rooms unbidden. He was the last person Ronan wanted privy to his conversation with the bishop.

"What the Hell are you doing in here?"

John's lips curled into a greasy smirk. "Watching your demise."

Ronan grasped his face in one hand and squeezed. "If you breathe a word of this to anyone, I shall drive my blade through your gullet so fast you will not even feel it."

John laughed. "I will not have to tell anyone. They already know. And you, bastard, will no longer prance around here undoing all the good your father did."

Christ's blood. This was worse than he thought. He had suspected some mutiny from those loyal to his father's madness two years ago after his death. When they quietly fell in line to Ronan's new and more tempered methods, he had accepted it. What a daft, green lad he had been. Was no one loyal to him at Dunrobin now? Allain surely still was. Always had been.

Ronan released John's face and left the great hall in search of his captain. If there was one person he could rely on to help unravel this mess, it was Allain.

"We have trouble," Ronan said, when he found Allain in the stable.

"Do we not always?" Allain grinned. "What now?"

Little ruffled the man, a trait for which Ronan was most grateful. He handed over the letter the bishop had delivered. His only ally at Dunrobin scanned the missive. A more legitimate heir to the Sutherland Earl's title and clan chiefship had presented himself and was bent on tossing Ronan out on his ear. He had so many questions he did not know where to begin and thoughts of waiting around for a sennight to meet his usurper did not sit well.

7

Still, he had to find out who this man was.

"There are only so many possibilities as to who this person can be." It was as though Allain guessed Ronan's train of thought.

"Aye. A brother or another son. And since another son would also be a bastard like me, it can only mean my father's brother has returned from the continent."

Bile rose in Ronan's throat as he said the words. Alexander Sutherland made his older brother, Artair, look like a spring lamb. He had been banished years ago for his cruelty by Ronan's grandfather and no one had heard from him in more than a decade.

Now, it seemed the prodigal son was set to return and claim that which Ronan had worked hard to reform. His own father had been a cruel, hard man who enjoyed the pain of others. If the truth of Alexander Sutherland's own evil was half of the legend, Ronan feared the entire Highlands would be laid waste by fire and steel.

Allain folded the letter and passed it back. "What do you want to do?"

Ronan paced. He did not know. The news had come so suddenly he hardly had time to wrap his mind around it let alone formulate a plan.

"I will be here when he arrives. I have no intention of abandoning the people here to another madman. But, I cannot help them in the long run if my head is on a pike."

Allain scraped his hand over his beard. "What do we know? I mean, did your father put anything into writing when he named you as heir?"

"Unfortunately, no. And I did not think to ask him as I slid my blade across his neck."

"You know as well as I do, he deserved it. But as I told you that day, say those words where the wrong ears can hear, and you shall have more to worry about than a challenge to your title."

Allain was right. Ronan had not spoken the words since the day he killed his own father. Thinking back brought Fergus MacKay to his mind; he had not thought of him in a long time. The man owed him a debt for releasing him from his father's torture chamber. Those two had been bitter enemies for years. Surely, the people Ronan was responsible for, were grateful for the two years' peace that had since followed.

A second vision passed before his eyes as he thought back to that day. The only woman he had ever loved had walked away from him. Ronan shook his head. He would not let himself dwell on her beauty, for the yearning in his soul was too much to bear. No, he would focus on this current problem and find a way to solve it.

"The letter says he will be here in a sennight," Ronan said.

Allain's brows knit together as he frowned. "Ronan, did you look at the date on the letter?"

His guts lurched. The bishop had led him to believe he had seven days from this day. Unfolding the parchment, Ronan glanced at the top corner. His heartbeat kicked up. It was dated eight days ago. His replacement would be on his doorstep at any moment.

Ronan left the stable just as a group of riders thundered up the path to the castle keep. He ducked in behind the armoury annex and watched John Sutherland step forward to welcome the party. Those twenty men he had considered loyal to his father, capable of terrible cruelties, were with him. Damn them all for bringing this upon Dunrobin.

"Well, this is a fine turn of events then," Allain said, suddenly beside him.

Fine indeed. By the time all the riders had gathered and dismounted, Ronan was certain there were more than sixty men—a large war party then, if the weaponry they carried was any indication. They were not interested in a peaceful takeover by the looks of the heavy armour they wore, and the trebuchet.

"Do you think 'tis your uncle?"

A tall, white haired man dismounted and scanned the area, his armour clanking. He was more like a giant than a man. The silver helmet he wore shaded his eyes, but his teeth were visible as he approached John, towering over him. The man reached down and grabbed John by the tunic.

"Where is the bastard?" His voice boomed over the crowd.

"My lord, I know not. He scurried away as soon as he saw the letter." The tremor in his voice was unmistakable.

The man drew his broadsword from its sheath on his hip and slid it into John's guts. Ronan would not mourn the man, but the lack of compassion or even patience for an explanation, was telling.

"I want the bastard!" the man bellowed. He stepped forward to address the other men.

The other guards, who had stood so confident moments before, now cowered. Their gazes dropped to the ground. Had Ronan not feared for the good people inhabiting Dunrobin, he would find their behaviour humorous.

"You promised me I would be served the bastard's head on a platter upon my arrival. I want him now!"

The man grabbed another of the guards and ran him through before he could open his mouth to answer. Christ's guts, would he kill every person here if he did not get what he wanted? Ronan straightened and clenched his fists. He was not loyal to those men, but how long before someone he was sworn to protect met the same fate?

Just as Ronan was about to move around the armoury, Allain grabbed his arm.

"Are you daft?"

"I care not for those men, but I am still responsible for them and everyone else here."

"Aye, you are, and what a marvellous job you'd do with a broadsword through your middle."

"What would you have me do?" Ronan pulled his arm out of Allain's grasp. "He will slay every man here until he gets what he wants."

"Aye, he might," Allain said. "But then what?"

"What do you mean?"

"When he kills those men and still doesn't find you, what will he do?"

"Kill everyone else."

"I don't think so—look."

Ronan turned his head. The man now addressed the stable hand and pointed to the horses as if giving instructions. Perhaps there was hope. Perhaps the man saw John and his men for the evil filth they were. Again he turned to go.

"Not so fast. I see what you are thinking and I admire your faith in mankind, but I still think you are in danger."

Ronan did not have time to question what Allain saw.

"Ronan Sutherland! If you can hear me, know this!" The man's hands were on either side of his mouth, but his voice was so loud it did not need the amplification. "I am Alexander Sutherland and I claim this castle, the earl's title, and the chiefship of clan Sutherland as rightfully mine. You have misrepresented yourself and I shall punish you accordingly. If you ever step foot on Sutherland lands again I will kill you where you stand. Any person who assists you is punishable by the same fate."

Ronan measured his options. If he revealed himself now, there would be no hope for him or anyone else to find peace. If he left to seek help, he would abandon those here to this man's cruelty.

"Christ," he whispered. "I have no options."

"Aye, I admit, precious few good ones come to mind."

"I need an army." He glanced at Allain to gage his reaction. The smile on his friend's face was reassuring.

"We do, but we need to know what we are fighting against first. For all we know he has thousands of men at the ready to protect what he thinks is his."

Allain's use of the collective 'we' was appreciated.

Ronan frowned. "As my father's brother, technically, it is his."

"Not if he is dead."

Murder? Ronan would go far to protect his clan and had already risked much. As much as he despised his father, killing him had haunted him ever since. Slaying a man on the battlefield was another matter.

There was nothing Ronan could do to help anyone here now but go in search of an army.

Ronan watched Alexander scan the area again and then march

his men into the castle. By the time they had all passed, Ronan realized he had seriously underestimated the number of those loyal to his uncle. Dozens of men followed, and Rowan shuddered to think of the turmoil they might cause. He could do nothing for his people at the moment.

"We need help."

"Aye, but whose?"

"You know who. There is no one else who could raise an army large enough."

Fergus crossed his mind again. They had enjoyed a strained peace over the past two years. Many on both sides had difficulty with a truce between the clans, but with both chiefs determined, at least no further attacks had occurred.

"But . . . the MacKay?" Allain's eyebrows were nearing his hairline.

"He owes me his life."

Allain shook his head. "Ronan, I was happy to see the back side of Fergus MacKay. He is a boarhound at the best of times. What makes you think he will come so quickly to your aid?"

"Once he understands this threat is worse than my father's, he will help." Every fibre in his being was certain Fergus would help. "Come, we must acquire horses and make haste. I am certain it will not be long before a search party is sent."

Once on their horses, they ducked through the back end of the stable and sneaked through the woods so they could circle around toward the main path into Dunrobin. The road connected northwest toward Tongue. They had no provisions and the light was quickly fading so they would need to make good time in order to find a safe place to spend the night.

How had everything gone to Hell so quickly? His father had tortured, beaten, raped, and slaughtered so many. Ronan had spent a lifetime watching in disgust. Life at Dunrobin had finally shifted into some semblance of order after his death. He could not count the number of times in the past two years he had been caught off guard by a smile from one of the maids or the kitchen staff. Dear God in Heaven, what would they endure now?

He urged his horse on harder. He felt the air forced from his lungs with each footfall, beating in time with his racing heart.

He had to reach Fergus and get back again before too much damage was done. His stomach clenched at the thought of that monster harming those people—his people.

Thundering along the road brought back memories just as painful, albeit not horrific. Far from it.

Engaging Fergus meant he would have to encounter the man's sister. Freya could be a problem. She had been his lover and almost had his child—she should have been his wife.

Circumstances were never in their favour, however. Thoughts of her fiery hair and passionate kisses sent his head spinning. Had it really been that long since he held her and lost himself in her sweetness?

Their lovemaking had been almost savage. A chance meeting on the road had sparked a fierce fire between them despite the bitterness between their clans and particularly his father and her brother. Back then he was certain nothing could stop them.

But something had stopped them. And in the end, despite the pain he had buried, he was not so sure it was not for the best. Had he brought Freya to Dunrobin, she would have been subject to his father's abuse and now Alexander's. As much as he hated to admit it, she had been safer with her brother all along.

Somehow, those musings did not soothe the ache in his chest or the tightness in his loins at the thought of her radiance. To have her beneath him and hear her cry out his name at her release was his most precious memory.

Ronan drove his destrier harder.

The MacKays were key to everything. Ronan smiled inwardly. Surely, his father grimaced from Hell, and he hoped Alexander caught a case of the running guts.

Nearing dusk, Ronan spied an inn which would provide safe haven through the night.

Now, as he and Allain settled into their chambers, he allowed himself one moment to envision a day when perhaps he and Freya could stay here while travelling to Tongue for a visit. Peace, perfect peace would see her in his arms, lying in this exact bed where he know rested, her curves moulded into his body and her breath steady on his chest. He could almost feel her there with him as his loins tightened with the image.

He sat up and put his head in his hands. While his last parting with Fergus had been more than cordial, and subsequent meetings since, fair and productive, he had not seen Freya in two years. Her parting words were, "*Ronan, I cannot marry you. Not now and not ever!*"

His heart had clenched so hard he was sure he would drop to the floor. How could he see her on the morrow and not claim her again? She was his. Always. Somehow, he had to make her see that.

CHAPTER TWO

Tongue, Scotland

The clouds in the distance were almost black. From her vantage point, at the top of Castle Varrich, she could see for miles. Freya MacKay held fast to the stone wall as she scanned the mountains to the east; the wind tugged her hair in the opposite direction. She estimated they might have an hour before the storm hit.

"Here you are." Her brother, Fergus, emerged from the belly of the watchtower. "It is nearing time to go to the chapel."

Her stomach clenched. Was that a sign?

She let out a deep sigh. "Fergus—"

"Freya, not this again." He crossed his arms over his chest. "Rorie is a good man and your betrothal strengthens our bond with the MacKenzies."

"I know that, Fergus. And I do not wish to cause trouble. It is just—"

He gathered her into his arms and rested his chin on top of her head. "You were reckless back then."

She nodded.

"And your heart was broken."

"Aye," she whispered.

"But that is all in the past. You made the right choice by letting him go." He squeezed her tighter. "The best way forward, lass, is with Rorie."

"I know you are right. I just cannot shake *him* from my mind today. I have spent so much time trying to forget him and for

15

some reason today feels like all that time has been wasted."

"How so?"

"I do not know." Freya paused, thinking, then pointed to the east. "Look, Fergus. A storm rolls in."

"Aye, and yet another reason to get you inside. Come, we must share the noon meal with the MacKenzies."

A loud, thunderous boom resonated around them. Fergus took her hand in his and urged her toward the steps leading below.

Freya scanned the village once more. Rain had just begun across the plains to the east. She squinted. Was it her imagination, or could she see something moving ahead of the rain?

"Fergus, I think there are riders coming in."

He leaned forward across the stone wall.

"Who would chance getting caught in that?"

They watched as the riders moved through the town and on toward the road leading to MacKay House. For one brief moment Freya was certain one of them was Ronan.

But that could not be.

"Let us return to the house and find out who our new guests are."

Freya followed her brother down the winding stairs, her trepidation growing by the second. She dared to wonder what she would do if it *was* Ronan.

She shook her head. There was no possible way it was him. She had made her intentions clear the last time she had seen him at Dunrobin. And besides, even if it was him, why would she assume his presence had anything to do with her?

Fergus and Ronan had mended much of the torn fabric between the MacKays and Sutherlands over the last two years. Not all was resolved, but at least no one feared surprise and savage attacks from either side anymore.

They entered the castle and went straight to the great hall. There, by the stone hearth, stood two men warming their hands.

"Sutherland," Fergus said. "Welcome."

Freya froze as a man turned and locked gazes with her brother.

"Fergus," Ronan said. "'Tis no pleasure visit I seek. I come bearing grave news."

Freya stood rooted to the floor. He looked so different from the young man she had called her lover. His hair was shorter and his eyes were harder. The face she knew so well, that once held a carefree demeanour, had been replaced by a hard, almost angry, expression. His body was more heavily muscled as well.

Two years had turned him into a grown man. Freya's belly fluttered and her pulse quickened. Entranced, she moved toward her brother.

"Freya," Fergus said. "Ask Alice to prepare a trencher and some ale for our guests."

Ronan continued looking at Fergus as he spoke. Freya stared hard at him, willing him to meet her gaze. After an age, he slowly shifted his attention to look her. A great surge washed over her.

Who did she think she fooled? She could never forget the way he had made her feel; his hot breath on her neck, his hands cupping her backside as he thrust into her body, chasing his release.

She felt her cheeks flame. The fire in his eyes cracked the ice wall she had built around her heart.

"Freya!"

Fergus's urgent tone startled her out of her trance. Ronan's gaze was still upon her as she turned to leave.

This was bad.

As she made her way to the kitchens, Freya contemplated the change in him. She had always loved how his dark eyes appeared almost black.

She could almost feel his arms around her again; muscular and powerful. She had been denied the security and passion he gave her for far too long.

This was very bad.

In the kitchen, the cook, Alice, yelled at Hugh MacKay.

"Will ye move yer big lout self out of my way before I boil ye down for stew!"

Hugh winked at Freya. "I am not going anywhere until you let me help you carry those platters over to the great hall."

Alice slammed her hand down on the table. "And why do you think I'd need help from the likes of you? I have been running this kitchen for longer than you can remember. I drop one pot of stew and everyone treats me like a wee bairn." The woman thrust her hands on her hips, lifting her chin high. "So, get out of my kitchen or you best be careful of what I put in yer food."

Hugh shook his head. "Fine. You can tell that to Fergus when he sees you carrying the platters yourself. I am only doing what he told me to do."

For a moment, Freya was certain Alice might relent, but then she pursed her lips.

"Out!" she said, pointing to the door.

"Daft, stubborn woman." Hugh's mutterings followed him out the door.

Alice turned and looked like she might pitch into her next, prompting Freya to raise her hands in defence.

"Do not look at me like that. I know better than to challenge you, and if Fergus wants to take you on, then that is up to him."

Alice smiled. "Very well then, lass. Thank ye for that. What is it ye want?"

Alice was well aware of her affair with Ronan two years ago so she was not sure what the woman's reaction would be regarding his return.

"Fergus wants me to bring a trencher and ale to the great hall." She paused. "We have unexpected guests."

"More! I thought that MacKenzie lot were all here by now."

"Aye, they're all here." A great knot crept into her belly. "These two men are not MacKenzies. They're Sutherlands."

Freya held her breath.

"Sutherlands? Lass are you unwell? You look like you've seen a spirit." Alice's mouth then formed a silent 'Oh.' "Do you know why *he* is here? Now, of all times?"

She agreed. The timing of his arrival was a bit much to absorb. What could she do? Set to become betrothed to Rorie MacKenzie on the morrow, how could she promise herself to another with *him* present? She could not bear the thought of it now. How would Ronan react once he discovered she would soon belong to Rorie? The day she had left him she told him it could never work.

There had been too much damage between their clans for an alliance of marriage to cause anything but more grief.

Her heart tightened as she recalled the pain in his eyes when she said goodbye. Now there was no pain; just heat and anger.

"I do not know why he is here. All he said was that he had grave news."

Alice smiled. "Well then lass, let's get that trencher and ale over to the great hall. Perhaps we will learn what has occurred then."

* * *

Ronan paced. He had to shove away his urge to run after Freya and take her in the nearest dark corner. His passion for her had not waned one bit in the last two years, and seeing her again ripped the old wound wide open.

She had been sixteen summers when they met and secretly carried on the affair for several weeks as tensions escalated between their clans.

His father's threat upon her life had been the breaking point for Ronan's tolerance of the man's evil. After he had killed him, he was certain he and Freya could be together, but she would not have him.

And he had let her go.

When she left, she had taken his heart with her.

Ronan shook the painful memories away. He had come for another reason and it needed to be addressed.

"My father had a younger brother," he said to Fergus. "If you think Artair Sutherland was evil, there exists no fitting word for his little brother."

He saw Fergus's fists clench. "I cannot believe there is anyone as mad as your father."

"I understand why you feel that way, Fergus." His father had been responsible for accusing Fergus of a horrific attack on the MacKenzies which landed him in the Edinburgh Castle dungeon. He had also been responsible for the death of Fergus's brother, William. Both events were terrible and worth the fury emanating from Fergus MacKay at the moment. "But I assure you, Alexander

Sutherland is worse—much worse."

"Tell me everything."

"My grandfather banished him. I do not know much about what exactly occurred, but his cruelty was said to be such that they drove him off Sutherland lands altogether. He has been gone for a dozen years or longer. Yesterday, Bishop de Strathbrook arrived at Dunrobin and handed me a writ of bastardy. 'Tis been validated and signed by King James. My uncle has successfully claimed the earl's title, the chiefship—everything."

Ronan found the words incredible even as he spoke them. His uncle posed a great danger to the entire region and he needed Fergus to see that. "I watched him run his sword through two men without blinking. Fergus, if he gets it in his head to pick up where my father left off, there'll be nothing left of the Highlands to claim."

"How many men?"

"Several dozen, and a trebuchet. By the looks of his armour, I'd say he has amassed a small fortune, so my guess is, he could pay for many more men and weapons. Add to that, those still loyal to my father? Aye, I'd say he is a real threat."

Fergus moved to stand by the fire.

"Christ. We are only now recovering from the damage done by your father. What do you suggest?"

"I say we hit him fast and hard before he gets a chance to settle in."

Fergus nodded. "I agree. The MacKenzie is here and I expect he will agree as well."

"The MacKenzie is here?"

"Aye." Fergus approached Ronan and placed his hand on Ronan's shoulder. "He is here for Freya's betrothal to his son Rorie."

Ronan's guts dropped. He had not considered her with another. Part of him had hoped to one day rekindle the intensity they once had.

"'Tis a good match lad; he is a good man."

"Fergus, you do not owe me an explanation. Freya made her

wishes quite clear when we parted. I came here with no expectation from her." *Liar.* "'Tis your help I seek to bring my uncle down before he burns us all to the ground."

"Aye, and you have it. I'll collect the MacKenzie and meet you back here."

Ronan let out a great sigh as he watched Fergus leave.

"Are you well?" Allain asked.

"Aye. I am. Fergus was easy to convince, and for that I am grateful. We must stay focused on this task. Any distraction could mean our downfall."

Right on cue, his biggest distraction entered the great hall with servants in tow, carrying food and drink. Ronan's guts rumbled in approval.

"My lords, please eat," Freya said, lowering her gaze.

How he longed to take her in his arms.

"We are indebted to you, *my* lady."

His address to her caught her attention. She glanced up and a brief smile passed over her face before she masked her expression and dropped her gaze again. He had broken through, just a little, but he had chipped away a sliver of the mountain of awkwardness between them. He could not have been more pleased.

Allain needed no further invitation and had already heaped a trencher full of meats and bread and cheese. Ronan's belly reminded him of his own hunger. As the succulent juices of roasted boar slid down his throat, he became more and more aware of Freya's presence. She had taken a seat near the stone hearth and though she was behind him, but he sensed every shift of her body, every sigh on her lips.

Without turning, he was certain she had turned around and was staring at his back. Considering the position she was in with the impending betrothal, he would not openly challenge her intended or do anything to bring dishonour to her. Still, he desperately wanted to get her alone and let her know he still wanted her more than his next breath.

Ronan pushed his trencher away, its contents half eaten. He needed to say something to her but did not want to draw anyone's attention. He pushed back his chair and turned toward the hearth. She had already gone. Damn!

Movement to his left caught his attention. The hem of Freya's gown was visible just underneath a tapestry. He glanced around. Allain was still face and eyes into his trencher, and the servant attending him had all her attention drawn there.

Ronan crept toward the tapestry and, pulling it aside, realized it hid a corridor. He turned and caught Allain's sidelong grin.

The corridor was narrow and led to a short, winding staircase ending in a small chamber with narrow slats on the walls backing onto the great hall. A guard's hideaway. Dunrobin had one just like it, as did most castles. During large gatherings in their great halls, spy-holes cut through the stone wall allowing the guards to watch the crowd for trouble and stop mayhem before it happened. He envisioned many of these chambers surrounding the great hall at MacKay House as they did in his home—former home. His chest tightened at the reminder.

He spotted Freya standing in the far corner of the small chamber looking down upon the hall. He cleared his throat, capturing her attention.

"My lord," she said placing her hand over her heart. "You startled me."

"No, I did not. You knew I would follow you. Just as you know I will always follow you."

Her flushed cheeks complimented her flaming hair. Freya had always been the most captivating woman he had ever seen; her blue eyes now flashed with a heat his body remembered. His loins tightened. He needed a taste, just one, then he would walk away.

He moved forward until his body caged hers into the corner. Her lips had parted with her silent gasp, and his entire attention had focused on her pert and luscious mouth.

"You are killing me, Freya. You always have."

"I do not mean to," she said, frowning.

"I know about the betrothal."

Her gaze flicked up to lock with his. Her surprise evident. "I did want you to follow me so I could tell you."

Ronan leaned toward her and placed his hands on the wall on either side of her head. "Then tell me," he whispered.

"I—"

He closed the distance between them, stopping when his lips were a mere breath away from hers. "Let me taste you once more."

Her gaze dipped to his mouth. She looked more than ready to comply.

He had just brushed his tongue across her bottom lip when a boisterous cacophony of voices from the great hall broke the spell. Freya gasped and then ducked under his arm, fleeing from the chamber.

Ronan bumped his head against the stone wall. His body was on fire. One taste? What had he been thinking? There was no way an eternity of tastes would ever satisfy his craving for her. Alexander Sutherland was now only one of his problems. He needed to break a betrothal between two clans without starting an all out war.

But break it he would. He had to, for she was, and always would be, his.

CHAPTER THREE

Freya closed her chamber door and leaned against it, panting heavily. She was in far more trouble than she could have ever imagined.

She breathed deeply to calm her racing heart. Standing so close to him, she captured his scent—leather and sea air. Her pulse quickened . He was everything she remembered, and so much more now. There was an air of danger about him that she had never sensed before, like he could snap at any moment.

She sat on the edge of her bed and rocked. What could she do? The betrothal between her and Rorie had been agreed upon for a long time. Would breaking it dissolve the bond forged between her clan and the MacKenzies?

A knock sounded at the door just before her sister-in-law, Nessia, poked her head around the door.

"What are you doing up here, Freya? Are you unwell?"

"No. Aye. I cannot say." Freya urged her inside. "Nessia, did you happen to see our guests?"

The woman's brows knit together as she stroked her heavily pregnant belly. "Of course, I saw them. We greeted them yesterday." Nessia placed the back of her hand on Freya's forehead. "Are you certain you are well?"

Freya lightly swatted her hand away. "Not those guests. The ones who arrived just a short time ago."

Nessia shook her head. "Who is it?"

Freya opened her mouth to speak but could not bring herself to say his name. Had it really been two years since his name escaped her lips?

24

"Freya, you are scaring me. Who has come?"

Freya held onto Nessia's shoulders. "Ronan is here," she whispered.

Nessia pulled back. While Fergus and Freya had long absolved Ronan of his father's crimes and their affair, she knew Nessia never had.

Nessia paced back and forth then stopped, only to add each new question or point.

"What is he doing here, Freya? What about tomorrow? Did you know he was coming? Do you know what this will do to the bond between us and the MacKenzies? A broken betrothal is not to be taken lightly."

"I have no intention of breaking my promise to Fergus, or to Rorie."

Nessia paused. She should understand Freya's situation, having been intended for Fergus's brother and married to him before he was killed and eventually marrying Fergus. She had later confessed to Freya she had had feelings for Fergus all along, though never would have acted on them.

"Oh, Freya. I am so sorry. I cannot even imagine what this is like for you. I know you loved him."

Freya did not want to think about it. Nessia was one of the few people who knew that Freya had become pregnant from her affair with Ronan. She had never fully recovered from the loss. Add losing Ronan to that sorrow, and she had taken a long time to heal.

At least she had thought she had recovered. If she had gone the rest of her days and not encountered him, she could have convinced herself it was true.

Nessia placed her arms around her shoulders. "Freya, you must ask yourself what you want. You are a woman grown." She squeezed her tighter. "What do you want?"

What did she want? That was easy. She wanted Ronan. But she did not want to disappoint Fergus or Rorie. It was not like she had a say in the matter anyway.

"I still love him."

"Then you should talk to Fergus. Tell him the truth and let him help you find the best way forward."

Freya shook her head. "You know, as well as I do, Fergus will explode if I tell him this." Her brother did not like complications. "And look at how he handled the situation with you, which had been complicated from the start. He knew he wanted you, but he let you marry William anyway."

"It had been the honourable thing to do, Freya."

"Aye, and how is my situation any different?"

Nessia did not say anything, but Freya knew what she had to do. She moved to the door and reached for the latch.

"What will you do?" Nessia asked.

"What is honourable."

Freya left her chamber and made her way to the great hall with Nessia in tow. When she entered, it was to find dozens of MacKenzies, including Rorie and his father, Kenneth, the laird of the MacKenzies, and a formidable man with his great size and fierce countenance. Rorie was almost as tall and well built, but his face was kinder. He had a humorous way about him that was pleasing. If only he stirred the same kind of feelings in her that Ronan did.

Just the thought of his name brought a fresh flutter to her belly. She did not even have to look for him to know he, too, was in there.

She moved to the side of the large table to where her brother, Fergus, and Nessia's brother, Colin, were gathered with maps laid out.

Fergus looked up and noticed their approach. His brows knit together when his gaze landed on Freya, but then softened when he saw Nessia behind her.

"Freya, I have bad news," he said.

She could not even fathom what he meant and so she said nothing.

"We all have agreed that a quick strike is necessary to stop a new threat to the east."

"What new threat?"

Ronan's voice was solemn. "My father's formerly exiled brother, it seems, has found a way to strip me of my titles and lands"

"Is that why you are here?" She dared to ask the question she had wanted to from the moment he arrived.

"Aye."

His expression gave away nothing. None of the heat appeared behind his eyes from earlier, and he showed no sign there was anything more at play. Very well then. Her earlier inclination to go through with the betrothal had been the correct one. He had not come for her.

"I see," she said turning to Fergus. "And what is the bad news?"

"We must delay the betrothal ceremony until we are certain Alexander Sutherland does not march here to burn us all." He placed his hand on her shoulder, his other reaching for Nessia, who slid her arm around his waist. He reached around her body to settle his hand on her belly.

"You are leaving?" Nessia asked.

"Aye, but it will take some time to gather enough men. The spring has been easy on us so the ground will be easily covered. Ronan is already here, so he can show us the best route to take with the numbers we will need."

Fergus leaned down and whispered something in Nessia's ear. She blushed crimson.

"Aye, Fergus," she said.

"When do you leave?" Freya asked.

"A fortnight. And every moment must be taken up with preparation and training. We cannot take any time to properly celebrate, lass. Are you terribly disappointed?"

Freya did not know what she was with Ronan standing so near and everyone else watching her every move. She had to admit she was troubled by her reaction to Ronan after so long, but she had made a verbal commitment to Fergus that she would honour the betrothal, and honour it she would.

Ronan coughed.

Freya lifted her chin. "I am disappointed, Fergus. I have made a promise to you, and I intend to see it through." She looked around until she met Rorie's gaze. "And to our neighbours, we have waited this long, and as all parties are in agreement, know that we will all meet back here to celebrate once this deed is done."

Freya turned back to Fergus who smiled.

"That is a smart lass," he said.

Freya noticed from the corner of her eye how Ronan's countenance had now broken into a scowl. He had been somewhat passive before; now his brow and mouth were drawn downward.

The MacKenzie came forward, along with Rorie.

"Thank ye, lass, for understanding," he said. "Some women throw fits and insist on having their feasting time."

"You did not know her a couple of years ago," Fergus said. His gibe earned him a jab in the ribs from Nessia. "Ow!"

"He is right," she said, her heart pounding. Back then, she had been reckless and put herself and others in danger for the intense passion she had shared with Ronan. She would have walked through fire for him then. "I am not the same foolish girl I was then."

She locked gazes with the man who knew her better than she knew herself, and watched a barrage of emotions cross his face. Surprise. Hurt. Anger. They were all there.

Rorie came to her side and placed his arm around her shoulders. He leaned down and kissed her cheek. "Thank you for waiting, Freya."

Why did his kiss have to feel cold? It should have sent butterflies loose in her gut, but instead it only made her stomach knot. She glanced over at Ronan again whose fists were now clenched by his sides. What did she want from him? A declaration before everyone? If he did, the new threat to the east would not be their only worry. No. He had to let her go, and she needed to find a way to convince him of it.

* * *

Ronan watched the MacKenzie whelp slobber over Freya. She was *his* woman, and while he would do nothing to cause trouble in Fergus's home at this critical time, he vowed to find a way to remind her that she could never, ever belong to another man.

He stared at her, with her gaze downcast and her hands wringing around and around. She looked miserable. Did she feel the strain of the sticky web they were caught in as much as he? If she did, it appeared she had already made her decision as to which path she would take. Well, let her think she could decide. There was no way she would end up married to anyone but him.

A large body moved in front of him, blocking her from his view, fierce eyes boring into his. "Is aught amiss, Ronan?" Fergus asked.

Ronan shook his head. "No, nothing is amiss." He could not let Fergus guess his train of thought or else he would be run through before the sunset. "I am just thinking about my uncle and the mess we are in."

"Is that all?"

Ronan looked deep into the man's eyes. Did he know how Ronan struggled? He opened his mouth to ask, but thought better of it in front of the current company.

"Aye, Fergus. That is all. I will feel much better once we have a firm plan in place to deal with him."

The great man's little wife placed her hand on his arm, softening his stance. The two appeared to share a very strong bond; it was something Ronan ached for as well. He had to bide his time. Fergus had said a fortnight and much could happen in that span. Perhaps a proper solution could present itself, and in the meantime, he had get the support he desperately needed to regain what was his. Uncle be damned. He had lived at Dunrobin and put up with too much to walk away from it all now.

"Good. Then let us make our plan."

Fergus turned toward the table and the maps. The MacKenzie and his clansmen joined him. When Ronan turned again, Freya was retreating from the hall. She glanced back over her shoulder and locked gazes with him, frowned and then left the hall.

Ronan turned back to the maps Fergus had laid out. They were well sketched and had more detail than he could have imagined.

"If we take this road," Ronan said, tracing his finger along a thick line, "we will run into trouble with our great numbers. But if we take this one, we will be travelling a little longer, but will have better road to work with. While a more southern route is the usual path to take, tracking east first, and then south, would be better in the long run and we can expect less trouble. There are many in Caithness who would certainly support our cause. I have spent much time helping rebuild the damage there that my father caused."

"'Twill take us at least three more days going that route, lad. Are ye sure?"

"Aye, I am, Fergus. My uncle will anticipate an attack straight on. He will not see it coming from the north or from the sea."

MacKenzie stepped in closer. "The sea you say?"

"Aye. Dunrobin is perfectly accessible from the sea and I know where we can find a ship."

Fergus looked back and forth from Ronan to the map. "The sea," he whispered.

"It makes good sense," the MacKenzie said. "I have men who have been to sea many times and can navigate well."

"Myself and Allain as well," Ronan said.

"I am not worried about navigation," Fergus said. "We have all spent our fair time at sea. But I wonder if we should go by land at all. Why not just sail from here?"

"How many ships do you have?"

"The one, but she is a beauty. Had her built this past year, and she is quite sea worthy. She will only hold two dozen men, though."

"I can solve that problem," MacKenzie said.

"We can be back on our lands in a day. We have ships aplenty and can be back here in three beyond that. Will that give ye enough time to gather your men, Fergus?"

"Aye, most of them." Fergus glanced back over the map. "If we take so many by sea, and send so many by land, we have a better chance of success, do we not?"

Ronan had to give the man credit. He possessed a solid strategic mind.

"By land and by sea it is then," Ronan said.

For the first time in days, the weight pressing on his heart lifted. At least one of his problems had potential for resolution.

CHAPTER FOUR

Freya followed Nessia to her chamber. The woman would bear her second child any day now, and it could not be easy for her to learn her husband would go into battle at this crucial time.

Nessia stopped in the hallway just before her chamber door and bent over, gasping.

"Are you unwell?" Freya asked.

She breathed deeply several times, in through her nose and out through her mouth, before stretching upright again. Placing the back of her hand on her forehead, she said, "I fear the babe comes early." Her cheeks were flushed and her jaw set. "Go, fetch the midwife to be sure."

Freya assisted Nessia into her chamber and onto her bed, then ran as quickly as she could toward the village and to Old Bridget's cottage. Her feet pounded the hardened ground in time with her heartbeat. There was never a moment to lose when it came to childbirth. Freya knew that all too well. Sudden memories of her own lost child caught her breath, but she kept running.

She arrived at Bridget's and knocked hard on the door. Shuffling from inside reminded her just how old Old Bridget was. It would take some time to get her to MacKay House.

"Bridget! 'Tis Nessia. Her pains have begun."

No doubt mention of the laird's wife would liven the old woman's step. The door swung wide and Bridget emerged with her cloak wrapped around her shoulders and her satchel already packed.

"You were expecting me?"

"Always be ready, lass. When you get to my age, you realize the

32

value of time. Now, bring me to her."

Freya helped Bridget to MacKay House, marvelling at the life in the woman's step. She had underestimated the strength the old woman still possessed.

Once inside the chamber, Bridget felt Nessia's belly from top to bottom and side to side. She placed her hand on Nessia's brow and frowned.

"The bairn is well and ready to come, lass. But I fear you are not. When did you start feeling feverish?"

In between panting Nessia said, "Last eve. But the pains only started this morn."

Bridget turned to Freya, "Get me fresh linens and water, and go fetch your brother. Tell him the bairn comes early."

Freya tugged on Bridget's arm until she was well away from Nessia's bed. "There is fear in your eyes? What is it?"

"All is well lass, the bairn is only a fortnight early, but I do not like her pallor.. Now go, get me my things, and for the love of all that is holy, do not put any fear into your brother. He will be hard enough to deal with as 'tis. He ordered me last time was to alert him the moment we know the bairn is coming and I will not challenge his order."

With that, Bridget ushered Freya out the door and firmly closed it behind her. Freya recalled the day Nessia's first babe was born just a year ago. Since Nessia had been previously married and widowed, there had been some speculation as to whether or not she was barren. When she became pregnant shortly after she and Fergus married, the entire village had come to pay their respects and bring gifts. That was a joyous day.

Her birthing day had not been so joyous.

With a tiny frame, Nessia had laboured long and hard to deliver her beautiful little girl, Rhona. Her recovery had not been easy either, and Fergus had been like a man possessed. Considering the faltering health of his first wife, Elizabeth, after their son was born, none could blame him.

Bridget was right, she could not risk bringing fear upon him again, as he would question everything the midwife would need to do to ensure both mother and bairn came through unscathed. Thankfully, Nessia was much healthier than Elizabeth had been.

Freya shook away thoughts of her own pregnancy and miscarriage two years earlier. She and Ronan had never had the opportunity to discuss it, as the battle that had occurred between their clans separated them until it was over. By then, Freya was certain no alliance would ever be possible.

She found Fergus in the armoury speaking with the MacKenzie and Ronan. Her pulse quickened at the sight of Ronan's muscles flexing as he sharpened a broad sword. She lowered her gaze and moved to Fergus's side.

Placing her hand on his arm. "Fergus, Bridget bids you to your chamber. She believes the babe comes early."

Fergus whipped around to stare at her, his mouth agape. "What? When? Is Nessia unwell?"

Freya smiled through her fear. "She is well Fergus. Bridget has checked her and believes the babe to be just anxious to meet us all."

She happened to glance at Ronan who stared at her with an intensity that nearly knocked her over. Did he also think of their lost child?

"Fergus, lad, go," the MacKenzie said. "We will be off within the hour. Look for our ships in a fortnight, or earlier if possible."

Fergus nodded. "Aye, we will be ready." Freya's heart constricted at the low and strained tone in Fergus's voice. He turned to leave, collecting Freya by the elbow in the process.

She felt Ronan's gaze on her back as she and her brother left the armoury. With all the MacKenzies gone for the next fortnight, she would no doubt see more of him. Could she maintain her resolve?

"Where do you go?" Fergus asked as she veered off.

"To the kitchens. Bridget asked me to fetch water and linens."

His eyes widened. "She is close, then?" He did not wait for an answer, rather raced for the stairs and took them by threes.

Freya gathered all required and made her way to Nessia's chamber. She did not need to rush, Nessia would no doubt be in labour for hours. Caring for Fergus's first child and helping with his second had helped her heal from her own loss. Bridget had said she did not think she could not conceive again. Still, approaching Nessia's chamber brought fresh anxiety she must bury, else she would not be any good to anyone.

"Fergus, lad, you must let me see to her."

Fergus was practically wrapped around Nessia's right side, stroking first her cheek and then her belly. "Why is she so warm?" he asked, ignoring the command. "Why does the babe come early?"

"I know not lad. Sometimes bairns come early. Sometimes mother's catch a summer cold."

"But 'tis not normal, Bridget. The fever I mean. 'Tis not normal for her to be burning up like this while she is in labour. Tell me what is going on!"

Fergus's desperate plea made Freya's eyes sting. She had never seen two people more devoted to one another than her brother and his wife.

Bridget straightened her shoulders. "I'll tell you what is going on, Fergus. Your wife is about to have her second child and she doesn't need a big lout like you up here upsetting her. She needs to find the strength we all know she has in order to see this babe into the world, and then she needs to rest. This wife is not fragile like your first one and you need to remember that. Comfort her instead of hanging onto your fears."

Fergus kissed Nessia's head and blinked several times. Freya moved forward and placed the linens on the side table along with the water. She wrung cloth in the cool water and wiped Nessia's forehead. Her sister-in-law blinked and seemed to become a little more lucid from the effect.

"Fergus," Nessia whispered. "Go."

"I'll not leave ye, lass. You kicked me out last time, and I'll not go through the hell of listening to you in agony from the other side of this door again." He looked at Bridget pointedly then. "And you'd best be getting used to that. All of you."

"Oh, that is wonderful," Bridget said under her breath. "I have two bairns to deal with over the next few hours then."

Her irritated comment brought a smile to Nessia's lips. A welcome sight. Freya continued wringing cloths and wipe Nessia's forehead and neck. Before long, the glaze in her eyes had cleared some and the flush in her cheeks subsided.

Bridget had just finished checking her progress when Nessia doubled forward in pain. When she cried out, Fergus was there to give her his strong arm to hold onto. Freya's gaze to shot to Bridget who nodded.

"She is ready." She then turned to Nessia. "Love, your bairn wants to meet you. Are you ready?"

"Aye!"

Fergus helped her into position.

"Push!" Bridget commanded.

Freya sat on Nessia's other side and held her arm as Nessia started to push a new life into their world. Something about the desperate look in Nessia's eyes struck Freya differently than the last time the woman had given birth. She looked afraid. An iron determination welled up inside Freya. She was so helpless in this situation and could not even imagine what it must be like for Fergus.

"Nessia, you are doing wonderfully," she said.

"Aye," Bridget agreed. "I can see the head, love. Your wee one is almost here. Just a couple more pushes now. Push!"

Nessia did not cry out this time, her focus fixed on Bridget as she tucked her chin into her chest and did as she was bid.

Two pushes later and the infant's cry echoed through the chamber. A girl.

Everyone gasped. They had come through it. Freya smiled at the sight of Fergus and Nessia laughing together.

"Oh, love, we're not done yet."

"What?" Fergus said as his face lost all colour.

"I mean, there is another wee one in there awaiting its mother's help to meet us." Bridget swaddled the little lassie and handed her to Freya.

The newborn's tiny hand worked its way out of the bundle and reached for Freya's hand. Little fingers wrapped around hers and held fast. Freya's heart was so full of emotion, she was sure it would burst.

"Nessia, love, I need you to push again, now," Bridget said, breaking Freya's moment with the newest MacKay.

Nessia cried out louder this time. The tension in the chamber changed with the sound.

"What is wrong?"

"There is a second child but it is coming bottom first." She shook her head. "'Tis breeched, lad."

"Can't you do something?" The fear in his eyes was heart-wrenching.

Nessia had gotten that glazed look again. This was not good.

"Fergus, come hold your daughter," Freya said. "I can help Nessia.

"No! Tell me what to do," he whispered, his look beseeching.

She understood his desperation, so if he was willing to help, then she would hold him to task.

Freya nodded. "Very well. Take those cloths, dip them in the cool water and wipe her brow."

Fergus was around the bed in moments doing exactly as he was told.

"Ahhhhhhh!" Nessia's cry was weak. It appeared, the swift first labour had taken her strength.

"Fergus, talk to her," Freya said. "She needs to push when told or the babe will be in danger."

"I'll first need to turn it," Bridget said. "Hold her, Fergus. This will be painful."

Freya closed her eyes and rocked the wee bairn in her arms as Bridget tried her best to turn the baby in Nessia's belly. She prayed to the good heavens above that both the babe and Nessia would come away unscathed, but she did not hold out much hope. The more time that passed, the less likely it would be that either survived.

After an age, and many tears and agonized cries from Nessia, Bridget said, "'Tis done. The babe is turned. I need you to push, Nessia. Now!"

Nessia pushed and Freya watched in horror as a lifeless little form slid from her body. Bridget placed her fingers in the babe's mouth to clear the airways, but nothing would bring the babe to make the sound everyone desperately longed for.

"Fergus, where are my babies?" Nessia asked, her voice a mere whisper.

Bridget shook her head and frowned. Fresh tears flowed down her cheeks as she wrapped the babe in the same way as the first child.

"Bring the babe to her mother," Bridget said to Freya.

An ache she had not experienced in two years welled up within her. Her tears could not be contained as she moved to Nessia's side and placed her daughter in her arms.

Fergus appeared only to then notice the boy's lifelessness.

"No, no, no, no!" He looked at Bridget. "Please, no," he whispered. He picked up the bundle and rocked it.

"Aye lad," she said, placing her hands over his arms. "We could not save the little laddie. God has called him home again. You must focus on your daughter and her mother now, for they are well."

"What do we do with him?" Fergus asked.

"We'll give him a proper burial," Bridget said, through her tears. "One befitting a laird's son."

"Do not take him just yet."

"I will not lad."

Nessia held her daughter and cried. Fergus wrapped his arms around them both and closed his eyes, nodding to Bridget.

"Freya, fetch Father Morris. The bairn will need blessing."

With a heavy heart, Freya left the chamber.

"Father," she said when she found him in the chapel. "Nessia's bairns have come early—"

"Bairns?"

"Aye, and one—" Freya choked on her sob.

Father Morris was beside her in an instant. "Oh, love, I am so sorry." He shushed her when she whimpered. "Only our Lord knows why such things happen. 'Tis part of the great mystery."

Freya was not ready to hear this yet. "Father, please, they need you."

He nodded and left the chapel. Freya knew what it was like to lose a child, but not one full term. Her heart was ready to break in two with anguish for Nessia's loss and the memory of her own. The sadness had nearly consumed her. Then came the guilt. Had she done something wrong to cause the miscarriage? Surely, Nessia had not.

Freya left the chapel to seek the place of solace she knew best.

Heading up the footpath to Castle Varrich was like drinking something cool on a hot day. Knowing the peace she found sitting at its base and looking out over the kyle quickened her steps. Strands of her hair had come loose during the birthing and she had not bothered to rebraid. She must look a fright!

The closer she came to the watch tower, the faster she climbed, so that by the end, she was almost running toward it.

When she reached the summit, her tears flowed like a stream after spring rains. Her chest ached, both from her run, and from pent up emotion. She doubled over on her favourite rock and let the anguish take over. For two years she had suppressed the agony of dealing with such a loss alone. She really did not know if she was capable of helping Nessia as she was close to falling into darkness again.

"Freya!" Ronan's voice rippled through her.

She did not want to have to face anyone now and especially not him.

He wrapped his arms around her, the action bring with it a fresh wave of agony. Why could not they have been together? Losing him in addition to their child had been too much to take, so she had suppressed it. Today's events seemed to have broken the dam.

"'Twill be well again, love. I have you," he whispered.

She would know that voice anywhere. "Oh, God! Ronan, she lost the babe!" She cried for Nessia and Fergus, for herself, and for Ronan.

"Shhhh. I am here."

Ronan's strong arms enveloped her and rocked her, bringing the comfort she craved until her tears subsided. Once her tears were spent, she leaned back to find that he, too, had red eyes. Had he wept as well?

Freya tried sitting up, realizing their contact was dangerous and inappropriate. "Thank you, Ronan."

His arms tightened around her. "You are not going anywhere."

"Ronan, please. I am well now."

"You are not, and we have much to discuss."

"What do you mean?"

"I know you weep for Nessia and Fergus and their loss. But you also weep for our loss as well." He said, his gaze downcast.

Did he really grieve too? How could she not have assumed he would? So caught up with her own feelings, she never assumed anyone else felt the same way.

"Ronan, 'twas a long time ago and much has changed since then."

"Aye, 'twas a long time ago. Some things may have changed, but not you and I." He reached up and stroked her cheek with his thumb. "You are mine, Freya. You always have been, and you always be."

A flutter began deep in Freya's belly. Being in his arms moments before had been for comfort, but now brought out other feelings; carnal ones.

"It can never be and you know it."

"I know nothing of the sort. True you are promised to another, but hear me, love. I will find a way to break that commitment."

Freya gasped. "Ronan, you would risk the bond between the MacKay and MacKenzie clans for your own wishes?"

He smiled and her belly coiled. "I would. And do you know why I would?" He leaned in close to her brushing his lips across hers.

"Ronan—"

"I would risk it because you are more concerned about it than the man for which you are intended. Had your first thought been of Rorie MacKenzie, I would not be so certain of your feelings. Your wish to prevent a clan feud is honourable, and believe me, I do not wish that either."

Again he leaned in and brushed his lips across hers, this time his other hand came up to cup her face.

"We cannot do this," she whispered.

He leaned back and searched her gaze. "You are right. We cannot. Not until I find a way to break your bond and retain the friendship between the clans." Despite his words, he claimed her mouth.

Freya's heart drummed in her chest as he explored her mouth. Her core clenched in anticipation of the passion her body remembered between them.

Without warning, he broke the kiss. "You want me as much as I want you, Freya. I am on fire for you. I want nothing more but to bury myself in your sweetness again and again until neither of us can stand it anymore." He trailed kisses down her neck and nipped her collar bone with his teeth.

Just then, a breeze swept up over the embankment, reminding her of where she was and what she could so easily let happen. She broke free from him, trying hard not to focus on his desire filled eyes or his sensual lips. He was pure temptation and made a whore of her.

She leapt to her feet.

"No, Ronan. I belong to another. You cannot have me!" Before he could react, she dashed back down the path and ran all the way back to MacKay house, and did not pause until she was inside her bedchamber with the door bolted. She closed her eyes and let her head fall back on the door. How in heaven's name could she possibly get through the next fortnight with him in proximity?

CHAPTER FIVE

When Ronan entered the great hall, he was surprised to discover it crowded with people in the midst of what appeared to be a celebration. A child had died and yet everyone appeared happy about it. What strange custom was this?

Allain caught his eye and moved toward him, the man's countenance solemn. "Where have you been? You have missed all the excitement."

"I went to the watchtower to think our plan through." He was a terrible liar and Allain knew it.

"Aye, and a certain flaming haired lass had nothing to do going to that location to think, I suppose."

Ronan did not even try to pretend what his captain said was false. He told him of their encounter, leaving out the very personal details, and said that he had only meant to comfort her on her loss.

"Aye, there was a short time when the place was about to be consumed in grief over the child's death. But all is well, you see, a miracle has happened."

"Aye, Ronan," Freya said from behind him, her voice washing over his skin and exciting him to his very core. He turned to see her smiling face and his heart ached at the sight. God how he wanted her! "I neglected to tell you that a wee lassie was born just before the laddie. He had not taken breath and so we thought the worst. Turns out he just needed his sister to lie near him and when his mother did just that, he screamed the house down."

Her eyes misted as she recounted the tale. "Fergus and Nessia have two new bairns to celebrate and the entire village is here to celebrate with them. Come," she said taking his hand. "Let me show them to you."

Ronan thrilled at the heat stemming from where their hands made contact. He squeezed his fingers around hers and she responded by tossing a grin over her shoulder. His loins tightened. He must speak with Fergus to help figure out a way for them to be together. There was no way she could ever belong to another.

When they arrived at the hearth, his heart constricted. Fergus, the great giant of a man, sat with a bairn on each arm and a smile from ear to ear.

"Congratulations, Fergus," Ronan said with genuine appreciation.

Fergus's gaze flicked to where Freya and Ronan's hands connected, his brow furrowing. "Thank you, Ronan. 'Tis a good day."

"I am pleased all has turned out well."

Fergus laughed. "As am I, lad. It seems my bairns wanted their father around when they came into the world."

Ronan risked a glance at Freya who still held fast to his hand. Her gaze was fixed on the babes. She squeezed his hand and he did the same. It was as though this event could heal the terrible loss they had both endured.

"Freya," Fergus said. "Help me bring them back to their mother now. We don't want to wear them out."

When Freya released his hand, the immediate loss of contact was measurable. She took the lassie in her arms and cooed to her. Ronan could easily envision this woman bearing their children. In that moment, he wanted nothing more.

His gaze followed her out of the hall as she stopped to let villagers have a peek along the way. Fergus stopped beside him with his own squirming bundle.

"I see it in your eyes, lad," he said. "But she is promised to another."

Ronan locked gazes with Fergus, his biggest ally right now and the one person he could not betray or whose allegiance he could not jeopardize.

" I know that, Fergus," he said. "I just—" He just what? What could he say? There was no solution he could think of that would not end in a damaged bond between two clans. He could kick himself in the backside a thousand times for letting her go. He raked a hand through his hair and looked at Fergus who eyed him curiously.

"I know," he said and left the great hall. He needed to figure a way out of this mess or else he had have to leave. He could not be here wanting her, but never having her.

* * *

Freya placed the babe near her sleeping mother and watched them both. Nessia's pallor had improved greatly. When Freya had returned earlier to the house, the place had been in uproar. She raced to Nessia's chamber to find her, Fergus, and Bridget, all crying tears of joy. She learned that after she had left, Nessia insisted on placing the babies together, and as soon as that happened, the wee laddie screamed his first breaths.

No one had any idea how he would fare, but for now there would be no funeral, and for that she was very grateful.

Nessia's eyes fluttered open. She smiled when she spied her daughter nuzzled into her side. Her gaze rose to meet Freya's. "Thank you so much, Freya, for everything you did here today."

"'Twas nothing on my part and you know it," she said, wringing another cloth for Nessia's forehead. "How do you fare now?"

Nessia tried to shift and winced. "I am a little sore. But I expect I shall come along well enough. I assume Fergus is still showing off his new son?"

"Aye, that he is." Freya smiled. "I have never seen Fergus in such a way, Nessia. Ever."

Nessia's eyes welled up. "Aye, I have not either. When the fever was on me, I could not tell him I knew in my heart I would be well. And I have suspected for some time there was more going on in my belly than just one bairn." She looked at her daughter and smiled. "Is she not the sweetest wee lassie you ever saw?"

Freya's heart squeezed anew. "She is that." An unexpected sob escaped her lips. The last thing Nessia needed to worry about right now was Freya's fresh grief. She left the bed and stood to look out over the fields through the window.

"Freya, love, I know now how you must suffer," Nessia said. "I lost my son for mere minutes; you have lost your bairn forever. How can I help ease your burden?"

Freya turned to her with blurred vision. "Oh, Nessia, your children are healing me, not hurting me. Every time I am with any of them my heart mends just a little more. Someday," she said as she returned to Nessia's bed, "I will have a family of my own."

"Aye, you will, and you will be a wonderful mother and wife," Nessia said as she grasped Freya's hand. "You have been through much, Freya. You have to believe all will work out as it should."

"In order for that to happen, an alliance may break between two clans, Nessia. You know as well as I do, I cannot have what, or who, I want." Her gaze shifted to the babe. "Perhaps I was foolish all that time ago, when I told him it could never be. Or perhaps I was right all along. An alliance between the MacKays and the Sutherlands would be foolish and cause nothing but grief and bloodshed."

Nessia shifted her gaze over Freya's shoulder. She did not have to turn her head to know her brother was behind her and had heard her lament.

Fergus stepped forward and placed his son in his mother's arms. He sat on the bed on the other side of Nessia and looked squarely at Freya.

"Freya, there is too much at stake for you to reconsider this alliance. You know this."

"Aye. I do Fergus. I will do my duty and see the betrothal through with Rorie MacKenzie. I was only telling Nessia the same thing." She bent her head low.

Fergus reached across and lifted her chin with his finger. "I know you understand, love, and I cannot imagine 'tis easy. Nessia and I understand better than anyone what 'tis like to marry for duty rather than love."

"But it worked out for you in the end did it not?" Freya asked.

"I mean, look at you both. How much agony would you have both been in for the rest of your lives had fate not intervened and brought you together?"

Nessia shook her head. "It would have been very difficult." She paused and looked at Fergus. "William and I would not have been able to live here."

Fergus lifted his gaze to hers and frowned. "Aye, I don't suppose you would have."

"Don't you see?" Freya asked. "Will I go through my entire life doing my duty with Rorie but pining for Ronan? How am I supposed to just walk away from the only man I will ever love?" Fresh tears welled in her eyes. She knew the answer, but somehow her heart did not want to hear the words duty or honour.

"It will not be easy, love. But for the sake of the alliance between us and the MacKenzies, you must follow through with our agreement. 'Tis not my wish to cause you pain, but this agreement has been in place for two years. Breaking it now, especially with a new threat from the east, would weaken our best chance to reinstate Ronan to his rightful place. The fate of all the north Highlands depends upon it."

Fergus stood and went to the window. "Freya, do you realize that had you stayed at Dunrobin with Ronan, you would be in serious danger at the moment? And what if you'd had children? What would have stopped Alexander Sutherland from driving a blade through you all at the same time?"

Freya had not thought of that. And Fergus was right. Had she married Ronan back then, he would not have been able to leave so easily to seek help. No matter which way she turned it, there was no future for her and Ronan. He was and always would be lost to her.

Fergus turned around. "Now, I believe 'tis time for my wife to get some rest. She did, after all, give me two bairns today. Freya, come, let us take the babes away so she can sleep."

"Must you take them?" Nessia asked, her eyes drooping almost closed.

"Aye, love, we must. They will need their mother soon enough.

46

In the meantime, their nurse will see to them." Fergus kissed her on the forehead then ushered Freya out the door, a babe in each of their arms.

Once the wee ones were settled in with the nurse, Fergus placed his hand on Freya's back and directed her toward the stairs. "Come, love, let us talk of happier topics. I have much I wish to ask of you in my absence. There is no one I trust more with my wife and my bairns than you."

Freya smiled. Of course, she would do anything her brother asked of her. They had many preparations to make before sailing to Golspie. If she were very fortunate, she would see little of Ronan in the coming days, and once he left, she prayed he would be successful—and not return.

* * *

Ronan paced before the hearth in the great hall. Allain and he had gone over the plans again to try to find any possible flaw that could inhibit their success. There was much about the plan to go by sea and land that made sense. First of all, his uncle would not anticipate an attack, and secondly, he would not anticipate it coming from two directions.

"What about the MacDonalds?" Allain asked.

"Aye, they owe us too, but I don't trust the MacDonald as far as I can throw him. The man is more like my father's ilk, and even though we stood side by side with his allies and had him released from the king's dungeons last year, the man is no less obsessed with usurping King James now than he was when he first hatched his scheme."

Two years prior, the MacDonald and Ronan's father had orchestrated a vicious attack on the MacKenzies and made it appear the MacKays were responsible, all in the hopes that King James would blame the wrong clan and prove his uselessness. Ronan had no time for such schemes and was certain the MacDonalds were best kept at arm's length.

And they would not need them anyway. Between the MacKenzies, MacKays, and possibly the Sinclairs, they could form a substantial army that could take down Alexander Sutherland in one swift blow.

"I agree with you, lad," Fergus said entering the hall with Freya in tow. "We will not need any MacDonald on our side, and if I see any of them, I may very well run them through as well."

Freya sat at the table, as did Fergus. Moments later, servants entered with trenchers of food and tankards of ale.

Fergus beckoned Ronan toward the table. "Will you not join us?"

"Aye, I thank you, Fergus," Ronan said, he and Allain taking their seats. Ronan tried not to pay too close attention to Freya, but could not help himself when he bumped her foot under the table.

Her gaze flew to his, and for a second, she looked like she might play along. Her expression soon masked and she cast her gaze downward again.

"Ronan, may I speak freely?" Fergus asked.

"'Tis your house. I expect you may do or say anything you wish here."

"Aye. But I am about to overstep my bounds as it pertains to your personal business."

Ronan shook his head and looked from brother to sister and back again.

"Fergus, this is not necessary," Freya said.

"Aye, it is, lass. We all need to know where we stand here so there is no confusion."

A knot crept into Ronan's gut, for he was fairly certain what was coming.

"Ronan Sutherland, I would follow ye into battle anytime and anywhere. I consider you a true ally and friend. I owe you my life." Fergus paused and leaned back in his chair, crossing his arms over his chest. "But my sister is about to become betrothed to another man. I know you two share a past, and I do not blame either of you for wondering if an alliance between you could ever be."

Ronan looked at Freya. She had wondered too? Her cheeks turned a bright crimson. Obviously she had. If she had spoken to Fergus, that must mean she still harboured feelings for him.

His heart felt a little lighter in that moment.

Fergus leaned forward and placed his hands on the table flat down. "Ronan, lad. It can never be. We need this alliance with the MacKenzies. I do not wish to bring unhappiness upon anyone, and especially my own family, but breaking this promise would end badly for all of us. Do you ken?"

Ronan understood. Fergus had laid it out clear enough. There was not now, nor would there ever be, a chance for them to be together. He had suspected as much, but now that he knew it, his heart sank. She is his. His!

He pushed his chair back and stood. Freya had still not lifted her head to meet his gaze. "I ken, Fergus. But know this," he said pointing at Freya. "There sits the vessel which holds my heart. I will never stop wanting her, no matter how many alliances are at stake. And until a priest blesses her as married to another, I will not give up hope that somehow, someday, she will be mine."

Freya's head shot up, her gaze locking with his. Her eyes were wide and a smile slowly spread across her features telling him everything he needed to know. She was his. She knew it and would not deny it.

Just then, a flurry from the entrance to the great hall caught his attention. A young lad tore into the hall and ran straight to his master. Fergus stood and placed his hand on the lad's shoulder as the lad bent over to catch his breath.

"Christ's teeth, lad. What is it?"

"'Tis the lass, the one we captured two years ago," he flicked his head in Ronan's direction.

Ronan's guts lurched. Muren?

"Aye, she and your mother have been taken by a large number of men on horseback. The villagers said the leader was head to toe in armour, like a great iron beast, they said."

"I ride," Ronan said, striding toward the door.

Fergus caught up with him before he reached the end of the table.

"You are going nowhere, yet," he said. "Not until we amass our army as planned. He wants you to come. Do you not see? He is using your sister and mother as bait."

"Just like you did," Ronan said before he could think the better of it.

"We never had any intention to harm her and we did not."

"No, you did not, because she," he said pointing to Freya, "helped free her." Ronan broke free from Fergus's grasp. "You cannot keep me from going to help my family, and you have made it quite clear I have nothing to protect here."

With one look back at Freya he left the great hall in search of his horse.

CHAPTER SIX

"Did you need to drive the dagger further into his heart?" Freya practically screamed her accusation at Fergus. She paced, trying to decide if she would follow Ronan or not.

"Freya, there was no point in giving him false hope."

"By God, Fergus, the man has lost everything, and now possibly his closest family too? You could have shown some compassion."

"What would you have me do? Leave my two new bairns and tear off across the country with half the men required to do the job properly? I cannot stop him if he feels duty bound to go after them, but I can advise him. And from where I stand, he is being lured!"

Freya winced when the last part of Fergus's argument ended in a roar. He rarely raised his voice to her, though he had done so many times to others. She stared her brother down. He was laird here and knew the ways of war much better than she, but he did not know Ronan like she did. He was not reckless, but he was, no doubt, hurting like no other time in his life and she was helpless to ease his pain.

But what could she do? If she followed, what assistance might she provide? She was good with a bow, thanks to Nessia, and her uncle Hugh had taught her to wield a small sword. But she lacked the physical strength to do much more than scrape her enemy. Still, Ronan and his captain were no match for what awaited them at Golspie if even half of what Ronan had said was true.

Freya thought about Ronan's half-sister, Muren. Fergus had agreed she be held captive for a short time in retaliation for a brutal assault on a MacKay tenant's daughter. Though he had ordered no harm come to the lass, he had not been aware of her delicate nature. Freya could not bear the thought of her in the watch tower and so had freed her. Unfortunately, Fergus had misunderstood the scenario and blamed Nessia for the deed. Thankfully, it all ended well in the end—except for Muren. Her gentle nature had not improved over time, and Freya feared the girl would never survive this abduction. Especially at the hands of those who would not be gentle with her.

"Fergus, we must do something," she said. "I know not what, but I cannot sit here and do nothing."

"I know, lass, but if we stick to our original plan, we will be successful in the end. Sometimes for the greater good there are—"

"Do not say it!" She moved past him and on toward the door. How could he be so cruel to consider them casualties already? She raced to the stable in the hopes of seeing Ronan; Fergus, shouting her name, followed her nearly the whole way.

When she got there, Ronan was just about to mount his horse. Thank heavens she had caught him. She approached him with caution. As if he sensed her, he turned and locked gazes with her. She raced to him.

"I could not let you leave like that," she said.

He smiled, deep creases appearing in his cheeks. How she longed to trace them with her fingers.

"I am pleased you did, Freya."

Her heart hammered at the sound of her name on his lips.

"I wish to go with you. I believe I can help."

His eyes widened and then his jaw set. "As much as I would love to take you away from here, there is no way I would put you in that man's path. He does not know what you mean to me and I would not have him discover it."

"Ronan, I wish things were different."

"As do I, my love, but for now you must stay and I must go."

Allain coughed behind her, prompting her to release her hold on Ronan.

"Freya, I want you to return to the house and help my wife with the bairns," Fergus said, his tone firm.

She turned to glare at him, expecting to see fury in his eyes. What greeted her instead was closer to sympathy. "Say your goodbyes, love, and go to the house—please."

Fergus never said please. Ever. She turned back to Ronan and mouthed goodbye and I love you. Heaven help her, she had to fight back tears. Would she ever see him again? Her heart thudded hard in her chest when he mouthed the same back to her.

She turned away from him with an ache in her chest, retreating to the house before she changed her mind and went anyway. Fergus was right, she could not help him. She only prayed to God now that someone could.

* * *

Freya's figure faded in the gathering mist as she retreated to the house. Ronan turned back to mount his horse and attempt to steady his heart when a large hand grasped his shoulder.

"Not so fast, lad," Fergus said. "I am asking you for one night to let me figure out what I can do to help you. I cannot raise the numbers we need to defeat him any earlier, but I might be able to assist you and your captain. Will you give me one night to form a plan?"

Ronan's head began to spin. Was there more Fergus could do? Was it right for Ronan to ask it of him? All of this trouble was because of him. All of it. Here before him stood a man who had almost lost a child today and still he offered to help.

"Fergus, I cannot ask it of you. You must care for your own and I will care for mine. When the army is ready, bring it and I will gladly stand by your side while we defeat this enemy together. But I cannot ask you to do more than you have already committed."

"You can and you will. Allain, take the horses back to their stalls then fetch Neville and Colin. We will sort this out," he said, facing Ronan again. "As sure as there is breath in my newborn babes, I am certain Alexander Sutherland will not harm your mother or sister. But if you tear across the country without a plan, I assure you, the blood spilled will be yours. Now, come inside and we shall solve this together."

Ronan followed Fergus back into the great hall and took a seat near him. Before long the hall was filled again with men arguing about the best approach and the best plan of attack—immediately, and later with the army.

His thoughts drifted from time to time to Freya and her declaration. The barrier between them was not breached, but at least he was certain she felt the same way for him as he did for her. He could face anything, or anyone, as long as he had her love to return to.

* * *

Freya paced in her chamber. Ronan had stayed.

Her belly churned as she weighed the decision before her. Never had she been at such a crossroad—honour versus love. She put her head in her hands. Ronan would leave here on the morrow and she might never see him again.

Looking out over the kyle from her chamber window, a tear tricked down her cheek at the thought of anything happening to him.

Voices at the end of the hall drew her attention to the door. Footsteps stopped and then a chamber door opened and closed. Fergus had gone to bed. She was about to turn back to the window when another, more distant door opened and closed again. Someone else was sleeping up here?

To whom would Fergus offer a family chamber? Unless the MacKenzies had come back—or he had offered it to Ronan. Her belly fluttered. She would never sleep now with visions of him lying on a bed just a few feet from her.

She paced again. This was harder than envisioning him gone. Her skin tingled and her pulse quickened as her thoughts drifted to him undressing to ready himself for bed. Freya walked to the door and reached for the latch—her hand was poised mid-air. Should she go to him? How could she consider such a thing when it would dishonour both of them. True, she was not yet betrothed to Rorie, but she was promised to him.

She spun around and dashed to the window. She leaned her

54

cheek against the cool stone to temper her heated flesh. It did not help. Nothing would help except the incredible release she experienced when she was in Ronan's arms.

She wanted him. Needed him. Honour be damned! Could she live with herself if he was murdered by his uncle upon arrival at Dunrobin? Knowing they could have shared their love for one another just one more time? Circumstances may have worked to keep them apart up until now, but she had one night to make him hers—to brand him on her skin for all eternity.

She straightened her gown and turned toward the door. Decision made, she reached for the latch with trembling fingers. Outside her chamber, she waited for any signs of movement in Fergus and Nessia's. All was quite so she crept on toward the chamber she suspected Ronan had been given.

Freya placed her ear to the door for signs of movement inside. She heard a loud sigh and footsteps. Whoever was inside was awake. She grappled with knocking versus opening the door a crack, and decided on the latter since knocking might alert Fergus.

Lifting the latch to his chamber, Freya pushed the heavy door open a crack and peered inside. Ronan stood with his back to her, gazing out the window. Soft light bathed him from one candle burning low on a table near the bed and the embers from the fire in the hearth.

She pushed her way inside and closed the door without making a sound. He did not move as she padded across the chamber and slid her arms around his torso. Thick muscles flexed under her hands and his sharp intake of breath told her he had not heard her approach.

"Freya," he whispered. "Are you really here?"

"Aye, Ronan. 'Tis me."

"You should not be here. 'Tis not right."

She stiffened. Would he reject her? She had not considered that. Instead of letting go, she held on tighter and buried her face in his back, inhaling deep. His scent, so clean and intoxicating to her, always made her belly flutter, as though that one sense alone was enough to make her ready for him.

"You will be gone from my life tomorrow and I may never see you again," she said. "If this is the only night we ever have under the same roof again, I want to spend it in your bed. I want you, Ronan."

His heart thudded beneath her hand, steady and hard and increasing with each passing second; his breath grew deeper and faster.

Ronan grasped her fingers and peeled her hands from his chest. Freya could not measure her disappointment. He was rejecting her. She fought the tightness in her throat and the burning in her eyes.

He released her hands and turned around, lifting her chin so she could look him in the eyes. She did not know what she expected to find in his gaze, but her blood surged in her veins when she discovered the passionate heat she remembered. His eyes were black with passion and his mouth was set in a hard line.

"Freya," he said, inching closer. "You have my heart and soul. I would give you my body if it is your wish."

Her heart soared. She smiled and reached up to draw him toward her. Their lips parted and she sucked in a deep breath as his mouth brushed across hers. She tugged on his head to seal the kiss but he resisted. Instead, his tongue darted out to trace her bottom lip before taking it between his teeth.

She shuffled her body closer to his and rubbed against him. He was hard and ready for her, and she ached to feel him inside her.

He responded by gripping her hip and pulling her closer, grinding himself against her. Freya moaned as he held her head in his other hand and pulled her in. His tongue thrust inside her mouth in search of hers. She grabbed the sides of his head and tasted him, their tongues tangled and their breaths coming faster.

Freya's thoughts fled until only one remained—him. All of him, on top of her, and inside her. Her heart pounded as she poured all the heartache and sorrow and love she felt for him into that kiss. If they never got another chance, she had make sure he would never doubt her love again.

The back of the bed bumped her legs and only then did she

realize he had moved them toward it. He released her hip and head and unfastened the ties at the side of her gown in record time. His mouth broke from hers to trail hot kisses across her jaw and down her neck. She turned her head and moved her hair to give him better access.

"Christ, you taste as good as I remember," he said. "I am going to have you all night, Freya. You do realize this."

"I have no other wish," she said in a breathless voice.

He pulled her gown up over her head and tossed it behind him. Her nipples hardened under his hot gaze. His near growl sent a fresh wave of heat to her core. Ronan leaned forward and touched the tip of his tongue to her nipple. She quivered in response.

He bunched up her shift, and in one swift movement, that too was discarded. He stood back and gazed upon her naked flesh. While he stared, he removed his tunic and boots as well. His shirt was last to go, and while his gaze drifted over her body, she took the time to do the same to him.

He was bigger than he had been when they parted. He was still a large man then, but now his muscles were thicker and more defined. She could hardly get her arms around his chest earlier and now looking upon him, she understood why. Thick and curved, she reached her hands out to torso. He sucked in his breath when she leaned forward and flicked her tongue over one taut nipple. When she grazed it with her teeth, he groaned.

"Freya, I want to go slowly, but will not be able to if you keep doing that."

Go slowly? Not if she could help it. She wanted him to ravage her, to unleash the intensity and desperation she knew was just beneath the surface. She gently bit his nipple. His body jerked and his breath hissed through his teeth.

Freya's feet then left the floor and her back made contact with the bed moments later. Ronan spread her legs wide and rubbed the tip of his erection against her moist heat before sliding inside her until she was completely filled with him. She gasped at the sensation.

"Have I hurt you?" he asked in a strained voice.

"Only if you stop," she said, rocking her hips to prove her point.

He took her invitation. Ronan pressed his lips against hers and began to thrust until his rhythm was faster than her breath. He filled her so completely. Her passion coiled inside her and grew as he pounded into her.

She gripped his shoulders and his slid down to cup her bottom.

Her release swiftly overtook her in intense waves. She arched upward and trembled all over, muffling her cries against her fist, lest her brother hear her in the next chamber.

Ronan fell forward and softly grunted against her neck as he stiffened. His erection pulsed inside her. Chest to chest their hearts beat at the same cadence. For a moment, they were one being.

She stroked the damp hair from his face. His breathing leveled and his heartbeat slowed. He lifted his head to gaze into her eyes. When he smiled, her heart fractured. This was the man who owned her very soul. How cruel were the Fates to put them at such odds in life that they could not find their path together?

"I love you," he said.

"Aye." She smiled. "And I love you, Ronan."

His face changed then and sadness crept into his eyes. He opened his mouth to speak but she placed her fingers over it.

"Do not say anything. We have one night and I will not waste it on words unless they are 'come here', 'turn over', or 'I want you now'.

Ronan chuckled. "You are right," he said as he slid from her body.

He walked to the fire and returned with a tankard and a trencher of food. They ate in silence. His body was glorious in the soft light. Though he would be glorious in any light, the fine sheen of sweat he had just worked up cast a smooth effect over him. She stared at his chest and the fine matting of hair dusting his nipples. Her gaze continued across his chiselled abdomen and beyond to where his erection was already stirring again.

She watched as it elongated and thickened. Her body hummed in anticipation when he lay on the bed beside her and it grazed her thigh. She was ready for him again.

Ronan placed the trencher and pitcher on the side table and turned back to her. "Come here," he said.

She grinned and scooted toward to him.

"Turn over," he said.

She flipped onto her stomach and giggled. He pushed her hair from her shoulders and trailed his fingers down the length of her back, making her shiver. His lips touched the small of her back while his fingers smoothed over her bottom. She closed her eyes at the sensation. Surely this was more pleasure than one woman deserved. Perhaps that was why they would never be together, because what they shared was more than any mere mortal was permitted.

Ronan stroked every inch of her body, and when he was done, he flipped her over and began the same ritualistic adoration with her front. He flicked his tongue across her nipple then sucked it hard between his lips. Freya arched off the bed, letting him know she loved this and craved more. She squirmed beside him and tried wrapping her legs around his waist but he stopped her.

Instead, he pulled her to sit astride him, with her breasts in perfect alignment with his mouth. He looked up into her eyes and smiled.

"I want you now," he said.

Her heart melted. It was everything she could do to keep her tears at bay. She slid onto his erection; her body quivering as she thrust her pelvis forward. Ronan gripped her hips and buried himself deeply into her, she was now completely impaled by him. The sensations racing through her veins were almost too much to bear. He grasped her hips and repeatedly impaled her while at the same time tugged on her nipple with his lips, extending it and flicking it until white hot heat shot to the junction where their bodies were joined.

As suddenly as before, she climaxed around him.

Her body still shuddering, he flipped her onto her back and thrust back into her, deep and hard. His erection hit a place deep within her which coiled her passion once again. When she felt his body stiffen, she was right there with him, her body convulsing with a climax so hard she feared she would faint.

Ronan panted into her neck and held her tight. She wrapped her arms and legs around him too for fear he might disappear if she did not hold fast.

Hours later, just as the first streaks of grey crossed the sky, Freya slipped from the bed, dressed, then padded to the door. She turned to look at Ronan's crumpled bed and the sleeping form of her love. Her eyes burned and her chest constricted, thinking about her future on the other side of this door.

She had to be strong. She had to let him go.

With that thought, she quietly returned to her chamber and to her own cold and unused bed. Freya turned her head into her pillow and wept.

CHAPTER SEVEN

Ronan approached Strathnaver with caution, followed by the men Fergus had sent with him: his wife's uncle Neville, and brother Colin. His mother's cottage was down by the sea and not visible from the road.

He shifted on his horse. His night with Freya had left him depleted and weary, as though he had been in battle. Her passion had barely doused when she had become aroused again. Not that he had a problem seeing to her needs, but it had been a long time since he had bedded a woman through the night.

When he turned his head, could still smell her faint scent in his skin. His loins tightened. How was that even possible? He had woken thirsty and ravenous from their intense lovemaking and sought out sustenance in the hall. He had hoped to see Freya breaking her fast, but she was not there, and he had not seen her upon his leaving. It was probably for the best. After the night they had shared, he doubted he had the strength to walk away from her. He was now more determined than ever to find a way to have her and prevent the inevitable feud that would ensue should she break her promise to her brother and Rorie MacKenzie.

Rounding the turn before his mother's house, Ronan brought his horse up short. Allain nearly collided into the back of him. The roof of his mother's cottage was nothing more than charred pieces of thatch still smoldering. He had burned them out? Ronan clenched his fists.

"Whoreson!" He was off his horse in a heartbeat and running. Inside, the table had been tipped over and shelves were knocked down so that their contents had spilled and smashed onto the floor. He spied a dark spot on the floor beside the bed and walked toward it. Reaching down, he brushed his fingers across the stain, his stomach lurching. He turned his fingers over and rubbed his thumb across them.

Blood.

Ronan met Allain outside.

"We ride hard," Allain said.

"Aye to that." Neville agreed. "How do you wish to approach the castle?"

"From the beach," Ronan said. "We can come in from the north side and follow a path they may not have guarded. 'Twas how I helped Fergus escape."

"Aye, I recall that lad. So you expect to gain entry through the dungeon then?"

Ronan nodded and pointed to the cottage. "That I do. If the mess in there is any indication, I doubt they have offered them guest chambers." He gritted his teeth. If that bastard had hurt one hair on his mother or sister's head, he would gut the man and then gouge his eyeballs out.

Ronan mounted his horse and spurred the horse back to the road as fast as he could. Once there, he was able to make better time. They would not make it to Golspie before dark, so he chose to find a secure place to sleep for the night.

Now, lying on the cold ground and wrapped in his plaid, Ronan's thoughts drifted to Freya. He did not need to concentrate too hard to feel her warm body pressed against his. He turned to his other side to hide his growing erection. She had been glorious in her passionate abandonment.

He dreamt of having Freya in his arms, but she then turned into Muren screaming while several men surrounded her, taunting her.

Ronan tossed and turned, trying to settle, but all he could think about was either Freya's passion or his family's torture. His dreams melded the two and he woke time after time bathed in a cold sweat and shaking with rage.

By morning, he was ready and on his horse before anyone else.

Now on the road, he kicked his horse's sides hard and leaned his body forward. The sky had cleared and he could see for miles ahead.

Before long, he led the party onto the path that would take them around the castle and to the beach. They led their horses to an enclosure. Ronan peered inside and caught sight of a man pitching hay.

"Hamish?" Ronan whispered the man's name hoping he would guess at the need for discretion.

The man's face lit up with a smile as he turned. "M'lord, you've returned!" He rushed to Ronan and knelt in front of him, holding onto his hand.

Ronan grasped his shoulders and pulled him to his feet. "Hamish, there is no need for that. I need your help."

"Aye, m'lord. I will do anything to help you. The other one," he paused and furrowed his brow, frowning. "I do not mean to be impertinent, m'lord, but the other one is surely a monster."

Ronan's stomach burned. "What has he done, Hamish."

The man shook his head. "'Tis awful at the castle. My poor Shannon works in the kitchen."

"Aye, she started there last year."

Hamish smiled. "That you would remember a wee kitchen maid speaks to your greatness, m'lord."

"Hamish, tell me what has happened. Has my uncle hurt anyone?"

"Oh, aye," he said and cast his gaze downward. "And worse, m'lord. His soldiers have done ghastly things to the chamber maids. One of them was beaten badly and has been sent back to her family."

"By God's blood, I'll rip him apart!"

Hamish looked around Ronan and narrowed his eyes. "Are these all the men ye have, m'lord?"

Ronan turned to regard Neville, Allain, and Colin. They were all battle trained and would bode well, but there was only four of them in total.

"For now, Hamish. I have come to collect my mother and

sister, and once I see them to safety, I will return with two large armies."

"We wondered what had happened to ye," he said. "Some said ye deserted us, but I told the lassies ye would be back and ye would help."

Ronan placed his hand on Hamish's shoulder. "You are right, Hamish. I witnessed his arrival. Allain and I realized we would need to get help since the men still loyal to my father had arranged my uncle's arrival."

Ronan sized the man up. His reaction seemed genuine. Could he trust him? He had no way of finding out for certain and realized he had no choice.

"Hamish, how many men do you think have bent under Alexander's rule? What I mean is, do you think they would help our cause?"

"None that I know of have pledged fealty to him in their hearts. The men you spoke of who were loyal to your father have all been executed. It was the first thing he did. Shannon said he had them all slain within an hour of arriving at Dunrobin, saying he did not tolerate traitors."

Ronan stepped back. Well, that was an interesting twist.

"M'lord, do not think there is an ounce of good in him. While he may have executed your common enemies, he has made it quite clear you are to be killed on sight. He holds you responsible for his continued banishment after your father died."

"Aye, Hamish. Worry not. I have every intention of seeing the inside of that man's chest for his crimes. Can we leave our horses here? I do not want to alert anyone to our presence. I shall return for them by nightfall."

Hamish pulled himself up a little straighter. "It would be my honour, m'lord. You are welcome to anything I have."

Ronan smiled. Once the horses were secured in the stable, he led them down a path toward the beach. Crags rose high above. He secure the horses and followed the path until he came to a narrow cave and slipped inside. He would not chance lighting a torch and so used his hands to feel his way forward until jagged rock smoothed out and became formed hallways connecting the entire dungeon. He knew every nook and cranny of this cave from the times he had snuck in here as a child.

Ronan stopped to listen for any sounds coming from a chamber to his left. He only heard a drop of water falling in a steady rhythm nearby. Then something brushed his leg. A rat. A big one too, by the weight of it against his boot.

"God's teeth. Rats!" It sounded like Colin uttering the expletive.

"Quiet. Do you want to get us all killed?" Ronan asked under his breath. Rats, be damned, they could not risk being caught.

Inching forward, he led them to a door with light pooling underneath. Ronan placed his ear to it, listening for movement on the other side. Something. A muffled drip. When he pushed the door open, they stepped inside and came to a dead stop.

Four torsos hung from the walls by the arms. Their heads were missing as was the lower half of the bodies. The stench was unbearable. Rotten flesh and sticky blood covered the floor. A long string of guts slid out from one of the unfortunates and hit the floor with a splat. Ronan glanced around, there was no one alive in the room and so the noise must have been falling body parts. He turned and ushered the men out of the room.

"Are you unwell lad?" he asked Colin, forcibly pulling him along.

Colin shook his head and swallowed. The natural lump in his throat bobbed up and down as though he worked hard to keep the contents of his guts inside.

"Hold it together, lad, we will get in and out as quick as we can," Neville said, grasping Colin's shoulder.

Ronan turned back to the hallway and stopped when it forked in three directions. The hallway on the right wrapped around and met back up to where they stood in the form of the one on the left. The stairs to the upper floors of the castle were at the far end. The hallway in the middle led to a large circular room containing additional torture chambers and the oubliette and other prison cells.

As they made their way down the middle hallway, the air

thickened with the stench of blood and rot. He had only been away for a sennight and already his uncle had done such carnage. He prayed those harmed were his father's loyal guard and that their deliverance into Hell was long and painful.

They came to the large round chamber that was encircled with other small chambers. All of the chambers were open and dark within, except for one. Light emanated from the hole in the door and underneath. Ronan's father had this room designed for security so that when in use, anyone would know of an approaching person. There was only one way in and one way out.

He had only barely crossed the threshold into the circular chamber when whimpering caught his attention. It appeared to be coming from behind the closed door and was high pitched like that of a woman.

Forgetting his caution, he crossed to the chamber and peered inside a square hole in the door. In a heap on the floor sat his mother who was rocking his sister in her arms.

His mother looked up to the hole in the door and blinked. She closed her eyes and shook her head and then opened them again.

"Mother, 'tis Ronan. Your eyes do not lie; I am here." He released the latch and swung open the door.

She scrambled to her feet and went to him, clutching him by the arms, embracing him quickly before gazing into his eyes. "Ronan, you cannot be here. He will gut you where you stand! Please, please, leave here at once!"

Her frantic plea made Ronan's heart tighten. She had always put him and his sister before herself. Her affair with his father all those years ago had changed him but not her. He had often wondered what had passed between them and how she could have ever loved the monster his father had been.

"Mother, I am here with some men, and we are getting you out of here," he said. He then looked over her shoulder at Muren, still crouched on the floor. "Have either of you been harmed? And why are there no guards?" He looked back into his mother's eyes. She could not lie to him even if she wanted to, for he knew her too well.

"No, Ronan, we have not been harmed. The guards do not come until after the noon meal. Not that they're needed. By the time they arrive, they have caroused all night and smell of sour ale and piss."

Ronan grunted with disapproval. That would buy them some time, though. "I was at your home. There was blood on the floor."

He could not breathe as he watched confusion pass over her face. Then her eyebrows rose and a smile played around her lips. "One of the guards tried to force himself on Muren and I stabbed him. Before anything else could happen, Alexander snapped the man's neck then ordered the other guards to hoist the dead man onto a horse before we left." She paused, then said, "He said he will not harm us if you turn yourself over to him. Ronan, he is completely mad. I do not know what to tell you except that you must leave here at once. There will be no trial—only judgement."

"And it is because I, too, believe him to be mad that I will not leave you here with him. The longer you banter with me, Mother, the more time we waste."

He released his mother and went to Muren. She was clearly weak so he carried her while Neville assisted his mother.

Ronan was careful as they left the round chamber and made their way back through hallway, past the chamber of dismembered bodies and to the door leading into the cave. They took great care feeling their way in the dark cavern that lead to the beach.

They inched forward and stopped frequently to listen for approach. Something was not right. It was all far too easy. He suspected that if Hamish had betrayed them, guards would be waiting for them at his home. So when they reached the beach, they turned to the right and southward instead of left and north.

"We do not collect the horses?" Neville asked.

"No. We do not. This is too easy," he said.

"Aye." Neville agreed. "We will need horses though."

"We will get them, just not anywhere near Dunrobin Castle."

Neville nodded and they continued creeping along the crags until the land flattened out and they could turn inland. They stopped to rest in a thicket that gave them a good view of the beach and the forest ahead.

"My name is Morag," she said, extending her hand to Neville. Ronan beheld his mother's appearance for the first time in a long time.

"I am Neville Stephenson, my lady."

"Oh, I am no lady," she said with a grin.

Ronan chuckled lightly. "She would not let me bestow anything upon her that had belonged to my father, including a lady's title which I could have secured."

"The only thing of his that I am entitled to is his son. Other than that, he made it quite clear I was not worthy of his wealth," she said and bowed her head.

Her hair was deep brown like Muren's and his, her eyes the same dark color as well. She was a beautiful woman. Ronan had always thought so, and now it was clear Neville did as well. He watched the man lift her chin with his finger and looked into her eyes.

"That was his loss," Neville said.

His mother smiled through her flushing cheeks. Ronan turned away. It was too hard to watch them.

"Enough of that you two; we need to travel far and fast if we are to put any distance between us and the beast dwelling within the castle."

Ronan gathered them all and they set off westward. There was a village not too far away where he could secure four horses. His mother would have to double with Neville and he was sure neither would disagree. Muren would ride with him.

He was concerned about his sister. She had always had a fragile countenance and had not recovered quickly from the MacKay abduction two years prior. He glanced back at her. Her gaze was cast downward and her skin was pale.

"How do you fare, Muren?" he asked.

"I am well, Ronan. You need not worry about me, brother. I can keep up."

The conviction in her words was weakened by the softness of her voice. She would need to muster every ounce of strength she had if she were to make it. Ronan had every intention of returning to Tongue with them and placing them directly into Freya's care. He did not doubt her strength for one second.

A short time later, they stopped to rest just outside the village. Ronan bent to check on Muren. She swiped her tears away from her cheeks but not quickly enough for him to miss them.

He cupped her face. "You will be safe again, Muren, I promise."

She surprised him then by smiling. "If anyone can do it, Ronan, 'tis you." She leaned forward and kissed his cheek then gave him a hug.

"Neville," Ronan said, "stay here with my mother and sister. Colin and Allain, come with me to find some horses."

CHAPTER EIGHT

Her neck hurt and her ears rang. She had been walking with the wee laddie for an hour. His wails did not cease and she prayed she could get him to quiet before his mother returned. Freya had offered to help with the bairns as soon as Ronan left to give her something to occupy her body and mind so she would not focus on the huge ache in her chest.

She had managed to keep their night a secret, but Nessia hinted she knew something.

Freya shifted the laddie to her other shoulder and hummed in his ear. "Sweet darling," she said. "Your mama will return in a minute. I have you, my sweet." When he stopped crying altogether she turned to the door to find Nessia and the wee lassie just coming in. She too was wailing.

They placed the babes side by side and the crying stopped. "I have never seen anything like it," Bridget said from behind Nessia. "They're too small to recognize one another, but the second they are separated, they wail."

"They sense one another," Nessia said. "One heart in two bodies. 'Tis nature's way of always ensuring they have someone who loves them."

Is that what Ronan was to her? The keeper of the other half of that one heart? If so, then the Fates were surely cruel.

Freya rubbed the back of her neck as she walked to the window. Gazing out, she had a perfect view of the village. Her gaze drifted to the road leading into the centre of the village and four sauntering riders. Before long, she recognized Neville and Colin. Her heart sped up as she then recognized Ronan riding

70

with a woman seated in front of him. Muren!

Freya dashed to the hallway and down the stairs. She darted into the great hall to collect Fergus who'd been studying the maps again.

"Fergus, he is returned! He has rescued them!"

Fergus looked up with confusion on his face.

"Ronan," she said. "He is back!"

Fergus followed her to the front of the house to where some clansmen practiced with wooden swords. They paused and watched the riders approach. Freya's pulse quickened when she made eye contact with Ronan. *The other half of her heart.* Her cheeks heated when he smiled at her.

"I see you have been successful," Fergus said.

"Aye, we have. I do not understand why though. It was all far too easy, in my view."

Fergus cocked his head to the side. "Do you think you were followed?"

"No," Neville said. "We came by a different route and stayed off the main road as much as possible."

Fergus nodded. "Very well then. Come inside so the women can be cared for and I can show you our progress. I have had word from the MacKenzie. There has been a delay with the ships because of stormy seas."

"I thank you for your hospitality," Ronan said. "Fergus, this is my mother, Morag Grey, and my sister, Muren Grey—but you've already met her have you not?"

Freya nearly choked at Ronan's comment. She chanced a look at Fergus to gage his reaction and caught the grin on his face. She had to remind herself that these two men had been bitter enemies longer than they have been allies.

"Aye, and were it not for my meddlesome sister, she would not have escaped." Fergus reached up and helped a pale looking Muren down from her horse. "You have nothing to fear here, lass. And so that you know, you had nothing to fear then, either."

"Thank you, my lord," Muren said.

"I will have none of that," he said. "I am Fergus." Muren tipped her head in acknowledgement.

"Thank you, Fergus," Morag said. "My son insisted on bringing us here for safekeeping or else I never would have dreamt to impose upon you in this way."

"Nonsense." Freya linked arms with the two women and guided them inside. "There is nowhere you'll be safer than here. Come, let us get you a bath and some fresh clothes. You must be exhausted after your abduction and journey here."

Freya sensed Ronan's gaze on her. She chanced a look over her shoulder and caught him staring at her backside. His eyes snapped up to her face and he blushed. The heat she gloried in was back in his gaze and moisture pooled between her thighs. She turned back to the two women and led them toward the kitchens.

Once there, she introduced them to Alice and arranged for a bath in the upstairs guest chamber. She helped them bathe and ensured they had plenty of food and drink.

"I cannot thank you enough for your kindness, Freya," Morag said as she finally tucked Muren into bed, then sat beside her near the fire.

"You are more than welcome and entitled to it."

"True, our families have become intertwined, but you do not owe us anything." After a short pause, she added, "I have always hoped things could have been different for you and Ronan."

Freya said nothing. What could she say? By agreeing, she dishonoured her commitment. By denying, she dishonoured herself and Morag by lying.

Morag leaned forward and grasped Freya's hand. "Freya, I know he still loves you."

"I am promised to another," she said. Morag opened her mouth as if to say something, but closed it again. "Fergus has made an agreement with the MacKenzie for his son, Rorie and I am to become betrothed. It would have already occurred had Ronan not arrived with his terrible news."

"Do you love this Rorie MacKenzie?"

Freya shook her head. "No. But he is a good man, and the marriage will do both our families honour."

"And what about your heart?"

"My heart has nothing to do with marriage." Freya had a hard time believing her own words. "I have agreed to the commitment, and to break it now would cause a rift between the clans we cannot afford."

"'Tis true it might be difficult, but you do not need to be the sacrificial lamb in this. Men are men, and they will always make bargains and break them. Why should your life and happiness be the cost for the clans to continue as allies when they have always been so?"

Morag had a point. Could she talk to Fergus? Should she? Her head spun with the implications.

"I appreciate your point of view, Morag, but you do not know Fergus, or Kenneth MacKenzie. They are the most bull-headed, determined men I have ever known."

"And so is my son," she said. "I do not think he will give up so easily, love. I just thought you might want to know what you are up against."

"What do you mean?"

"As I said, Ronan is still in love with you, and I believe is determined to have you for his own. You share real love, Freya. That is not something to toss away lightly."

Freya stood. "Toss away? You do not know how much I have suffered, knowing I cannot marry the man for whom I would give my last breath."

Morag smiled. "So, you do feel the same way."

Freya opened her mouth to speak and realized the clever trap she had fallen into. She grinned. "You have a mischievous way about you, Morag."

"Please, sit and talk with me some more. I do not wish to upset you. The truth is, I lost my love many years ago and never recovered it. That man caused much harm to those around him, yet there was still something in him that connected us. I would not see you go through the same pain I have because you would not be completely honest with yourself."

"You are a very wise woman, Morag Grey."

Morag laughed. "You don't get to be my age without learning

a thing or two. Now, tell me everything you know about Neville Stephenson. That man has caught my eye and I plan to explore a little love myself."

"You have good taste," Freya said with a smile. "He is Nessia's uncle and Fergus's captain. He has a strong mind and is loyal and devoted to this family and this clan. Aye, I would say you could have chosen far worse than Neville."

"Has he ever been married?"

"No. He hasn't. I have never heard him talk about a woman either, which is odd for a man of his age."

"A man of his age is also my age," she said with a wink.

"I meant no disrespect."

"Fear not, dear Freya. I am teasing you." Morag yawned. "I feel very weary all of a sudden. Perhaps we can continue this conversation on the morrow."

Freya stepped over to her and kissed her cheek. "Thank you for your words of encouragement, Morag. You are right. I must be honest with myself about what I want."

Freya left the chamber and walked to the great hall. All was quiet so she sat by the stone hearth and thought about what Morag had said. Memories of their night together filled her mind and awakened that need down deep in her core.

Just then, a shiver spread across her back. She did not have to turn to know it was Ronan. Her body was so in tune with his.

He stopped before her and stared. Her breath quickened as their gazes locked.

"Freya," he whispered.

They stared at one another a long moment before she broke the silence. "You will be happy to know your mother and sister have been well looked after."

"I never doubted it for a moment."

Her pulse picked up as she watched him step a little closer. His gaze roamed across her body like a caress. His eyes heated and his lips parted.

"I prayed for you."

His gaze snapped up and locked with hers. "I dreamed of you."

Her throat tightened at the desire etched across his face and the strain in his voice. "Ronan, we cannot be together."

"And we cannot be apart. You are mine, Freya, and I will find a way to make it so. There is no way I will see you married and giving your body to another man. Not now. Not after our passion has been rekindled."

His words washed over her, simultaneously sending thrill and fear rushing through her. He reached forward and lifted a length of her hair with his fingers. He brought it to his nose and inhaled deeply, closing his eyes.

"I could smell you on me the morning after. I want that again. Every day. Every night. Forever, Freya. I want you for myself forever."

If she did not leave now, she could not say how far she would go. Her body hummed with anticipation of having him claim her again.

She stood to leave, but he caught her by the waist and drew her into his hard embrace. His lips instantly covered hers and all reservation fled. His tongue tangled with hers and his fingers bit into her sides. She slid her hands up his chest and linked at the nape of his neck, pulling herself against him. She could not get close enough. It was as though his body provided what she needed to survive, for without him, she would wither and die.

All too soon, Ronan broke the kiss and tugged her into the secret passageway used by the guards. He drew her inside and closed the door then bolted it. They always had to do this, sneak around and hide their love. True, there was a certain thrill at the thought of getting caught. Her morals seemed to go into hiding when she was in his arms.

His mouth was on hers again as he slid down the wall to a sitting position, taking her with him until she straddled his hips.

"I need to be inside you, Freya. Right. Now." His words caught as he fumbled with the opening at the top of his tunic.

The urgency he displayed was intoxicating. She was not sure who was more desperate for the other as she watched his member spring free; the engorged tip of his erection grazed the inside of her thigh, making her tremble.

His shaking fingers pulled at the strings of her gown then tugged them loose, pulling open her bodice. His mouth captured hers as his thumbs brushed her nipples trough the fabric of her shift. The sensation had her arching against him. She reached between them to hold him at her entrance, then quickly slid down onto him.

"Ronan." She gasped his name as he filled her. He groaned against her lips, his hot breath fanning her face as she rocked her hips. He tugged hard on her nipple, making her cry out with the pleasure-pain. The sensation quickened her pace. She plunged herself onto him, meeting his upward thrusts into her trembling body.

She was on the brink of climax, looking over the edge. "Harder," she panted.

In one swift motion, he flipped her onto her back and drove himself into her. He slid out, just to the tip of his erection, then buried himself to the hilt. Then again, and again until she felt him swell insider her and knew he was ready.

Freya clenched around him in an explosive climax that seemed like it would never end. Ronan's entire body was rock hard, every muscle coiling, ready for release. He pound into her at such a pace she could barely collect her breath when her own sensation built again so suddenly. Her back arched toward him as he continued thrusting deep within her body.

"You are mine," he said, tensing above her. She felt his release, heard him gasp her name as he pulsed inside her. Freya responded with a second climax that shook her entire body.

Ronan's hot breath on her neck, and heavy frame pinning her to the floor, were sensations she never wanted to forget. This feeling of utter and total contentment was one of the truths she could not deny. She did not want to be anywhere else but in his arms.

"Freya, I cannot live without you," he finally said. "I must speak with Fergus. I loved you before, but this is a thousand times greater. There is no way you can marry the MacKenzie lad."

The sound of her intended's name was like water dousing a fire. She wiggled away from him and began straightening her clothes.

"Ronan, we cannot keep doing this," she said to the floor, unable to look him in the eye, for the shame that had set in her heart.

"We will not have to," he said.

"What do you mean?"

"I mean I intend to speak with Fergus and beg him to consent to giving you to me."

"Ronan, I am already promised."

"But you belong to me. Fergus should not have given away what was mine to begin with."

Freya shook her head as she tied the strings on her bodice. "'Tis not that simple, Ronan."

He grasped her shoulders and gazed into her eyes. "It is, Freya." He smiled and patted her bottom when she passed him to unlatch the door.

CHAPTER NINE

Ronan paced in front of the hearth. He had not slept one wink the night before. When he did not fantasize about Freya, he envisioned Fergus's broadsword spilling his guts onto the floor.

He needed to know where he stood. He prayed there was at least a chance Fergus would entertain his idea of resolving this issue once and for all.

"You look like hell," Fergus said from the doorway.

Ronan's guts tightened. "Aye, I feel like it."

"What has happened?" Fergus asked.

"This is not about my uncle." He shoved his hands through his hair.

Fergus's brow furrowed. "Oh? Well then, what is it about?"

Ronan had never suffered from a case of nerves before, but this morning, he was certain he would lose his belly at any moment.

"Good God, man, sit down before you fall down." Fergus sat, motioning for Ronan to take a seat across from him.

Ronan nodded and sat at the table. He swallowed the knot in his throat. "It is about Freya, Fergus."

Fergus's hands clenched into fists. "What about her?"

"She is mine."

"She is promised to another man."

"She was mine first and I want to wed her. Today."

"Have you lost your wits?"

"No. For the first time in a long time, I am thinking clearly. I should have never let her leave Dunrobin two years ago. We were lovers then, and . . . God helps us, we have rekindled that passion now."

Fergus stood, his chair toppling in the process. He put his fists on the table and leaned toward Ronan. "You have bedded Freya recently?" His voice was low and accusatory.

"Aye. I have. You cannot marry her to another man because she might be carrying my child. Again."

Fergus's hand closed around Ronan's throat and he squeezed just enough for it to be uncomfortable, but he did not fight the man he hoped would become his brother-in-law. "Do you realize her promise is to secure an alliance with the MacKenzies and this clan? What do you expect will happen when that promise is broken?"

Fergus loosened his grip when Ronan could only croak. "I have a solution."

Fergus released him. "You had better have a solution or else we will have enemies coming from all sides."

"My solution is, we defeat Alexander Sutherland, reinstate me as Earl of Sutherland, I take my sister to Dunrobin and befit her with a lady's title and a large dowry and we marry the MacKenzie lad to her. I have what was mine and the MacKenzie gets more money than he could ever spend."

Fergus blinked several times. Ronan watched as he thought over the proposal. "And if we cannot defeat your uncle?"

"Then we have bigger problems to deal with."

Fergus walked over to the hearth and placed his arm above it to stare into the fire.

"Tell me, Ronan. What does it feel like when you are apart from my sister?"

"Like every breath is filled with sharp blades."

Fergus turned to him. "Aye, I know that feeling well enough. Watching Nessia marry my brother was the hardest thing I have ever done."

"I am not as strong as you. I cannot do that."

"It cannot happen until the MacKenzie returns. I will not incite the man any further by acting without his agreement, which leads me to another matter. What does Freya want?"

When she was in his arms she was without abandon, but he

was not about to poke the boarhound in front of him any more than he needed to by telling him that.

"She feels the same for me as I do for her, but is set to do her duty as you have outlined it."

"Christ's teeth, she said that? Freya has never done a thing I have asked in her life and now she is willing to sacrifice herself for the clan? I find that difficult to believe."

"I have no reason to lie to you, Fergus. You are welcome to ask her yourself."

"Ask me what?" Freya said from the doorway.

Ronan noted the dark circles under her eyes. She too had clearly lacked sleep the night before. He found small comfort in that. He let his gaze drift down across her lush curves and smiled, delighting in the flush that kissed her cheeks.

"You had better sit, Freya," Fergus said. "You two have created quite a mess that will need some negotiation to fix."

Freya locked gazes with Ronan and gaped. "You have told him?"

"Aye, I told you I would, and I have."

Her eyes went wide as she looked from Fergus to him and back again.

"And you still live."

"He does for now," Fergus said. "But I cannot protect him from the MacKenzie's wrath if it rears its head. The man is a bear at the best of times."

Ronan grinned. A bear indeed. Had he ever considered his own countenance? Freya rolled her eyes at him. "I am being serious, Fergus. How do you plan to break the promise to the MacKenzie?"

Fergus jerked his head in Ronan's direction. "Ask him. He has it all worked out."

Ronan reiterated what he had said to Fergus, and had to swallow the lump lodged in his throat when, instead of smiling like he wished, she frowned.

"You do not seem pleased," Fergus said.

"Have you asked Muren about her wishes? By forcing her to marry Rorie, you give her no choice."

He had not thought of that. He took it upon himself as his responsibility to look after her and their mother, though the latter would accept no assistance. Ronan was certain Muren would welcome life at Dunrobin.

"I have not asked her, though considering her current lack of a home, I believe she will agree to this."

Freya turned to Fergus. "And you think Kenneth MacKenzie will agree to this?"

"One thing that man loves is coin. I do think he will be swayed by the dowry, aye."

Ronan held his breath and waited. Freya worried her bottom lip with her teeth as she searched his face. He clenched his fists. Perhaps she was not as taken with the idea of marriage to him as he had thought. He held his breath and waited.

"If you believe this will not cause a rift between the MacKay and MacKenzie clans, then I am in agreement," she said after what felt like an age.

Air whooshed from between Ronan's lips. When he smiled at Freya, her cheeks pinked. He wanted her again. Would his body ever grow tired of wanting her? He could not imagine so.

"Very well then," Fergus said. "The MacKenzie is due to arrive on the morrow and I will speak with him then." He then turned to Ronan. "If there is even a hint of a breakdown in our relationship, this agreement is forfeit and Freya marries Rorie as planned." With those words he left the great hall.

Ronan waited until he gone before moving to take the chair beside Freya.

"You made me nervous just then."

"When?"

"When it took you more than a heartbeat to jump at my solution."

"Ronan, you know I would not put myself above the wellbeing and needs of the clan."

"I do and it makes me love you and want you even more." He leaned in to kiss the sensitive place behind her ear. "I want you again."

"Ronan, you cannot seduce me here," she whispered and shifted away from him. "Until this matter is resolved, we must not be seen together."

"I understand your concern, but I cannot help wanting you. You walk into the room and all my thoughts turn to how and when I can get you out of your gown so that I can bury myself in your sweet flesh. You have possessed me, Freya."

Her breath quickened as she stared as his mouth. "We should be careful."

"Aye, we should and we will." He pushed his chair out of the way and knelt before her. "But first, I must ask you a question."

His loins hardened further when she smiled. "Will you be my wife, Freya? Will you let me love you and cherish you for the rest of our days?"

She flung her arms around his neck and nearly knocked him over. "Aye, Ronan. I will be your wife."

He buried his face in her neck and nipped her with his teeth. Her body's resulting tremble had his heart thudding and his erection straining against his tunic.

Freya flicked her tongue along his ear and he nearly came undone.

"We need to find privacy. Now."

Ronan stood and was about to drag her to their secret chamber again when Fergus returned with Nessia in tow. He groaned. There would be no way they could sneak off together now. No doubt Fergus had an inkling something might occur between them for Nessia headed straight for Freya and ushered her out of the hall.

"Was that necessary?" Ronan asked Fergus.

"You know damned well it was. If I have to chain you to keep you away from her until the issue is resolved with the MacKenzie and you are wed, I will."

"If he agrees on the morrow, can we be wed the same day?"

Fergus shook his head and laughed. "No, you cannot. She is my sister and deserves a proper wedding feast, Ronan. And so I suggest you cool off in the kyle if you cannot control your desires."

At that moment, Fergus's suggestion was probably the only

thing that would help him. Ronan left MacKay house to do just that.

* * *

"You cannot keep me prisoner in my own home, Nessia."

"I can and I will. Your brother is laird here, and as his wife, I tell you to stay away from Ronan until the matter is settled with the MacKenzies. I understand the burn of passion better that you realize, but having a tryst with Ronan while you are still promised to another man is not only shameful, it is also dangerous."

Nessia was right, but Freya could not believe restricting her movements throughout MacKay house was necessary. Then again, had they not been interrupted, she and Ronan would likely be ravaging one another in the secret chamber at that very moment. Her belly tightened.

"It was not our intention to dishonour our families or the clans, Nessia."

Nessia took her hands and squeezed. "I ken that, love. I remember when you were meeting with him two years ago. You were like a woman possessed, like your very next breath depended on seeing him."

"'Tis like that now. Nessia, I cannot think when he is near. I only want him touching me and I him."

"I know what that feels like too. Fergus and I share a powerful bond that I do not think anything could break, but we never betrayed William, Freya. This is what I am trying to get through to you. If everyone else found out about your behaviour with Ronan, you would be labelled and would bring shame upon us all. Surely, you can stay away from him for a few days."

Freya was not sure that she could, but she nodded to Nessia. "I shall try."

"Good. Now, you are to take your meals in your chamber and only come to me to help with the bairns when I bid you. I understand that will be difficult"

"I will not disappoint you, sister."

Nessia left the chamber and Freya heard a distinct click of the lock turning from the outside. She shook her head. She was not the same lass who would do anything to reclaim her freedom any more. She was a woman full grown who understood the gravity of the situation they all faced.

Freya walked to the window and stared out over the kyle. Tomorrow she would learn her fate and she prayed all would go in hers and Ronan's favour. Now that she had had a taste of him again, she was not so sure she could let him go, much less let another man touch her.

CHAPTER TEN

The approaching horses filled his gut with dread and excitement. He had never experienced such a surge of fluttering in his entire life. Ronan waited until the MacKenzie party was all inside and seated before looking sideways at Fergus. The man's scowl spoke volumes. He clearly did not want to break the arrangement.

Damn. Would he go through with it?

"Is aught well?" MacKenzie asked when Fergus did not offer libations or food straight away.

"Aye, all our plans still stand," he said. "But I do have a matter to discuss with you concerning the betrothal between Freya and your son."

Ronan noted Rorie sitting straighter, his brow furrowing. Not a powerfully negative reaction by any stretch, but his father was another matter. The MacKenzie slammed his fist on the table and stood.

"We had an agreement MacKay! Do you tell me you wish to break it?"

Fergus stood and leaned forward. "I wish to discuss an alternative which would benefit us both."

MacKenzie looked from Fergus to Ronan and narrowed his eyes, pointing. "Is it because of the bastard?"

Fergus turned his head and Ronan caught a hint of amusement in his eyes. "Aye, the bastard is a part of the alternative proposal."

MacKenzie slammed his other hand on the table. "Have ye dared touched what belongs to my son, Bastard?"

Ronan's heartbeat picked up. His face grew warm, and his cheek muscles clenched when he gritted his teeth. Fergus placed a hand on his shoulder and squeezed a silent warning.

"What I propose will be beneficial to everyone here, MacKenzie. You have my word on that."

MacKenzie turned his focus to Fergus. "Then out with it, Fergus. Before I lose my patience with the lot of ye."

"It is our intention to remove the threat of Alexander Sutherland and reinstate Ronan as Earl of Sutherland, is it not?"

"Aye," Kenneth and Rorie both said at the same time.

"And as you may or may not be aware, as the earl, Ronan is financially very well endowed."

Fergus paused. The MacKenzie's brow knit together in confusion for a moment.

"When I am Earl of Sutherland once more, I will bestow upon my sister, a lady's title and secure a very hefty dowry to be awarded upon her betrothal." Ronan turned his gaze to Rorie MacKenzie. "That man can be you, if you so choose it. Believe me when I say, I would not offer my sister to just anyone." He had yet to share the scheme with his mother and sister and anticipated a battle over it, however the lad appeared to be a decent sort.

"In return," Fergus said. "Freya's promise to Rorie is null and void, and she is free to make another choice without fear of harming relations between our clans."

MacKenzie's eyes narrowed again. "'Tis you she wants, is it then?"

There was no point in denying it. "Aye."

"I agree to the terms," Rorie said before his father could speak.

The father whipped around to square off against his son. "'Tis not your choice to make, lad."

"No, but I am making it anyway since 'tis my life we negotiate." He rounded the table, holding out his arm to Ronan. Both men grasped forearms. "I wish you and Freya every happiness." With that and before his father could protest, Rorie left the great hall.

MacKenzie's eyes grew wide and his mouth agape. Ronan surmised he had not had too many in his life who dared to not only challenge, but also remove the opportunity to enforce his authority.

Fergus chuckled. "We are in agreement then?"

MacKenzie regained his composure. "It would appear so." To Ronan he said, "The lad did not ask what the dowry would be, however I am a more practical man."

"Two thousand marks."

MacKenzie's eyes rounded. It was a great deal of money, but securing his future with Freya was worth it.

"Aye lad. I will accept that and raise a goblet of ale at your wedding feast."

"But first we must defeat Sutherland," Fergus said.

"What happens if we do not reclaim my seat?"

"Then this arrangement is forfeit and the original one stands," Fergus said.

Ronan turned toward Fergus. "You will not allow our betrothal to occur immediately?"

He shook his head. "I am afraid not, lad. I cannot risk it."

Ronan was certain his guts were about to spew from his body. Claiming Freya for his own was within his grasp but still far enough away to prevent it from ever happening. Would they ever find a path that led them forward together?

"So be it," Ronan said. "MacKenzie, I trust you are ready to sail?"

"I am, lad," he said. "Are you ready to put on your sea legs, then?"

"As I am the only one who can show you where to weigh anchor, then aye, I am ready." To Fergus, he said, "Can I at least say good-bye to Freya?"

Fergus smiled and crossed his arms over his chest. "Aye. With a chaperone."

God's blood.

* * *

While Freya was thrilled with the news that the MacKenzies had agreed to the new arrangement, she was not thrilled with thoughts of Ronan going to sea with them.

She had never sailed, but had heard many tales from those who had. The North Sea could be treacherous and unforgiving, and it was much easier to perish on the water than it was on land.

Nessia had come to collect her an hour before the men were to leave. She selected Freya's gown, and now fussed with her hair. She was to say good-bye to her love in the great hall. For a fleeting moment, she wondered if perhaps Fergus had relented and would allow them to make their formal committal now instead of waiting. But Nessia had assured her this was only to give them an opportunity to say farewell.

Nessia tugged the ties of Freya's gown tight, enhancing her curves. The green velvet gown was new and she was certain Ronan would like how she looked in it. Or would he prefer to see her out of it? She hid a smile. Their lovemaking was as fevered as ever. Would they ever tire of one another?

Her carnal thoughts fired her blood. "Nessia, is all this fuss necessary?" Freya asked. The truth of it was she only wanted to see Ronan and all this time making herself up took away from her time with him.

"Aye, Freya. It is necessary for his memory of you over the long voyage to Golspie and back. He will need warm thoughts of you for what he is to face in the weeks ahead."

Freya had been so consumed with her own needs, she had not considered Ronan's. If they would give her a few moments alone with him, she was certain she could provide him with enough distraction to warm him for the rest of his life. She grinned.

"You are not permitted any time alone with him, Freya." Nessia tucked a stray copper curl into mesh netting.

"And who is to watch over us children while we say our good-byes?" Freya could not keep the bitterness from her voice. She had been desperate to see him since speaking of the arrangement in the great hall three days earlier and was like a wild cat holed up in a cage too small for it to exercise properly.

Nessia stopped her task. "Freya, your brother insisted you be kept apart and I will not taunt him any more than is necessary these days." She smiled. "With the wee ones keeping me going, I do not have the energy to disagree. If you wish to challenge him, then so be it; I, however, have better uses for my energy."

Freya turned to Nessia. "I am sorry, Nessia. I do not mean to drag you into my problems. It is just that I will not see Ronan for who knows how long. Now that I know he and I will be wed, 'tis even more difficult to say farewell."

Freya's heart was in her throat as she walked to the great hall. She wanted to race into Ronan's arms and touch and taste every inch of him until his departure, but Fergus forbade it. She could only allow Nessia to guide her to the opposite side of the table from Ronan and her brother.

Her gaze locked with Ronan's and he smiled. His face had none of the stress and strain from the last time she had seen him. In fact, some of the old, carefree Ronan shone through now. Her heart beat faster. By the heavens, he took her breath away. He wore a leather jerkin with a white leine underneath. His plaid was wrapped underneath his sword arm and he was rigged out with enough weaponry to defeat an army himself.

Moisture pooled between her thighs as his gaze slid down the length of her body and slowly back up again, as if he memorized her.

"I will give you five minutes," Fergus said.

Freya whipped around to see Nessia literally dragging him from the hall. She gave Freya a knowing smile, whereas Fergus scowled.

She herself grinned—a lot could be done in five minutes. When she turned back, Ronan's seat was empty. She frowned. Then powerful arms enveloped her, hauled her up, and familiar lips descended upon hers.

Ronan's insistent tongue parted her lips and dove inside in search of hers. She reached up and tangled her fingers in his hair, pulling him closer while he gripped her hips and drew her forward to press her against his erection.

In this moment, words were meaningless, for none existed to describe the delicious sensation surging through her. She poured every ounce of love and passion into her kiss. And he returned it wholeheartedly. Would they ever exchange another?

Somewhere behind her, a door opened and closed. No one

spoke. It could only be Nessia for if it were her brother she would have been ripped from her lover's arms by now.

She retreated as did he. Staring up into his eyes, she studied each line on his face and the curve of his mouth. She inhaled the scent of his skin and let his hair slide back and forth between her fingers. Every part of her needed to remember every part of him.

"You own my soul, Freya," he said. "Keep it safe."

She smiled. "I will, as long as you keep mine safe."

"Ronan, 'tis time to go," Nessia said from the door.

Ronan looked over her head. "Thank you." He looked down into Freya's eyes again and grinned. "When you lie in bed at night, I want you to think of me."

"I assure you, I will."

"Think of me here." He brushed his chest across hers bringing her already taut nipples to further attention. "Think of me here." He leaned down until his mouth was a breath away from hers. "And think of me here." He pushed his hips forward until his thick erection pressed against her."

She gasped. She would surely alight with flames any moment now.

"I will always love you, Freya. Never forget that."

A heartbeat later, he was gone and cool air rushed into her body at the loss of his heat. Would she ever feel warm again?

CHAPTER ELEVEN

Somewhere on the North Sea

Sea spray hit his face like a blow from a man's fist. Ronan's head jerked back and he stumbled, holding fast to the ropes tied to the sails. A strong nor'wester had picked up an hour before and threatened to run them off course if they did not get the sails tied down.

He had been to sea with his father a few times in his youth and had been fascinated by the mechanics of a ship's crew, learning a small bit by observation and practice.

He walked toward the mast, wrapping the ropes around his arms tighter as he approached. Once there, he waited until another seaman tied the loose ends below him and then he slipped his arms free. His hair was matted to his face and his clothes were soaked from heavy rain and violent seas.

At least he was not sick. The reason he was above deck in the gale was because of the number of heaving bellies below. The MacKenzie had assured him his men were sea worthy. Now, he was not so sure.

"'Tis all secure now!"

Ronan turned his head, barely able to hear the man shouting from not six feet away. He nodded and stepped away from the mast only to slide toward the side of the deck as the ship rocked to port and scooped up a crashing wave.

He wrapped his arms around the railing and held on for dear life as the wave pushed his body and then pulled it again, begging him to join it forever in the sea's depths.

Christ's teeth, this was surely Hell! Those who chose to live their lives on the sea deserved a special place in Heaven for their courage. He smiled. Fergus MacKay, the bravest man he knew, had quickly opted to lead the army by land when they had divvied up the tasks. Perhaps there was some fear in the deep recesses of that man's soul after all.

Carefully, he made his way below deck to his quarters. The captain had been kind enough to ensure a cabin be fitted for him and the MacKenzie and Rorie. Once inside, he squeezed the sea water from his hair and reached for the pitcher of mead one of the crew had left him. It was secured in a wooden cup fastened to the table preventing it from spilling unless the ship turned to an unimaginable degree. The amber liquid warmed a path to his belly and helped him regain his courage.

Alone in the cabin, he planted his legs apart and let his body sway with the rocking ship. Boards groaned and creaked under the sea's pressure. Ronan wondered if his body did not protest in the same way.

As a boy, he had viewed the sea as a great living thing with its own soul that only allowed passage to those who respected it. Once that respect was taken for granted, the sea rebelled and claimed lives.

Would now be one of those times? Their intent was to destroy a man and his army. There was nothing noble in that, unless one considered the lives that could be saved in the process.

The ship pitched hard to starboard as the door flew open. The MacKenzie and Rorie tumbled inside. The latter clicked the latch in place.

"I see you've been out there too," MacKenzie said.

"Aye, the sails needed securing and too many men were down here below deck, heaving." Ronan raised his eyebrow and awaited explanation.

"A sorry lot, those men." He took a seat at the table and poured mead into a goblet. He drew a long draught and wiped his mouth with the back of his hand and then slammed the goblet down on the table. "We lose time with this storm!"

"That we do, MacKenzie. But it will be worth it, I assure you. There is no way Sutherland will expect that half the army sails this way, while the rest cross the moors on foot. When he sees Fergus's war party, he will think he can win by easy numbers. That is when we surround him."

In theory, the plan was brilliant. The biggest challenge was getting messages to and from the men on land to the men at sea with his uncle between them. Ronan prayed the lad Fergus suggested, who Ronan had just seen heaving his guts into a barrel, really was the fastest rider in the Highlands. Andrew something or other.

"Aye, well you just remember your end of the bargain when all this is over and Sutherland's head is on a pike. You will remember your promise of the dowry and your sister's hand in marriage when you are Earl of Sutherland once more, aye?"

"I have given my word, MacKenzie. I intend to keep it." He glanced at Rorie, whose mouth was drawn into a frown. "What is it lad? Do you think my sister is not good enough for you?"

Rorie's head snapped up and anger flashed in his eyes. "You do not need to worry about my part in this, Sutherland. I appear to be the one with the least say in any of it."

For a moment, Ronan pitied the lad. He had been promised a betrothal to Freya for nigh on two years only to have it ripped away from him. Then his father is the one asked to agree to an alternate arrangement on his behalf. Ronan was more than familiar with having no control. He respected the lad for doing his duty.

"I assure you of this, Rorie MacKenzie. I would not offer my sister unless I was certain of the kind of man who could care for her. She is not feisty like Freya, nor half warrior like Nessia. Muren has a delicate nature and if I thought for one moment you would mistreat her, I would never have offered her in the first place."

Rorie's gaze locked with Ronan's. His brows drew in and he frowned. Was he now only realizing the differences between the women? Ronan watched him for signs of aggression of any sort. If he showed the slightest anger, the deal was off and he had find another way to claim Freya. He would not sacrifice his sister to come to harm as 'twas only for the good he had viewed in Rorie that the idea had come to him in the first place.

"I am well aware of her nature, Sutherland," Rorie said.

"You have spoken to her?" MacKenzie asked.

"Aye, briefly. A man would have to be daft not to know she has a gentle nature."

Rorie's countenance softened, and Ronan wondered if he were not attracted to his sister after all.

"And a lovely face too," MacKenzie said.

Ronan turned to the older man whose eyes had crinkled around the edges. Well, it appeared his sister had made an impression on both men. The tightness in his belly loosened. As much as he wanted Freya, he needed to be sure his sister was in good hands. The reaction before him was reassuring.

* * *

The ruckus in the great hall was deafening. Freya listened from the secret guard chamber. Her belly had tightened into a fierce knot, and she placed her hand over her mouth an hour ago so she would not make a sound to give away her presence.

Her brother was angrier than she had ever seen him. She could scarce believe how things had turned sour so fast. No. She would not believe Ronan would set them up like this.

"I have you surrounded, MacKay," Alexander Sutherland said. "You will pledge fealty to me or I will lay your village to waste and personally bed every female in this house including your wife—that is, after I dice you to bits and serve you to your hounds."

Freya's belly heaved. There was no stopping its contents from spewing onto the floor. She retched until there was nothing left but the sound of Fergus's battle cry and then silence. Was he dead? How could Ronan really have set them up? Was it true?

"Well, well," a deep menacing voice said from behind her. "A hideaway and a lass to warm my men."

Freya slowly turned and nearly retched again when she came face to face with the Devil himself. Her breath caught in her throat as he grabbed her arm and pulled her toward the door and into the great hall. She whimpered when Fergus's lifeless body came into view, blood pooling from his mid-section.

Her captor shoved her forward. "Now, lass. I wonder if your name might be Freya. It appears my nephew insisted you not be harmed and that you are to be returned with us to Dunrobin."

He waved his hand around the chamber and looked at his men. "Burn it all," he said and grabbed her by the waist flinging her over his shoulder when she screamed for Fergus to wake up. She screamed and screamed until her throat burned and nothing but death and destruction lay behind her.

Crossing Tongue Village on a horse with her hands tied before her, smoke from the many fires burned her eyes and lungs, and a heaviness fell over her. The Devil said that Ronan did this; that he had arranged it so that their defences would be down when Alexander attacked. She thought back to when he had returned from rescuing Morag and Muren. He had said it was too easy and she guessed now it was. Had he played them for fools? Her heart told her no, but her head told her aye.

She choked on a sob as she thought of the love they had rekindled—now sullied by the lives lost this day. Her captor broke into a heavy gallop and the effort squeezed her body until little air could enter her scorched lungs. Stars formed in her eyes and before she could protest, blackness enveloped her.

When she awoke, it was dark and she was lying on the ground, a fire crackling beside her. Freya blinked but could not soothe the stinging sensation in her eyes. Whether from smoke or weeping, she knew not.

She took in her surroundings and assessed several men moving about. They had made camp. What did they intend to do with her? And what of her family? Fergus. Did he live? What about Nessia and the bairns? And Morage and Muren? Gut wrenching sobs threatened to erupt from her and it took everything in her to keep them at bay; the result was a tremor in her body she could not control.

"She is awake, my lord." The man's voice beside her was cold.

Footsteps drew closer. She was afraid to open her eyes. Would they slay her right there, lying on the cold ground, or worse? Her body shook harder. She could not control the burn in her belly, nor the cold wash of fear splashing over her. Never before had she felt such terror as she did now.

"Take her to him. Carry her if she cannot walk." The second man sounded angry.

The first man laughed. "He doesn't normally take such an interest in them."

"He certainly seems to want this one. Said he would tear any man limb from limb who touched her."

Freya's hair was moved away off her face.

"Aye, she has a pleasing look about her. 'Tis a shame. I would have had a go at her later when she awoke. Perhaps I will take my chances with one of the other two."

"You know he said to leave them alone too?"

"What he doesn't know will not hurt him. Unless you decide to tell and then I will drive my blade into your gullet."

Shuffling sounded around her. She kept her eyes closed and prayed to God someone would help her.

"You there!" A third man said. "You were told to bring the lass to his lordship when she wakes. Does she?"

"Does she what?"

"Wake, you fool! His lordship will stick his sword through you without remorse if you do not smarten up."

Freya sensed someone closer. She opened her eyes a slit. Two large knees were before her face and then hands scooped underneath her. Her body was lifted into the air by large arms and carried for several minutes before being placed on something softer—and warmer— more comforting than the cold ground from earlier. As she came fully conscious, her tremors returned.

"I know you are awake, lass." She immediately recognized the voice. "You will come to no harm until you are at Dunrobin and we face your lover together."

Her lover? What exactly had Ronan told his uncle? Freya's belly lurched. She was going to be sick again. She opened her eyes and tried focusing on something to help her stop her mind from spinning and the coiling in her belly.

"Come, lass," the Devil said. "You will dine with me this eve, and tomorrow we shall talk about the future."

The future? Did he not mean to kill her then? She tried piecing together what she had overheard from the great hall. He had said Ronan told him they would attack as soon as he could draw the MacKenzies away. The MacKays were the only thing lying between Alexander Sutherland possessing the entire Highlands and so they must be destroyed. He said the whole plot was Ronan's idea.

Freya's head pounded. How could that be? Was everything they had ever shared a lie? No, it could not be! They had shared passion and declared their love. Surely that could not be falsified?

She lifted her body up to a sitting position holding her knees with her arms. Freya worked hard to control her shaking limbs but to little avail. A piercing scream of terror and rage sliced through her. Morag? Or Muren?

Freya drew a deep breath and thought about her loved ones back home. What would they have her do? What would Fergus say to her right now if he could speak to her?

The Devil laughed. "You are a spirited one, lass, I'll give you that."

His words were enough to remind her just who she was and the family from which she hailed. Her captors may be stronger than her in form, but they would not break her spirit and they could not take her soul. Those were her possessions, and no betrayal from Ronan or physical abuse from these beasts would take that from her.

"You may glare at me all you like, young Freya, but you cannot harm me. I alone hold all the power in the Highlands now. Your brother, the only real threat, was easily duped and even easier to kill, I might add."

Freya flew at him then. Her body would not be stayed. She grabbed his hair and toppled him to the ground, managing to slam his head once before he grasped her by the arms and flipped her over.

"I see we have found your weak point, lass." His foul breath washed over her face reminding her of her earlier sickness. Her guts lurched anew.

He studied her face with a curious expression. She held fast to her courage by a thread. When he shifted, she felt his hard shaft against her thigh. Her heart raced, realizing the man was aroused by violence. Though she did not know what would happen next, she would keep that knowledge close to her. The more she learned about him, the more likely she may find a weakness in him to exploit.

He leaned down until his mouth was a breath from hers. She held her own breath to avoid the stench.

"My lord, you wanted to see these two as well?"

The voice was accompanied by whimpering. Her resolve arose. She shifted to try dislodging him, but he caught her movement and countered, keeping her pinned.

"Drop them on the furs," he said.

A thud and another whimper sounded to her right. Freya and he continued their staring contest until finally he grinned and lifted off her. He pulled her up with ease and then shoved her toward the other two, who Freya prayed were unharmed.

When she caught her balance, she examined the women. Kneeling, she brushed Muren's hair away from her face. It was matted, but there were no marks on her skin. The poor lass's eyes were wide with fright; she trembled much as Freya had moments before.

"Shhhh, Muren. I have you," Freya whispered.

Shuffling from behind her caused her to turn—she was not comfortable with her back to him, not even for a second. Morag moved to Muren's other side and wrapped her arms around her daughter. Freya locked gazes with Morag. Nothing added up. If Ronan was part of this then why were they all treated in such a manner?

Morag opened her mouth to speak but Freya shook her head slightly in warning. The only thing she knew for certain was that Morag and Muren appeared to be as rattled by this whole affair as she was. If Ronan was involved, why had he not insisted on their comfort?

"I know you are scheming, young Freya. I can already read you quite well," he said.

She whipped around. "Very well. If you wish to know. I am scheming. I will escape your grasp, and Ronan's too. If either of you thinks you can destroy my family or that I will come along willingly, you are mistaken."

He smiled. Though why he looked pleased, she knew not.

"I doubt it not, young Freya," he said. He waved his hand toward a blanket on which bread and meat was spread. "Please, come and eat. We have a long journey ahead of us tomorrow and all three of you will need your strength for what awaits you at Dunrobin."

CHAPTER TWELVE

Ronan gazed out at the sea. The storm had broken in the night, but not before forcing them to take safe harbour at Thurso. He stood on the shore and cursed the Fates who had driven them aground. It would take a miracle now for them to rendezvous with Fergus and his men as planned. By his estimation, if they left within the hour, and came in from the north, staying close to the beaches, the plan still had merit. He would need to be sure they only engaged those they trusted along the way, though.

"We will have to walk to Dunrobin with our gear on our back, MacKenzie," Ronan said to the man standing beside him, who appeared in much the same contemplation as he.

"Aye. We'd best be at it then." He turned toward Ronan. "Do you not feel an unease this day?"

Ronan raised his brows at the question. "Unease? I did not take you for a superstitious man."

He shook his head. "I am not, but something feels very off, Ronan. We had better be more cautious."

Good advice. Ronan turned to the other men; he had not noticed their countenance before, but MacKenzie was right. There was an uneasiness about them. They could not battle his uncle like this—they would not stand a chance.

He moved into the thick of the men. "We make ready to march within the hour." His voice was loud and clear. "Our plan has taken an unexpected turn, but we are all here and we are all able." He caught the eye of a few of the men who noticeably stood straighter. "Our journey will be long and our fight will be hard. But know this. You fight for every man, woman, and child who

100

is not here. You fight for their lives, and for their freedom from a man who will lay them in the ground without a second thought."

He now had everyone's attention.

"We must remember the faces of our loved ones as we march toward Dunrobin. It is for them we fight!"

A few men said 'Aye'.

"I said it is for them we fight!"

A few more joined in and MacKenzie came up behind him.

"Do you hear the man, lads? We go to war! The threat is real and we are the only ones who can save our homes and families now! We will not let one man take that from us!"

The men nodded their heads in agreement.

"To Dunrobin!" he said.

"To Dunrobin!" they shouted, pumping the air with their fists.

The atmosphere among the men transformed from solemn to determined. The men picked up the pace with the preparation, and before half of that hour was gone, they were ready to march.

Ronan and the MacKenzie led the men for hours, stopping only long enough for a brief rest and to eat. They had made good time. A village was ahead and he needed to make a decision whether or not to approach the bishop of Caithness for help. He would be located just south of the castle at Dornoch. This meant circling around, but he could see no other alternative. His family had always held the clergy in the region in the palm of its hand, and considering his endorsement of the writ of bastardy, Ronan was not quite sure if he could, or would, assist.

"We go to Dornoch?" MacKenzie asked with disbelief in his voice.

"I think 'tis the best solution. The bishop handed me the writ personally, and had endorsed it. Aye, there is that. But if my uncle has created as much mayhem as I believe he has, the bishop is the key to reversing the writ. Without it, my uncle is a man without the power of a piece of paper."

It all sounded ridiculous to Ronan. One piece of paper told a man he was elevated to this or that. That same piece of paper could strip a man of everything, including his right to live. There was much about the whole situation that did not sit right with him. He had worked hard over the last two years to build a strong community to replace the tyranny under his father's rule.

"Who will go with you?"

"I go alone with Allain. I will not risk you or your men. If the bishop is still on my uncle's side, I may be captured. You must still carry out the plan, MacKenzie. It is critical you surround his army. Only then will you and Fergus have a chance to defeat him. Stay here until nightfall. At dawn, if I am not back, march without me. Do you understand?"

MacKenzie shook his head. "'Tis madness, Ronan. Surely your uncle will have men on the lookout for you even here, as it is so close to Dunrobin Castle."

"Aye, that is a risk I must take. If I can sway the bishop, we have a better chance to reverse the writ. Without that, we have only our fists, and that pulls us into the conflict he craves. I wish to rid him of everything and drive him as far away from here as possible."

"Godspeed to you then, Ronan. We will see you in the morn."

Ronan grasped arms with the man. "If God is on our side, then aye, MacKenzie, that you will." He turned to Allain. "Are we set then, my friend?"

"Do you really think approaching the bishop is the best course of action at this time?" Allain asked, once they were on the road.

"Aye, I do. You do not?"

"With the army marching, are we not best served with them instead of on a fool's errand."

Ronan stopped. "Why would you say that? You know as well as I the writ gave my uncle all the power he wields. Stripping him of it is a logical first step in defeating him."

"You are the master here," he said. "If it is your wish, it shall be done."

"What do you mean by that, Allain? If you have something on your mind, then be out with it."

"Aye, I will tell you what is on my mind. You would not face Alexander in the beginning of this mess. Instead, you tore off across the country to seek a man's help who has been our worst enemy for decades. Now we are the best of friends and relying on them to defeat your family. It all seems a wee bit illogical to me."

"How can you say that?" Ronan could not believe his ears. "You believe we should have shown ourselves that day back at Dunrobin? You think my uncle would have welcomed me with open arms? Did you not hear his words?"

"Aye, I heard them, Ronan. But I believe that since you went to Tongue, you have thought more about bedding and wedding Freya MacKay than your clan's safety."

"Is that what this is all about? You do not approve of Freya?" Ronan could not have been more shocked.

"Aye, I do not approve. And I do not approve of you peddling Muren off to the MacKenzie in order to keep your bed warm."

Ronan's fist landed on Allain's jaw, sending the man's head jerking backwards. "You whoreson! How dare you speak of my reasons regarding either woman."

Allain held the back of his hand to his mouth which dripped crimson. He laughed and Ronan's heart filled with dread. What the hell was going on?

"Oh, I dare, and it is because I dare you will not succeed in this plan of yours."

Ronan grabbed him by his tunic and lifted him off the ground, growling, "What have you done, Allain!"

Allain struggled, but could not free himself from Ronan's grasp. "I have only thought about Muren's safety as you have. I do not trust Fergus MacKay as you do, so I have secured your mother and sister for you."

No. No. No.

"Allain! Tell me what you have done."

"Put me down and I will tell you, Ronan. Though it is no doubt done by now and all shall be resolved upon our arrival at Dunrobin."

Ronan had no choice but to release Allain when a blade stung the back of his neck, and another at his side, perilously close to his heart.

"You are in no danger from me, Ronan," Allain said. "I have secured protection for both of us by revealing our alliance with the MacKays and MacKenzies to your uncle's men. They have your mother and Muren by now and are no doubt returning with them to Dunrobin as we speak"

Ronan's head buzzed. His blood pounded in his ears and it took everything in him not to snap Allain's neck. He placed his hands on his knees and leaned forward to help him focus. His uncle at Tongue? Christ's guts! The man would burn the place to the ground! What of Freya? What of Fergus?

Ronan made to move toward Allain again, but four very large arms held him back. He struggled against them, his fury and fear rising to a pitch, threatening his sanity and his consciousness.

"Where is Freya?" he demanded. "What of our alliance with the MacKays? Allain you have set our fate!"

Allain shook his head. "I have secured our place at your uncle's side as it should be. Your vision of alliances is flawed, Ronan. No MacKay can be trusted. Your father knew it. Your uncle knows it. And you must learn it."

"Allain, I will ask you one more time, and then I will not be accountable for my actions. You have been a loyal and trusted friend of mine, and I do not wish to harm you. But I will drive my blade through you where you stand if you do not tell me, where she is."

Allain's eyes grew wide. "How can you say that to me when all I have done is help? Very well. Your beloved Freya was collected along with your sister and mother. They should be there by the time we arrive." He walked past Ronan. "Come, let us go to your uncle. A great feast awaits us."

The arms around Ronan loosened and he found his chance. Grasping the twin blades sheathed at his hips, Ronan opened his arms and drove them backward landing one in each neck of the men who'd held him. He released and turned, unsheathing his broadsword and kneeling low to slash their bellies open in one movement. They clutched at their spewing necks as they fell to the ground.

Still on his knees, Ronan looked up at Allain who'd come racing back to the scene. His eyes locked with Ronan's.

"What have you done?"

"The first step in fixing your mess, Allain. Believe me when I say you have destroyed any trust I ever placed in you." He grabbed Allain's hands and twisted them behind his back. In his ear he said, "If any harm comes to either woman, I will slice you apart piece by piece."

Ronan grabbed the loose ends of the rope holding Allain's tunic in place around his waist, and secured his arms behind his back. He then removed his own belt and secured it around the man's neck and drew his hands farther up his back to keep him from any arm movement at all.

"I was trying to help." Allain's voice was weak. Damn the man to Hell.

Ronan removed his blades from the men on the ground, wiped them and returned them to their sheath on his waist. He needed to speak with the bishop now more than ever. His desired favours from the man would far exceed reversing the writ; he needed the king's army involved. If the MacKays were already destroyed, and the MacKenzies walking into a trap, the balance of power had already tipped.

Ronan grabbed Allain by the belt at his back and shoved hard. Stumbling forward, the man straightened and shot one mournful look over his shoulder before walking toward the bishopric at Dornoch.

* * *

Freya's hips ached and her wrists burned. After a long night with no sleep, Sutherland secured all three women and placed them each on a horse in front of a guard.

They had been riding for hours and Freya was not sure how much longer she could sit upright. She did not recognize the road they took, and by the roughness of it, assumed Sutherland had decided to stay off the main road.

Her weariness played with her wits. At times when she was

close to sleep, her thoughts drifted to riding with Ronan years earlier and how they had met. A sudden jolt would snap her back to her present, and her heart would break all over again at the realization that she still could not be completely sure he was not involved.

Her anger surfaced. How could she have been so witless? What kind of man would be so convincing in his deceit? And what about his sister and mother? Freya's mistreatment was no greater than theirs. Everything she had known about his father was becoming a reality in the son. Fergus had always said the sins of the father must be shouldered by the son. Freya had always argued on the side of Ronan and eventually convinced Fergus of the man's honour.

Where had it gotten any of them? Her heart constricted at the thought of her beloved brother lying in a pool of his own blood. He had been the strongest and best man she had ever known— and now he was dead. She choked on a sob and the arms around her tightened.

"Fear not," the voice quietly said in her ear. "All is not as it seems."

"What?" The voice sounded so familiar, but she could not quite place it.

"Hush, Freya, 'tis me, Neville." *Nessia's uncle?* "I was able to sneak out of MacKay House with the guards and accompany you. If you draw attention, you risk revealing me and we will both be killed. Do you understand? Nod if you do."

She nodded. Thank the Lord in Heaven for bringing Neville as her saviour.

"You must stay strong. I was the only one who was able to get out. Luckily, Sutherland is more interested in stuffing his fat face than observing those of his men. And most of them are too busy keeping out of his way to notice anything out of the ordinary. I cannot help you much, but I am here, lass. Know that."

"Fergus," she whispered defying his order not to speak. "Nessia and—"

The body behind her stiffened and her grief welled up again.

"Nessia and the bairns were not harmed when we left. Fergus was—"

Freya shook her head. She did not want to hear—could not listen to the words spill from Neville's lips.

As a child, she had thought nothing could ever harm her brother. Fierce and strong, he was the one everyone cowered from, but also looked to for protection—he was feared by his enemies and trusted by his clansmen. She could not imagine what Nessia was going through having lost her first husband, and Freya's brother, William, to the Sutherlands two years ago. Losing Fergus on top of it, and to the same family, would surely turn the woman mad with grief.

They went along a bend in the road and before them stood the towers of Dunrobin Castle. Freya's belly tightened and her guts heaved. She would have to face Ronan soon. What would she say to him? Marry him now as Alexander had suggested? Not a chance in Hell. She would rather stick a blade him as soon as the opportunity presented itself.

Their horse meandered down the path leading to the castle and the land flattened. Once, she had thought Dunrobin was beautifully situated with the lush lands before it and the sea at its back.

What stood before her now was a vessel that had birthed evil and grown it into a seething, sickly mass of poison set to destroy everything in its path.

"Are you well enough to help the other two?" Neville's voice brought her back to the present.

She turned her head to the side. "Aye, Neville. I can help them. Do you have a plan?"

"I do not, but keep your eyes open, lass. I believe the Sutherland will use you in his schemes, but will grow tired of you soon enough. Remember that. As long as you are useful to him, I believe he will not harm any of you."

"What schemes?" she whispered.

"Oh, that one is up to a lot of no good, lass. All you need to do is keep your wits about you and listen to your heart. It will always guide you in the right direction, as it always has."

"You there!" Alexander Sutherland rode up along-side them just then.

He picked Freya off Neville's horse and placed her in front of him.

"You will ride into Dunrobin with me."

"As you wish, my lord," she said as evenly as she could. Attacking him last night and his resulting arousal was not in her plans to repeat. She prayed complacency would at least keep her from a beating—or worse. Neville was right, once he tired of her, she would be handed over to the guards. Then the real hell would begin. No. She needed to find a way to keep his attention without exciting his interest.

"Ah, lass. If you think you will win me over with pleasantries, you are mistaken. I have one purpose for you and one purpose only."

"And what is that, my lord?" she dared to ask, keeping her voice soft.

His arms squeezed tighter around her. "Do not think I am not familiar with the ways of loose women. I am aware of your affair with my nephew, young Freya, and so I am immune to your whorish ways. I will not fall into any of your traps."

Her stomach dropped. She had been forewarned often enough from Nessia of the repercussions of continuing an affair out of wedlock. At the time, nothing seemed to matter more than spending time with Ronan. Still, this man's words implied far more than censure.

"My lord, I do not mean to offend you. I merely ask what your intentions are."

"You will find out soon enough. My nephew has made his wishes clear; who am I to deny family?"

The menace in his tone made the hairs stand up on her neck. She did not know what was worse, marriage to Ronan now, or living under the same roof with the monster at her back.

When they arrived at Dunrobin, a scurry of activity greeted them. Men and women lined up to greet them, with their hands clasped at their front and their heads bowed low in submission. These were not people happily anticipating their laird's arrival. They were afraid.

Freya dismounted without his assistance after Sutherland. His raised eyebrows and smirk only made her chin lift higher. She looked around to find Muren and Morag being drawn forward. Neville was nowhere in sight. Good. She was comforted enough just to know he was nearby—one savior among a den of demons.

CHAPTER THIRTEEN

The scent of incense burned his nostrils as he waited for the chapel to empty. Ronan took stock of the people shuffling toward the door. Dornoch was a bustling hub, but the din in the sanctuary was so low, the crowd could be cut in half or less. A sombre crowd then. Was that a sign of just how bad life had become for these people?

He kept his hand over Allain's mouth to ensure he did not give away their hiding place in the shadows. As much as he would like nothing more than to snap the man's neck right now, Allain held important information necessary if he was to secure the bishop's assistance and free his mother, his sister, and Freya.

How had it all gone so wrong so fast? One moment, he was close to claiming Freya once and for all, and in the next, he feared he would never see her again. He shook his head. He would not let his thoughts go down that path. He needed to stay focused on the individual steps toward success.

Soon, the chapel was empty, save for the priest and the bishop. Ronan stepped out of the shadows with his prisoner and approached the men.

"Ronan, my son," the bishop gasped, his eyebrows nearing his hairline in surprise.

Ronan grinned. Was there also a little fear in the man's eyes?

"I wish I could say it is good to see you, your grace. However, since your endorsement of my uncle's campaign has cost me everything but my life, I fear you will earn no pleasantries from me."

Bishop Strathbrock frowned and held out his hand. Ronan

looked at it and shook his head. "You will get no such devotion from me either. Do you know what you have unleashed?"

Ronan shoved Allain forward. The man fell to his knees at the bishop's feet and stayed there with his head bowed.

"This man needs to beg forgiveness for his sins. Is there anyone here qualified to hear him?"

The priest, a man Ronan had never seen before, stepped forward.

"Now see here, young man—"

"I am not just any young man. I am Ronan Sutherland, and I tell you what I see," Ronan said. "I see men who would rather line their own pockets than consider the lives of those they doom in doing so."

The bishop stepped around Allain and grasped Ronan's shoulders. "I agree with you, young Sutherland. I have erred in my judgement of your uncle, and of you. The situation is grave and delicate and may take some time to rectify, however."

Not if he could help it. "Take some time? You cannot be serious. Time is the one thing we do not have. The MacKays have been attacked, the MacKenzies march into a trap, and I have blades pointed at me from all sides. How much more dire do you think the situation needs to become before you will act?"

"Your grace, does he speak the truth?" the other priest asked. Then to Ronan, "I am Father Sinclair. I have only been in these parts for a few weeks, but I have seen a great change in the people coming into the parish. There is desperation in their eyes and they speak of the earl's wrath." He turned back to the bishop. "If there is a way to stop this man, I would offer any assistance I can in order to speed it along. One life lost is too many."

Those were the sanest words he had heard in the last day and night. There was no time to lose. His uncle gained more ground with each passing moment, and the sooner he was stopped, the more lives would be saved.

"You must reverse the writ," Ronan demanded.

The bishop's face grew pale and he dabbed at a sheen of sweat on his brow with a cloth he pulled from inside his vestments. He moved to a pew and slumped down into it.

"It is not quite as simple as that, my son. You see the king has endorsed the writ—"

"You told me the king's counsel endorsed the writ. I am telling you that we not only need it reversed, but we may well need the king's army to contain my uncle, or there will be nothing left of the Highlands to rule, to hear your sermons, or to save."

"You suggest he travel to Edinburgh?" Father Sinclair asked.

"Aye. As soon as possible. 'Twill be a good three days for you to get there if you leave this night."

"I fear my bones will not withstand the journey." The bishop's pallor turned grey.

Father Sinclair looked between both men and frowned. "I would have to agree with him, Ronan. Look at him. He will never even make it to Inverness in his aged state."

"What do you suggest?" Ronan asked.

The bishop looked up. A serene look washed over him. "I will draft a letter to the king and Father Sinclair will deliver it. With my seal, he will be able to place it directly into King James's hands."

"And what will you write in this letter?"

"I will request immediate reversal of the writ, and your reinstatement as Earl of Sutherland. I cannot promise the king will agree, but I will do this, as I know it is the right way of things."

Father Sinclair provided parchment, quill, and ink. Within an hour, he was packed and ready to make the journey south.

"I can make better time than three days, Ronan. You must have faith all will be well."

"Thank you, Father. I am grateful for your clear vision in these dark times. Believe me when I say we fight the Devil himself here."

Father Sinclair nodded and left the chapel.

* * *

Freya had only been to Dunrobin once, and that was with her sister-in-law two years earlier, when they had tried to save Fergus from Artair Sutherland's clutches. At that time, she was young and reckless enough to be oblivious to the real dangers women faced when in the company of bloodthirsty men.

Anyone fool enough to provoke them would find out soon enough just how dangerous men can be. As she gazed down along the table at the hungry gazes of the Sutherlands, she shifted Muren's chair marginally closer to hers. The lass was smart enough to keep her gaze lowered and her mouth shut. Morag on the other hand had wailed like a banshee when one of the guards had approached them earlier, lifting a piece of Muren's hair and inhaling. She had attacked like the mother lion she was and had a bruised and swelling eye to prove the folly in her efforts.

The rest of the day had passed without incident. The three women were locked into a guest chamber and subsequently bathed, fed, and dressed. Sutherland had insisted they dress and join him for dinner each evening. Why he insisted on the guise of pleasantries, when clearly there were none, defied her understanding. He had yet to join them. And on that note, she wondered where Ronan was as well. Sutherland had said his nephew awaited them at the castle, but from what she gathered, he was absent.

Not that gathering information was easy. She gleaned as much as she could from snippets of conversation, but the only definite thing she could be sure of, was that Ronan was not at Dunrobin Castle. Then where the hell was he?

She did not have to wait long to find out. A hush fell over the table prompting her to turn in the direction of everyone's gaze.

Her breath caught in her throat as she watched Alexander Sutherland enter with Ronan by his side. Their gazes locked for one moment and she thought she recognized a flicker of the man she had loved, but then it was gone. His gaze hardened and he looked away. When they approached the table, Ronan bent low to kiss his mother's cheek and in turn Muren's. He did not bestow the same upon Freya.

"MacKay," he said to her, his tone tight.

She gasped. MacKay? He had never called her thus. Ever. The last inch of her heart split and she now knew she had lost him. She could not hide the sorrow in her eyes as she lifted her gaze to meet his. His jaw ticked, but his countenance gave away nothing.

"I see she is not the love of your life, as I have been told, my nephew. Perhaps she does not deserve to sit at a Sutherland table after all. Shall I return her to her chamber until we decide what to do with her?"

Long moments passed as Freya held her breath. Ronan's hard stare bore holes into her soul. It tore her apart from the inside out. How was it possible he had convinced her so thoroughly of their love?

"She should not be at this table, Uncle," Ronan said. "Nor should any of the ladies. We have much to discuss regarding the MacKay and MacKenzie alliance to attack us. The women will only do as women always do—get in the way of men's business."

Freya jumped to her feet knocking her chair back in the process. "You bastard!" She spat at Ronan and lurched at him with fists raised, but a guard caught her by the waist, holding her back. The tick was back in Ronan's jaw, and just for an instant, a flash of the man she knew was back in his eyes.

Morag and Muren stood beside her and Freya saw his glance fall on them. His expression softened.

"Take them back to their chamber," Alexander said. "See to it they are guarded and no one goes in or out." He then placed his arm around Ronan's shoulder and led him to the head of the table. "Come, my nephew. Tell me everything you've learned of the MacKenzie's battle tactics. It will aid us greatly in the coming weeks."

Freya looked over her shoulder as Ronan took his seat on his uncle's right hand side. He did not glance her way, rather filled a goblet full of ale and drank deeply. Her brow furrowed. Ronan did not usually drink ale. He slammed the goblet down and poured again. Somewhere in the back of her mind, she wondered if he was trying to tell her something.

* * *

After three goblets of ale, Ronan was feeling the effects enough to stay calm and stick to his plan. After leaving the bishop, he visited the sheriff and was assured Allain would be properly secured. The only logical place to go from there was Dunrobin and figure out what his uncle was up to.

He had succeeded in making Allain's arguments to his uncle and convincing him they wanted the same thing—MacKay and MacKenzie clans destroyed. His uncle seemed gleeful at the prospect of them working together—Ronan had to work hard to not throttle the man.

Walking into the great hall and seeing Freya again nearly made him forget everything and go to her. By doing so, he would reveal too much and they would all be hanged by dawn. No, he needed to convince his uncle he could be trusted until the king's army came to their aide. He just prayed Freya would keep her cool until then.

The hurt in her eyes drove daggers into his heart. Would she ever forgive him once this was all over? Even if she did not, at least she would live.

"Now, my nephew. You say they are seaworthy, these MacKenzies." He stroked his beard. "I may have use of ships when our campaign drives us southward."

Southward? Did the man covet all of Scotland?

"Aye, they are seaworthy. Though we could not make it 'round Duncansby Head."

Alexander chuckled. "No doubt because the men were soft in the belly and too unused to a flogging." He leaned forward. "You see, men, like women, need to be reminded of their place as often as possible."

At that moment a young serving girl came with another pitcher of ale and placed it before her laird. He grabbed her arm and twisted until her head was inches away from his groin.

"And kitchen wenches should know better than to approach a laird's table unbidden." He shoved her away and threw the pitcher at her, covering her with the draught. The silver pitcher clanked its way across the floor.

Ronan stood, his chair scraping the wooden floor and his uncle's attention honing in.

"We do ourselves no justice by wasting good ale, uncle." Ronan picked up the pitcher and placed it back in the maid's hands. "Now go and fill this up and do not be so clumsy next time."

Her eyes grew wide and he saw the hint of a smile on her lips. He shook his head in warning. She appeared to catch his meaning when she lowered her head and then bobbed it once as if to nod. Shannon. He recognized her and recalled her father, Hamish, recounting the stories she had told him. At least he had one in the castle he might the able to rely on.

He had almost given himself up in that moment and had to recover quickly. He would need to be smarter and more careful in order to pull this off.

"As you wish, my nephew," Alexander said. "I see no need to be kind to any of them, as they will serve me in the same manner, regardless if I waste good manners on them or not."

Christ's blood, his uncle really was a monster.

"The servants are the least of our concern right now," Ronan said. "As I told you earlier, the MacKenzies are a very real threat. You must make ready for attack. With all due respect, you have not been through a war up here in a very long time."

"You speak the truth, but if the so called formidable MacKay defences were any indication, I have nothing to fear from the MacKenzies. Their numbers may be significant, but they cannot harm me, or beat through my army."

This was what Ronan wanted most. A definitive account of just how much man-power his uncle wielded. Only then could he find a way to get word to the king's army and the MacKenzies so they could properly prepare.

"You are certain of your numbers, Uncle?"

Alexander cocked his head to the side and narrowed his gaze. He leaned forward, and for the second time that evening, Ronan was certain the man saw into his very soul. Ronan worked to keep his countenance calm, focusing on his even breath.

"I am very certain of my numbers, young Ronan. And if you think five thousand men is not enough to defeat those worthless MacKenzies, you must tell me what secret weapon they possess."

He sat back in his chair with a wide smirk on his face. Five thousand? He had estimated no more than several hundred upon approaching Dunrobin.

"Do you hide them in the bowels of the castle then?" he dared to ask. "For I only see a few hundred here."

"Ahh, you have much to learn, Ronan. One never places his entire army in one place."

He stood and motioned for Ronan to follow. They walked toward the back of the castle and climbed the tallest tower. Once there, Ronan had a fantastic view of the entire region. Inland and to the west he saw farmlands and mountains. Closer to the castle, the smaller portion of his uncle's army readied itself. But to the southeast and out to sea his gaze beheld several ships anchored and lying in wait.

Christ! Had his ships made their way around the tip of Scotland, they would have been discovered by his uncle's fleet!

"Now you know, Ronan, why ships are very appealing to me. I will defeat the MacKenzies on land but then I will take everything they have and we will sail into Edinburgh and claim the throne from those worthless Stewarts."

"I think you may have to deal with the MacDonalds of the Isles if that is the prize you seek."

"The MacDonalds are no threat to me. I have made sure the MacDonald will spend the rest of his days in prison. So you see there is nothing standing in my way any longer. It is only a matter of time before all this is mine. I must admit, Ronan. I did not anticipate your alliance. From everything I have been told, I expected you to work against me."

As he said his last words, his fingers bit into Ronan's shoulder in warning. Aye. It would take very little to lose this man's trust and then all would be lost. He must tread carefully to ensure the man's defeat. The ships would prove challenging. On land, they had an advantage, as long as the king understood the urgency of the matter. If not, all was already lost.

"When do you march against the MacKenzies?" Ronan asked.

"At day break. We will run them through and then begin the campaign south, hitting Ross and MacDonald, and farther past Inverness to MacIntosh lands. I understand the MacIntosh believes himself worthy of defending his lands, but he will discover the truth of it soon enough. They will fall. All of them, Ronan." His uncle's face twisted into an ugly sneer. "And they will all know the name of Alexander Sutherland by the time I am through with them."

The man was stark raving mad. There was no doubt about it.

Following his uncle down the winding tower stairs, Ronan contemplated his next move. Freya and his mother and sister appeared safe, as long as he kept his attentions away from them.

Earlier, he had spied Neville, among the guards and nodded to him. Ronan meant to seek him out to learn of what had actually occurred at Tongue and to what degree the MacKays were incapacitated. He prayed Fergus was not harmed and was doubling the MacKenzie numbers by the hour.

When he and Alexander entered the hall again, a ruckus had ensued and some of the kitchen maids, including Shannon, were being molested by the guards. A great surge of fury welled within him. He could not stand by and watch these women be raped. But if he ran to their aid, his guise would be lifted and all would surely be lost.

"What passes here?" Alexander's voice bellowed into the great stone chamber. "I did not give you leave to sport with these women when they have yet to feed me."

As twisted as his logic was, Ronan was grateful that Alexander's priority was his empty belly. At least that might give the maids time to make themselves scarce.

"First, we feast!" he said. "Then you may sport with any woman you wish, who is not under guard."

CHAPTER FOURTEEN

Freya paced while the others slept. They had all agreed to take turns keeping watch during the night, and her shift was nearing its end. She was exhausted and confused. Something niggled at her. Ronan's actions were confounding, but the ale drinking was new. Just how much of him did she really not know?

She stood at the window and gazed out across the sea. The moonlight shimmered on the water and lights danced in the distance. She squinted. Lights on the water? There must be ships out there. But according to the number of lights, there would have to be a whole fleet. As she leaned forward to see better, a shuffling from behind her caught her attention.

Footsteps from outside her door grew louder. She tiptoed to the door to listen for voices. The steps echoed through the hallway outside and stopped in front of her door. She held her breath and waited. A soft thunk sounded on the other side and she heard deep sighs coming from whomever it was.

Freya's heart pounded and she jerked her head back from the door when she thought she heard her name whispered. Ronan? Her pulse quickened. Should she open the door? What if it was not him? She leaned in and pressed her ear to the door again. Muffled whispers of words she could not discern made her reach for the latch. Just before she touched the cool metal, it lifted on its own.

She stepped back and waited for the door to arc open. Somehow, she was certain it was Ronan. Her heart beat like a drum in her chest. She held her breath. Would he enter her chamber? For what purpose? So he could seduce her again and then throw her to the wolves in the next instant? Not this time.

The door inched open and Freya peered closer at the door frame. There was an additional latch, one that would bolt the door from the inside. Before thinking any better, she shoved all her weight against the door and clicked the lock in place. A gasp on the other side told her the person did not expect it.

She waited to see if the intruder would persist, instead she heard faint laughing as the footsteps moved away.

Freya slumped against the door and let her head fall back against it. Her knees quaked. Part of her still wanted him so badly it was bound to drive her mad, but the logical side of her wanted to grab the nearest blade and drive it through him.

"Who was at the door?" Morag asked.

Freya jumped. "I thought you were sleeping."

"I was until the door slammed shut. I thought someone must have come in." She rubbed her eyes, sitting up.

"No, I thought someone was out there so I checked and then locked the door to be sure no one entered."

"I doubt a lock from the inside will stop them if they seek entry badly enough."

"You speak true, however, for now it appears Sutherland does not want us harmed. Any guard could sneak in here if he wanted to with the door unlocked. He would have to make quite the racket in order to get in, and then he would risk waking his laird. I don't know about you, but that is one man's attention I'd rather not attract."

Morag got out of bed and approached Freya, wrapping her arms around her. "He is not acting like himself, lass."

"Who?"

"You know of whom I speak."

"He has made his wishes quite clear, Morag. I see no reason to speak of him again."

She tutted. "Freya, he is protecting us, that is all."

"I appreciate, as his mother, you have to see the best in him, but I have looked into his eyes, and what I saw there tonight left me with no doubt there is nothing but disgust for me left in him."

She wrapped her arms around her middle as if doing so could change the cold, hard fact. Ronan did not love her, and she wondered if he ever did.

"Freya, use your head. What do you think would happen to us if Ronan showed us the real love he has in his heart?"

Freya shook her head. All she could see was the disgust in his eyes. Morag tightened her arms around her.

"Alexander Sutherland would have gutted the lot of us where we stood, that is what." She gave Freya a little shake. "Freya, look at me. You must not give up on him. I know my son and I would bet my life that he loves you more than his own. He distances himself to protect you. Please, for both of your sakes, do not give up on him."

"My brother is dead. You cannot expect me to forgive the man responsible. I cannot. I will not!"

With that, Freya broke from Morag's embrace and moved to take her place in the bed beside Muren. She flopped down on the pillow and drew the covers up and over her head. She heard Morag heave a great sigh as Freya shut her eyes tight. She did not want to see or hear anymore reminders about how much she had lost. No, she needed to formulate a plan to get back to Tongue and find a way to protect Nessia and the children. Please God, they were not harmed and had others there to help them.

Would Neville have gathered enough information to have formed a plan? Was he able to get information out? And if he could, exactly how was she to find him in a sea of soldiers she did not know if she could trust to keep from ravaging her?

As much as she hated to admit it, right there in the chamber, with Ronan's sister and mother, was the safest place.

Muren mumbled in her sleep and Freya turned over to regard her. She peeked out from under the covers and took in the young lass. Muren had been through so much as well. Freya recalled the screaming from the first night and then wondered if Muren had been attacked. She compared the scream to the one Morag had given when one of the guards had touched her hair. They were different.

Freya sat up and Morag turned her head.

"Why did Muren scream that first night we were taken?"

Morag came to the edge of the bed and sat. "One of the guards tried to haul her off for his sport," she said, frowning. "Freya, I have never been so afraid in my life, until I saw you and the fury in your eyes that night. I thought, if Freya can do this, so can I. We can both protect Muren."

"Aye, we can, Morag. But I tell you now, my priority is to return home to Fergus's wife and children. That is where I belong. You and Muren can come with me. I have a friend out there." She tilted her head toward the window. "He will help us return to safety."

Morag smiled. She really was quite beautiful. "You speak of Neville Stephenson."

"How do you know that?"

"Because he was with Ronan when they rescued us."

"Neville was there? Are you telling me you really were rescued?"

Morag's brow furrowed as she frowned. "Of course we were rescued. Freya, they burned out my cottage. Ronan and Neville and the others rescued us from the dungeon and we tracked back a different way from the one we came. I rode with Neville and we spoke a great deal of the MacKay and Sutherland feud. When I say my son has nothing to do with what is going on and is only trying to protect us, I speak the truth. I know you have your reasons for disbelieving me and I know you are in pain. But know this, Alexander Sutherland is a liar who toys with us all for his own sport."

Could it be true? Did Ronan pretend indifference and disgust to protect them from his uncle's attentions? She wished, more than ever, she had opened the door. Freya slumped back onto the pillow. Her mind raced with the possibilities.

"We should be asking ourselves what we can do to help him. I feel he is trying to get close to his uncle for a purpose, but I cannot fathom why. Other than trying to influence him on our behalf, I cannot imagine what he can accomplish."

"Have you seen the ships?"

Morag's brow furrowed. "What ships?"

"Out there in the bay. There must be a dozen or more. Go look, I saw them there not more than an hour ago."

Morag moved to the window and Freya waited for her affirmation. When she said nothing, Freya got out of bed and moved up behind her. She peered out into the darkness. The moon was hidden behind the clouds and everything on the sea was black. It could not be. She had seen them with her own eyes. How could they have simply disappeared?

"It makes no sense. They were there. I swear it," she said.

"I believe you, Freya. I think there is only one of two possibilities. Either your eyes tricked you, or the ships were there and now they have moved."

"But where could they have gone in such a short period of time?" Their chamber afforded an extensive view of the sea. Ships could not just disappear.

"Perhaps there is another possibility we have not considered," she said. "That they are still there."

"How can that be?"

"You saw lights correct?"

"Aye."

"And now there are none."

"Aye, Morag, we have established that much."

"So considering the time frame, I would suggest the lights are simply put out."

"But ships always leave some light on to assist in avoiding collision. The only time you would hear of a ship moving under complete cover of darkness, is if—"

Morag smiled. "If?"

"If they are about to attack." Freya looked out to the sea again and strained hard to detect any sign of the ships sailing closer to shore. Try as she might she was not certain if she saw black ships, whales, or a trick of what little light there was.

The wind picked up and moments later the moon illuminated the water again. Freya's belly tightened because now the ships sailing without the aid of lanterns were clearly visible. Morag grabbed her arm and gasped.

"Who are they?"

"I know not, but their destination is unmistakable."

Freya watched them for the next hour, between the moon appearing and disappearing again moments later. Silently they came. Friend or foe of the Sutherlands? And would that make them the opposite for her? When they neared the shore, dozens of smaller boats emerged from the larger ships. They rowed until the shore was dotted with intruders.

Just when Freya anticipated they were ready to attack, the party of men moved off toward the south and away from the castle, their destination unknown and her questions unanswered. An hour later still, all was quiet. Morag urged her into bed and despite the activity of the evening and the uncertainty of her safety, Freya fell into a deep sleep.

* * *

Ronan listened to his uncle relay his plans to the captain of his ship's fleet. He had every detail planned down to each soldier's duty. It appeared nothing escaped his notice. Despite his monstrous methods, Ronan had to acknowledge the man had a strategic mind that was unmatched.

"You will stay off shore until we signal your arrival. You've been too close lately and I fear you may be spotted, so you will have to take greater pains to hide the ships." The warning was clear.

"Aye, my lord. If that concludes your orders, we will be on our way."

His uncle nodded and the captain left the great hall. He then turned to Ronan and smiled. "You are in deep concentration, nephew. Do you have any questions about my plans?"

"No, uncle. I consider your approach thorough."

He chuckled. "Aye, I am thorough. It is how I am able to achieve exactly what I want. For example, when you were able to escape with your mother and sister."

Ronan sat up a little straighter.

"That is correct. I knew you were here. Did you not think

you were allowed to collect them with very little resistance and that was odd?"

"Aye, I did." Ronan was not about to share all details on what he had learned about that rescue. Namely the habits of the guards in the dungeon. Ronan had observed exactly as his mother had suggested. They filled their gullets at night and rarely moved before the mid-day meal.

"And yet you left a clear path to MacKay's door for me. Perhaps that was your intention all along."

"What do you mean?"

"I mean that perhaps you relate more to my attempts to rule over these barbarians than to roll around in the muck along-side them."

Ronan opened his mouth to deny it but his uncle put his hand up.

"You are not yet ready to accept the Sutherland blood that runs through your veins, Ronan. You were allowed to live with your mother for far too long. I told Artair he should have hardened you to the ways of a true leader from your birth, but he had put all his faith in his eldest, and we both know how that turned out. Your father was a mad fool."

Ronan knew that story all too well. His older half-brother, Artagan, had met his fate at his father's hand. A chance meeting with Fergus MacKay when they were lads would prove to everyone the importance of recognizing both friend and foe. His father had been wild with fury when he learned Artagan and Fergus had become friends. His brother succumbed to his lashings within a month of receiving them.

"I was but seven when my brother was—when he died."

Alexander grinned without mirth. "Aye, and if you were my son, your whore of a mother would have never had you for even seven days."

Ronan worked hard to hide the fury in his heart at the mention of his mother.

"You hide your feelings well, Ronan. But not well enough. I know you are here to protect them more than to ally with me."

Ronan's head snapped up. "Of course I wish to protect that

which is mine. But when I told you I am here to support your campaign, I meant it."

His uncle leaned forward. "Do you?" He cocked his head to the side. "Then let us test that shall we?" He waved one of his guards forward. "Bring the fiery haired lass to me," he said.

What in Hell's name? Ronan's fists clenched.

"For someone indifferent to the lass, you appear quite interested in my intentions right now."

Ronan slowed his breathing and worked to calm his thudding heart. "I am interested as to why you think I care about what happens to her. In fact, I wonder why she is still here? Why not send her back to her brother?"

"Her brother refused to die, and I suspect will be on my doorstep before long claiming vengeance." He flicked his hand to the side. "Or some such noble nonsense. The only thing that matters in these games of war is the individual pieces we have to play against one another. You are here and seemingly on my side. I need to find out just how loyal you are."

A sick ache filled Ronan's guts. Somehow he knew what was coming, and he prayed Freya had the strength to endure it. He prayed he did. Staying close to his uncle and privy to his plans was bigger than he and Freya, however, and they would both have to sacrifice for the greater good of the lives of all those at stake.

In that moment, having steeled his resolve to the task, Ronan was certain he was about to lose Freya forever and a numbness passed through him. He would never feel anything ever again.

The guard entered with Freya by his side. She did not struggle. She had no idea what was about to happen. Ronan swallowed hard. She had dark circles under her eyes and they were red rimmed. Had she wept? She would be the only one of the two now who could, for once he was done with this deed, there would be no going back. She would never forgive him and he would never forgive himself. From this moment on, she must be his enemy in every sense including in his heart.

CHAPTER FIFTEEN

Freya kept her eyes downcast. She had no idea what was going on, just that the guard had said the earl and his nephew had business with her. Sutherland had said she would be married to Ronan upon arriving at the castle and based on his cool reception last evening, she was sure he had now relinquished that wish. Would they let her go? Unlikely. What, then?

"It appears we need to establish the connection between your family and mine, lass," Sutherland said.

Freya's head shot up. She locked gazes with Ronan, whose expression was masked to a point she hardly recognized him. Did he play a game with her? Did he mean for her to deny their relationship—or former relationship?

"My lord, I know not of what you speak. Our families have no connection." She glanced back at Ronan again. Nothing.

Sutherland's brows raised and he smiled. "Is that so?" He stood and walked toward her. "You see, I am not convinced of it. I believe there is something very real between the two of you, and I cannot have my nephew, who has pledged his allegiance to me and my campaign, holding anything back from me."

Freya's belly dropped when he lifted a lock of her hair and held it to his nose, inhaling deeply. She recalled his arousal from the night he had abducted her. She could not help the terror seeping into her belly and coiling around her heart. Did he mean to take her with Ronan watching?

"Uncle, I assured you, the MacKay lass means nothing to me."

Ronan's flat tone was hardly recognizable to Freya. Was he truly indifferent to her then? If so, how far would he allow his

127

uncle to go to prove his so called allegiance. Damn the both of them! If they wanted to toy with her, she would not give them the satisfaction of her fear.

"What must I say to convince you, my lord?" She lifted her chin. "Your nephew means nothing to me either."

Freya watched Ronan's brows draw together slightly and then even out again. Bastard!

Alexander looked back and forth from Ronan to Freya and back again. "Very well. You have both made it clear you mean nothing to the other."

Freya's belly churned as she awaited her fate.

"Freya, sister of the MacKay, you shall marry me, the Earl of Sutherland, and we will unify the north through marriage." He leaned closer and the stench of him made her guts roll. "I cannot wait to hear you scream beneath me," he said in a low voice.

Freya gasped. Marriage to this monster? Sweet Lord in Heaven, she would never survive a night with him. His eyes sparkled at the horror she must be portraying on her face, if it was even a quarter of what she felt.

Freya turned to Ronan. He may not love her any longer, but surely he would not see her repeatedly raped by the man he himself considered the most deranged and savage beast he had ever encountered. She poured every ounce of fear and pleading into her expression when Sutherland turned around to fill goblets with sweet wine.

Freya beseeched him in silence. Though his gaze never left hers, there was no recognition that he understood, or cared. Sutherland returned and passed them both goblets.

He raised his in salute. "To a fine alliance." He tapped his goblet off hers and then Ronan's. He then drank deeply, urging her and Ronan to do the same.

Ronan finished his wine and placed the goblet on a table. "Congratulations." Then he left the great hall, leaving her alone with her future husband.

Sutherland licked his pale lips as he refilled his goblet. Freya pressed hers to her mouth and bit down hard. She needed to muster her courage and focus on something to bring her through this nightmare. She thought of Nessia and the barins, of her siblings. They would need her to stay strong. She prayed she could endure this—endure him.

Freya held out her goblet. He smiled and filled it again.

When she emptied it a second time, he tsked at her. "My dear, you really must slow down. We will be wed tomorrow and I want you in your full capacity when I take you." He walked around behind her and again smelled her hair. "Oh, how I will make you scream. Do you like pain, Freya? You can never know true pleasure unless you have known the full extent of pain. And I will give you both."

Freya held on to the contents of her belly by a thread. She would drive a blade in him before he showed her the extent of such pain. Aye, she had known true pleasure, even if the man no longer cared for her and would leave her with a vile beast. Freya knew enough of pleasure to distract Sutherland long enough to drive a blade somewhere deep inside his body where it would spill his life's blood and rid the world of his poison once and for all.

What she needed to do now was to ensure he trusted her enough to let her get close. If she came on too strong, he would suspect her falsehood. If she showed too much fear, she would arouse him too much and he would surely take her then and there.

She turned to face him with as much humility as she could muster. "My lord, as my husband, it is your privilege to teach me any lesson you feel is necessary. I cannot promise I will always be willing, as I have never had a firm hand when it comes to my behaviour."

His nostrils flared as he inhaled and a pleased smile spread across his face. Her ruse appeared have the desired effect on him. "You will learn your place, young Freya. I intend to make sure you crave the pain from me as much as the pleasure."

Freya forced a smile as he leaned down and placed cold firm lips against hers. When he leaned back, something like anger flickered in his eyes.

"You do not yet know how to kiss a man, but you will learn.

Have the maids bring your bath to your chamber this evening and you may dine there with the bastard's mother and sister. They may attend you until we are wed."

With that, he turned and left the great hall. Freya's knees buckled and she slumped to the cold stone floor. Her breath came in great gasps. Blood pounded in her ears, and the walls spun around her. She swore images from the tapestries dotting the walls mocked and taunted her, their jeers ringing in her ears. She was going mad. Freya focused on her breathing, searching for enough calm to provide some clarity to what had just occurred.

When she had entered the great hall, she had no idea what to expect. Nothing could have prepared her for the horror she had discovered and was about to face. She feared she would need strength she did not possess.

Freya placed her head in her hands and wept. She wept for her past and for her future. She wept for loved ones lost and for family she would never see again. She wept for the love she would never have again.

After her tears dried, she wiped her eyes and made to get up to return to her chamber. A noise from the doorway caught her attention and she looked up to lock gazes with Ronan. His expression was pained as he watched her. She opened her mouth to speak and he shook his head.

She needed him now more than ever and he would not help her. She was already dead.

* * *

Ronan turned away from Freya and the scene in the great hall. He had heard every word his uncle had said to her. Blood pounded in his ears at the thought of the man laying one finger on her, much less taking her to his bed.

He stalked out of the castle and onward until he came to the soldier's quarters. He hunted until he found what, or rather who, he sought.

Taking him by the arm, Ronan led Neville to the stables. "Do you think you can get out of here undetected?"

"Aye, I have done it twice already. No one seems to care about me. They're all too afraid of your uncle."

"Well, that is a good thing. I want to know if Fergus lives and I want to know the condition and location of his army."

Neville's brow furrowed. "And what assurances do I have that you do not betray us?"

That was a good question. "None. But if you find out this information for me, I will share what I know with you and then you may do with it what you will."

"That is a fair deal, Ronan. I will return here tomorrow. Meet me back here and I will share what I have learned. You have my word."

Ronan watched Neville slink out the back of the stable and prayed no one else saw him. His mind buzzed with the information he had acquired in the past day and the implications. If his uncle was to succeed, he would bring about the worst kind of devastation upon the land. Regardless of anything else, Ronan could not let that happen if he could help it at all.

He made his way back to the castle to find his uncle. Perhaps if he got the man drunk, he would not be able to perform with Freya. Christ, just the thought of it brought his meal close to spewing from his mouth.

Ronan eventually found his uncle back in the great hall, surrounded by his captains. They were bent over a map and marking off sections. When he spied Ronan, he waved him over.

"Here is where the battle will claim the MacKenzies, young Ronan. If you wish, I will let you rule over the north once I claim the throne."

Ronan found it to be a minor concession considering how much the north would lose in the process.

"You are too kind, Uncle," he said.

Without warning, he backhanded Ronan, snapping his head back. Ronan's cheek burned and blood dripped from his lip. He wiped at it with the back of his hand and stared hard at his uncle who pointed a fat finger in his face.

"You mock me again and you will not live to see the morrow.

Any concession I allow you will be at my mercy and from what you have earned and nothing more."

This was the kind of treatment Ronan had known from his father. He had let his guard down for a brief moment and was now grateful for the reminder exactly what he was dealing with. He would not even think of him as uncle any longer, merely a man, without title or deserving of that respect. Ronan knew how to play this game.

"I do not mean to mock you. 'Tis a generous gift you offer me and I am grateful."

Alexander's eyes narrowed. Ronan would not even swallow while under the man's scrutiny. He had learned from a very early age how to mask fear. Long moments ticked past while he waited for Alexander to either slay him or accept him into the inner realm of his confidence.

Finally, a ghost of a smile hinted at his lips. "You would do well to remember it."

Without another word for him, Alexander turned back to the maps and to his captains. Ronan learned that everything he had said the night before was in fact exactly what he had planned. With the element of surprise, the man actually had a chance to succeed which was the frightening part. What he did not know was how many people around him were not loyal. Even if he and Neville were in the minority of loyalty to Alexander Sutherland, Ronan was confident their efforts could trip the plans sufficiently to prevent any serious damage.

The evening passed without incident. Ronan, armed with Alexander's battle plan, longed to share the information with Neville and send it out across the land, but he would need to keep it to himself for one more night.

His thoughts drifted to Freya on many occasions. He had not needed to worry about Alexander's intentions that night, as it appeared the man had some sense of attachment to the sanctity of marriage before bedding her. Ronan nearly burst out laughing. If he only knew how little both he and Freya had respected that in the past he would slay them both where they stood.

Late that evening as he lay in his bed, Ronan thought about how he would react when forced to watch her marry the next day. Would he allow it to happen? Could he even stop it if he tried? If he jumped in and was killed, he would not be able to get word out about the planned attacks. But if he allowed it to go ahead, Freya would surely suffer tortures beyond reason at the hands of the worst demon who ever called himself a man. His hands were tied. He was damned if he did and damned if he did not.

He tossed and turned until daylight broke out across the ocean beyond the back gardens. The one person whose judgement he trusted the most was likely dead, so Ronan tried to imagine what Fergus would do if he were here. Damned man would find a way to save Freya and get word out.

Realizing the uselessness of his sleepless night and the lack of clarity hours of agonizing had earned him, he left his chamber to walk to the beach. Once there, he gazed out over the ocean as the sun rose. The sky streaked yellow and pale crimson, as though forewarning of the evil brewing in the day ahead. Would the sky not even give him respite from his worries?

Scraping his hand across his face, he cursed his cowardice. How could he let Freya go on believing he would not come to her aid? It was cruel and made him no better than his father. All he had to do was raise a finger to her and then he would be just as bad as Alexander.

Perhaps he fought a losing battle.

Perhaps he *was* as bad as they were.

He turned back to the castle and walked across the gardens toward the falconry, as a distraction, he told himself. The new hawk had broken its wing and the falconer was attempting to heal it.

"How fares our new hunter?" he asked Rob, the falconer.

"Fine this morning, my lord," he said.

Ronan stopped for a moment and looked at the man. He had addressed him as per usual and for a brief moment, Ronan was drawn back in time to a month ago when aught was normal. Though a month ago, when he did think things were normal, he had no idea how much he still loved Freya. Should he regret everything that had passed?

"Why do you address me so?" he asked. If anyone overheard the man, he would be flogged.

"No matter to me who is in charge, my lord. You shall always be the master here in my eyes."

"I was usurped and am no longer lord here. You would do well to remember that," he said. It would not take much for an example to be made out of the man.

Rob laughed. "I do not know the way of lords and usurpers," he said. "I only know how to mend broken wings and train unruly hunters."

Ronan gazed at the man as though he saw him for the first time. As though he saw everything for the first time. Did the man purposely speak in double truths or did Ronan simply need to find meaning in any form he could?

"Would you like to take him out, my lord?"

Ronan's gaze drifted from the falconer to the injured bird. Its leather cap prevented it from getting spooked and yet it darted its head from side to side. Seeking. Searching.

"Aye, Rob. I would like that very much. Do you think he is ready?"

"Aye. I do. His wing was well enough a sennight ago, but he would not budge. Like he is afraid to try to become what he was meant to be."

Again the double truth struck Ronan like a blow. Was he afraid to become the man he wanted to be? Or was he more afraid to discover the man he was destined to become   evil, like his family?

Ronan strapped leather to his forearm and waited until Rob placed the hawk there. It shifted on its feet and dug fast into his arm.

"There you go, strong one," Rob said. "Talk him through it, my lord. 'Twill help him."

Ronan had taken birds out many times so was more than familiar with how a soothing voice helped them. He stepped away from the other squawking birds and spoke in low tones to the hawk.

"You are a brave, strong lad aren't you?"

When they had moved far enough away, Ronan stroked the bird's chest. "Shhhh. You shall have your freedom soon enough. Hold still now."

Ronan untied the straps and gently lifted the cap from the bird's head. It fluttered its wings and shifted nervously on his arm.

"Hush now. You are doing fine. You can do this, great one," he said. "For there is no finer hunter in all the land than you."

The bird quieted and cocked its head toward Ronan.

"Oh, you like that praise do you?" Ronan chuckled and the hawk turned his head sharp left. "What do you see? Are you ready?"

The bird was fixated on something in the distance. Now was as good a time as any to see if he would ever get over the injury. Sadly, not all of them did.

Ronan dropped his arm a couple inches and then pushed upward. The bird spread its wings wide and leapt off his arm. Wings flapping, the bird rose higher and higher, taking Ronan's spirits with it.

It circled around a few times and then dove straight down mere feet from where Ronan stood, capturing a small rodent in its beak. The bird's high pitched call on its descent was music to Ronan's ears.

Once the rodent was consumed, the bird continued its hunt for the next half an hour before returning to Ronan's arm and pitching without hesitation.

"Such a great hunter you are," he said. "Did you enjoy your spoils, ya great greedy thing? You need to save some of those mice for the other birds, you know?"

Ronan's heart felt light. He was practically giddy when he returned the hawk to Rob.

"He did well," Rob said.

"Well?" Ronan smoothed the bird's chest again, surprised that it did not appear to mind. "He did marvellous. He just needed the chance to prove himself worthy of the task."

As though a lightning bolt raced through him, clarity emerged. He was so like the hawk, injured supposedly beyond repair. But the damage to his outside was not so much as to the self-inflicted damage to his insides. He did not need to wait to see if he would become evil like his father and uncle. He already knew who he was. Now, he just needed to show everyone else.

They would be in for a surprise—Freya especially. She would not marry Alexander. She would not endure one more moment of pain and suffering at the hands of anyone.

Ronan strode back to the castle with renewed vigour. The sun was still low on the horizon and he had time to plot and plan; time to make sure he saved those he loved, and bring those to justice who deserved it most.

CHAPTER SIXTEEN

Clasping her fingers together to keep from trembling, Freya sat near the crackling fire while Morag brushed her hair. Sutherland had ordered her below and given her one hour to prepare. It appeared he was anxious to wed her after all.

"You will make your lip bleed, lass," Morag said.

Freya had not even realized she worried it. She let her lip be for the moment, but still wrung her hands.

Morag stopped what she was doing and sat in front of Freya, grasping her hands.

"Look at me," she said.

Freya looked into the woman's eyes. Steely determination lay in them. Her lips were pressed into a straight line and her jaw was clenched.

"Even if he makes you marry him today, nothing will happen until tonight. That gives us plenty of time to find a way to get you out."

"Just me? No. I am not leaving here without you and Muren as well. With me gone, he will only focus his attentions on you instead. Better me to bear the brunt of his cruelty than either of you."

Morag shook her head. "You are brave but foolish, Freya. You cannot imagine the tortures he plans for you. I have heard the maids talking about the unfortunate few bidden to his bed only to be brought to the healer in the morn."

Bile rose in Freya's throat. Could she endure it? For the sake of those she loved, she would risk her life without question, but how much torture could she really endure?

"If only—"

"Do not say it," Freya said interrupting her. She would not hear one more word in lament over Ronan's turn of loyalty and lack of protection. Her heart could not stand it.

"What is done is done. Your son has made his decision. He will have to live with it." She squared her shoulders and stood. Taking a deep breath she said, "I will see this through, if only to protect you and Muren. But you must promise me that should the opportunity arise to leave, you will take it."

Freya waited while Morag's brows drew tight. She frowned and stood in front of her as if to block her path to the door. Morag grasped her shoulders and shook her hard.

"You will see the ceremony through because you have no choice. But you will *not* be here this evening to endure his torture." Morag shook once more. "Do you hear me, Freya? I will not allow this to happen."

Freya worked hard to deaden her emotions and prevent the terror swirling inside her like a tempest. She prayed Morag was right and that someone would come to her aid before it was too late and Sutherland damaged her beyond repair.

She smoothed her skirts and lifted her chin. He might be able to do atrocious things to her body, but he would never, ever reach her soul.

"I am required in the chapel. Will you accompany me?" she asked.

Morag nodded. "Muren, you are to stay here. The more out of sight you are, the better."

"I will not," she said. Muren had always been a quiet lass, and so such vehemence in her declaration was surprising. Both Morag and Freya turned to her.

"Muren, it is not safe," her mother said.

"And you think here alone is any safer than in the den of demons? At least there, I am in the open with both of you. Here, I have no one." Muren's voice was full of pleading.

"Well, aren't we a dire lot?" Morag said, drawing a deep breath. "Ready yourself quickly then. And for the love of heaven, do not pull your hair back from your face. The last thing we need is one of his men noticing you."

Muren pulled her hair down to hide her face and donned her crumpled gown. Her actions had Freya wondering if she were a meek lass or perhaps a very good player.

A knock sounded at the door, startling the three women. Freya moved to it, looked back once and nodded at the women, before lifting the latch and swinging the door wide. She was not prepared for the sight that met her eyes.

"You are ready?" Ronan asked. His eyes were bright and he smiled at her.

Freya's belly heaved. He looked pleased that she was going through with this. Could he be any more cruel? What in Heaven's name had she done to deserve this treatment from him?

"Aye, my lord. I am ready to marry your uncle. I trust he is ready to claim me as his?"

She watched as his smile smoothed into a straight line. His jaw flexed for a moment giving her some sense that he was not entirely ecstatic about the situation. Good. She had no intention of pretending this was a joyous occasion.

"Freya—"

"Ronan, how can you allow this to happen? What has gotten into you?" his mother asked stepping up beside Freya and wrapping her arms around her middle. "He will kill her," she said.

"No. He will not."

"And what will you do to stop him?" Morag asked. "You've done nothing to prevent our capture, nor our ill treatment since we were brought here."

"Mother, now is not the time. You must trust me."

Heavy footsteps prevented him from saying anything further. Three armed guards rounded the corner. Ronan grabbed Freya's arm and tugged her forward.

"The other two must stay here," he said to the guards. "See that no one goes in or comes out." He unsheathed his dirk and pressed the tip to one of the guard's necks. "On pain of death to you and everyone you have ever held dear, do you understand me?"

"Aye, my lord. We understand. We pledged our fealty to you and you may trust in it."

"Very well." He turned back to his mother and sister. "Listen to me. Do not attempt to leave this chamber. I will come for you when I can. You will be safest here. Do you understand me?"

Freya looked over her shoulder to see Morag and Muren nod and slip back into the chamber.

Ronan pointed the tip of his blade at all three of the guards again. "No one! Is that understood?"

When they nodded and took position outside the door, Ronan led her forward and toward the hallway leading to the stairs.

"Ronan, must you be so cruel?"

He stopped then and pulled her into an alcove and behind a curtain. Cupping her face in his hands he gazed deep into her eyes.

"You must trust me, Freya. No harm will come to you. Please, believe me."

"No, Ronan. I do not understand. I—"

More boots sounded from just beyond their position. Ronan leaned down and placed his lips to hers. "Hush," he said against her mouth.

Had she not been so concerned about the origin of the footsteps, she would have bitten his bottom lip right off. She hardly breathed until the heavy booted footfalls faded. When Ronan released her she shoved him away.

"Do not ever touch me again," she said, seething.

He took her elbow again and drew her forward. When she tried slipping from his grasp, his fingers held fast, unrelenting.

"I know you are angry with me, and you have every right to be."

"You have no idea how I feel. You vowed to protect us, yet you bring me into the belly of the beast, to await his ravishing. I know you do not care for me, but I had no idea you loathed me so much that you would see me abused in the manner in which he intends. You are as bad as he is."

That comment brought him up. He turned her so that she had

no choice but to look at him. "You have no idea how many times I have wondered just that over the past days." He leaned in close to her. "You will not be harmed, Freya. You may never wish to look upon me after today, but if you ever held any feeling for me in the past, I swear on it that you will not come to harm."

"As soon as I am able, I will leave this godforsaken place and you behind with a smile on my face. You are right, I will never want to see you again once this is all over with."

"So be it." He dragged her forward again.

Freya had to practically run to keep up with him. He led her out of the castle and to the side entrance of the chapel. She had to fight to keep her guts in their place and steady her breath when they stopped just outside.

"Keep your courage, Freya," Ronan said. "For just a little while longer and all will be well. Trust me."

"I do not trust you, nor any other Sutherland I have ever encountered. No wonder your mother left your father. My only regret now is that I let Rorie MacKenzie go. His loyalty was never in question. I wish I had never met you!"

She watched as a pained expression crossed his face. "You do not mean that." He shook his head. "What we have is real and you know it. You may not be able to see it today, but you will in time."

"The only thing I want to see of you and your kind is your back." She was more than ready to take his dagger and gut him with it. Him and his false words. "I despise you, Ronan Sutherland."

* * *

Freya jerked out of his hold and rushed into the chapel. He could not blame her for her anger, but it killed him to know he had lost her forever. At least she would live. She would take the vibrant part of his soul with her, but she would live.

Ronan entered the chapel to find Alexander holding Freya's arm and directing her to the bishop. He stepped inside and glanced around to ensure all was in order. Looking down toward the main entrance, he spied Neville and nodded. Thankfully, he had returned with good news just after Ronan had left the falconry. Fergus was alive. The MacKay's were at full strength and twice the army Alexander expected would be on the doorstep at any moment.

He had asked Neville to keep to the shadows so that Freya would not see him. The plan would run smoother if she were not alerted. Alexander had a clever eye for noticing changes in demeanour, Ronan had witnessed that enough times over the last two days. If he thought anything was out of order with Freya, he would suspect something was amiss. As it was, her not knowing how close she was to being saved made her performance more convincing. And Ronan needed Alexander's attentions on her and nothing else.

Ronan had accepted that even if the ceremony was concluded, they would never consummate the marriage. Ronan would die before he let that happen.

He moved to stand beside Alexander and waited for the ceremony to begin.

Alexander turned to him with a smirk that made Ronan bite the inside of his jaw. "I am pleased you were able to get her here with little trouble," he said. Then, leaning close so that only Ronan could hear, he added, "Though I doubt she will admit it, secretly I believe she is looking forward to our wedding night."

Ronan swallowed the bile that had risen in his throat and worked to show no expression. His gaze flicked to Freya whose cheeks had flushed full crimson. She had heard the comment.

"I am sure you are right, Uncle. Her wedding night will be one to remember."

Freya gasped and her eyes filled with tears.

I will never let him touch you. Just hold on a little longer. Ronan shouted the message in his mind, praying some spiritual being would carry it to hers.

A moment later, her head shot up and her brows drew tight. She masked her expression and quickly looked down again when Alexander turned toward her.

"Are we ready to proceed?" Bishop Strathbrock asked.

He was not so good at keeping a calm demeanour and the result of his nervous energy was in the form of sweat beads forming on his brow and upper lip. He swiped at it frequently and had practically soaked through the front of his robes.

"Are you unwell, your grace?" Alexander asked.

The bishop jumped. "Naught but a fever, my lord." His gaze darted to Ronan and back again.

Alexander turned to Ronan with raised eyebrows and smirked. "Well then, let us proceed, shall we?"

Alexander took Freya's hand. Ronan's gaze flicked down toward it and noticed her tremble. *Soon, my love. Very soon now.*

The bishop rushed through the vows. Though it was pure torture to watch the woman he loved marry another, it would be worse to have it dragged out.

Before the bishop could conclude the ceremony, a vibration shook the chapel. It rumbled through his body and into Ronan's chest. The sound escalated until the rumble became loud enough that the bishop's attention was drawn toward the windows.

Alexander released Freya's hand at the sound of the door bursting open. Ronan looked back to see one of his guard rush through.

"My lord, an army approaches."

Alexander strode toward him, unsheathing his broadsword. "MacKenzies? How many?"

The guard nodded. "MacKay too by the looks of it," he said. "Possibly other clans as well. There are too many to count."

Alexander halted mid-stride and turned back toward Freya. Ronan did not move toward her though he longed to. He just needed Alexander to take the last steps out of the chapel and his plan could come into play.

Alexander raised his sword and pointed it at Freya. "Go with the bishop to your chamber and stay there until I come for you." He then pointed the sword at the bishop. "Go now! Come Ronan, you are a foolish lad to be unarmed. Go quickly to the armoury and meet me out front. Today is the day we begin your reign over the Highlands."

Five heartbeats later he was gone. Neville slipped out from his hiding place and bolted the door from the inside.

Ronan heard Freya gasp beside him. "Neville? You are here?"

Neville came forward and gathered her into his arms. "Aye love, and I come to tell you that your brother is alive and well and fighting outside."

Freya doubled over and cried out. "Fergus is alive?"

Ronan could not imagine how much more she could take. This glad news on the cusp of escaping the worst fate imaginable was bound to send even the strongest mind into turmoil. She swayed and he knew what was coming. Ronan caught her just as her legs buckled.

CHAPTER SEVENTEEN

Freya blinked several times to get her bearings. The stone sculptures topping pillars inside the chapel spun around her and voices were muted. It took her several tries before her eyes came fully open and she was able to place what had happened. Strong arms held her. Ronan.

She jerked out of his grasp only to stumble, causing him to grab for her again. Once she was steady, he released her and held his hands up, palms out.

"Do not touch me!"

"Freya, you must let me help you."

She backed up until she was closer to Neville and said, "I do not need your help. My brother is outside and he will offer me all the protection I could ever need. It is too bad I did not have the sense to heed him about you in the past."

His brows drew tight and he frowned. "You do not mean that, Freya. You have been through much in the past few days. I understand you are angry, but all was necessary to make Alexander believe I had sided with him so that I could discover his plans and use them against him."

"I do not believe any filthy word spewing from your lips." She turned to Neville. "Please, get me out of here."

Neville shook his head. "That would not be wise, Freya. Until this is over, you are not going anywhere near Alexander Sutherland, in fact—"

Her belly dropped. She did not like the sound of that. "What?"

"Fergus suggested you and Ronan marry as soon as possible so

145

that Sutherland would not be able to claim you. At least that way, he could not place that kind of mark on you."

No. "No!"

"Aye, lass, 'tis the only way."

"No, there must be another way."

"While there are thousands of men out there fighting right now, there is no way to know if we will prevail. If Sutherland is victorious, he will come back for you. Marrying Ronan now is the only way you can be protected."

"Your grace," Ronan began, "if a couple had previously engaged in an intimate act and then married. Would the marriage be considered consummated?"

"It would, my lord. But I do not see how that is a relevant question."

Freya's heart sank. If she married Ronan, she would not have to bed him in order for the marriage to be valid. It would be binding and unbreakable. There was no way she could go through with it. Not now. Not after all he had done, even if he had done it for his so called right reasons. She had been through hell and back, and he was the cause.

"It is a relevant question, your grace, because Freya and I have the blessing of her brother and guardian and it just so happens that we—"

"Ronan!" she said. Her cheeks heated as though touched by flame. She glanced at the bishop and noted his rounded eyes and that his mouth had formed a circle.

"If this is true, then I must marry you right away before your souls endure any further harm."

Freya glared at Ronan. Thankfully, he did not look smug. His eyes had taken on a concerned expression but he still frowned. This was not the way she imagined marrying him way back when she thought they were meant for one another.

He reached out to her. She stared at his hand, hanging in mid-air. If she married him today, she would save her body from torture, but ensure her heart would never find peace.

How much had passed between them since that day in the

wood when they first met? He seemed so much older now than he did then. She too had matured from the young adventurous lass who had given herself so freely to him without care or consequence. *That* Freya would have longed for the day when circumstance allowed them to join their lives together forever. What had happened to her along the way? Did any of her remain?

A sudden pounding on the chapel door roused her back to the present. Her gaze flicked up to Ronan's.

"If I give you my hand, it does not mean I will ever give you my heart."

His lips set in a grim line. "I understand. We must do this now, Freya."

She lifted her hand as the pounding on the door increased and placed it in his. Together they turned to the bishop and he rushed through the vows. What seemed like seconds later, the bishop declared them husband and wife and Ronan's lips were on hers in a hard but searing kiss.

Freya blinked at him several times as he pulled away. A slight curl to his lips reminded her of the man she thought he was, the one with whom she had fallen so desperately in love. Was he still there? Would the old Freya fight for him?

"Come now, all of us," Ronan said, while moving to the side entrance, but not letting go of her hand. "We must find a safe place for the women and the bishop inside the castle."

The pounding continued as they slipped out the side door. They ducked back behind the chapel and onward through the dense brush until they arrived at the back of the castle.

The din of the fighting was almost unbearable. The roar of thousands of men, steel clanging against steel, and the stench of fresh blood was enough to make Freya's legs tremble. Though she did not fully trust or forgive him, she did not let go of Ronan's hand. He led the party to a set of narrow steps that led to an upstairs hallway. Creaking the door open, they moved quickly and quietly toward the main staircase, and onward to the third floor to where she had left Morag and Muren but an hour earlier.

When they turned the corner, her belly dropped when she

realized it was empty. If the three guards were gone, what had happened to Morag and Muren? She could not bear any more loss or heartache this day.

Ronan released her hand and practically ran to the chamber. He threw open the door and stood in the doorway staring inside. Freya caught up to him and peered in to find the guards sitting down looking like sheep to the slaughter and Morag pacing in front of them.

"What passes here?" he asked.

All four of them slipped inside and promptly closed the door.

"I am teaching these lads some manners," his mother said. "Just because they are soldiers does not mean they cannot be polite when asked a question."

They glanced at one another and then at Ronan with dumfounded expressions.

"And so you thought you'd bring them inside and lecture them instead of letting them perform the job for which they were brought here?" Ronan raised his hands in question.

For the first time, Freya glimpsed the undercurrent of his frustration. It softened her anger toward him. What if he really was trying to protect them all this time? He had placed them in awful positions in doing so, but what if she suspended her anger for one moment and allowed that he might have had the best intentions?

While that may be true, the unfortunate cost was her ability to trust him. And now she was bound to him for the rest of her life. Freya slumped onto the bed and stared at the wall. While Ronan and his mother bantered about the proper etiquette of guards outside a lady's door, Freya could not bring herself to get past the next moment, let alone what the future held for them both. Did he intend for her to live here with him or would he send her home to her brother? And did any of that even matter with a battle raging outside?

She moved to the window and gazed out over the ocean. The sight that beheld her made her gasp. "Ronan!"

He was by her side a heartbeat later, staring out through the window with his jaw set. "Christ's teeth! I must warn them." He turned to her.

His proximity heated her flesh. She was torn between meeting his scrutiny and looking at the dozens of ships about to make landfall. Reinforcements. This would be a bloody battle and there was no way to know who would emerge the victor.

"Freya, look at me."

Everything else fell away when he spoke her name. She squeezed her eyes shut and tried closing her heart to the sensations hearing her name on his lips brought, but she could not. Try as she might, she loved him now, and always would—him and no other.

Freya opened her eyes and turned her head. He lifted her chin so that she had to look up at him.

"I must go warn them."

"I know."

"I will return for you," he whispered.

She tried holding back, but a single tear escaped and slid down her cheek. Her emotions were a swirling vortex. She loved him, despised him, was furious with him, and wanted to bed him all at the same time, and she was ready to collapse with the weight of the burden.

He leaned down and brushed his lips across hers. "I love you, Freya. I always have. I always will. My beautiful, Freya, enchanting faerie from the wood. You stole my heart that day and I knew you would never return it."

His words made her heart squeeze tight. Air escaped her lungs in a desperate whoosh. The Ronan she had met that day, not quite a man full grown, had stolen her heart too. She wanted to tell him so, but the reminder choked her words.

"Can you ever love me again?"

"Ronan," she whispered.

He touched his forehead to hers. "I will return for you."

He brushed his lips across hers once more. A sudden surge of panic hit her as she realized he may never return. When she opened her mouth to speak, he took the opportunity to press his affections further.

Ronan swept his tongue inside and it quickly tangled with hers. It was as though no time had passed since they were last together at Tongue, stealing away in the secret chamber. Their bodies cared not that their minds had separated.

Wrapping her arms around his neck, she pulled him in tight and kissed him as though there would never be another opportunity. After several minutes, she finally pulled back to look into his eyes.

"I am still angry with you. I may always be angry with you."

He smiled and her heart broke. "When I return, you will let me begin all the ways I plan to make it up to you."

"Aye, I will. You will return."

He nodded. "I have a wife now. I have to return or else she will punish me. Perhaps even torture me."

His wife. Ronan's wife. She could not twist her mind around how much had happened in such a short time.

"Go now and Godspeed, Ronan. Please, be safe."

"I will, Freya. I love you."

"And I you, husband."

Her words drew a heartbreaking smile from him that had her heart pounding in her chest and other parts of her stirring to life. Consummation or not, if he did not leave soon she would drag him to the nearest empty chamber and finalize their wedding all over again.

Ronan broke from their embrace and then addressed his mother and sister. He gave instructions to his guards and the bishop, then left. He glanced back once toward her and winked—and then he was gone.

CHAPTER EIGHTEEN

Ronan's biggest challenge was to skirt around the battling Sutherlands to get to Fergus. With Neville tight to his heels, he crept along the outer wall of the castle, careful not to draw attention to either the fighting men ahead of them, or the reinforcements behind him.

They managed to secure weapons inside the castle so that they would not have to attempt going to the armoury. Thankfully, Dunrobin had always housed a grand weapons display in the great hall. He and Neville availed of his father's prized broadswords and dirks. They were now well equipped.

The din of battle pounded in his ears. Ronan's heart drummed together in time with the relentless clang of sword against sword. One life struggling against another. The warrior behind him, though aged, was strong and true. Ronan had heaved a sigh of relief when he encountered him earlier. And yet another when he learned that Fergus lived.

Ronan scanned his surroundings once again to plan his route. If he veered left, he would surely encounter the Sutherland army and risk capture. No good could come from it. Yet it was the fastest way to reach the MacKays and MacKenzies. Ronan tried brushing away thoughts of the men he would have to fight against today, only to rule once this was all over. In a matter of days, his uncle had undone the two years of hard work he had put into the clan. He was right back to where he had been with his father. With that realization came a certain clarity and determination.

Ronan recalled his outrage at his father's behaviour. His uncle's was worse, so why had he been less driven to stick a sword in his gullet? He wanted his uncle dead with every fibre in his soul. So, why did he hesitate?

"What is it?" Neville whispered.

"I am working out which route to take."

"There is only one logical option, lad."

Ronan sighed. Neville was right. If they went right they would have to work their way around the entire army and that could take hours. The only way was to the left and straight through.

"Are you ready for this?"

Neville looked at him and grinned. "Like you, I have someone waiting for me when all of this is over, and I do not plan to get myself killed and in trouble with her."

Ronan grinned. "So, you wish to court my mother, do you?"

"Aye, I believe I do."

"Well then, I guess we had better get this over with. If I let anything happen to you, I'll have to answer to her—no good can come from that."

Neville grinned. "We need to go fast and hard, lad."

"Aye. That we do." He pointed to a copse of trees just beyond the stables. "On my mark, we make a run for there. Are you ready?"

Neville nodded. Ronan held up three fingers and let them fall, one by one. When he brought his arm down he took off across the side gardens toward the stables.

Once out in the clearing, the back end of the fighting came into view. He did not risk taking the time to do more than glance, but in that one split second, saw blood spurting out from one man's neck. Friend or foe he could not tell. Again, he grappled with exactly who his enemies were in this battle.

Once they reached the stables, they ducked inside to remain undetected. Ronan was barely winded, but thought it wise to allow his breathing to slow some before moving forward again. One more sprint to the edge of the trees and they would be in the thick of it.

"If I fall or am taken, you must get to Fergus. Tell him where the others are and make him promise to keep all three safe." He grasped Neville's broad shoulder. "Do you understand?"

Neville nodded. "Aye. I understand. Now show me a man worth following."

Neville's words stuck a chord. All this time, he had focused on what he thought was wrong in a leader when he should have spent more energy on what was right, and show by doing. He drew in a deep breath.

Ronan turned toward the trees and sprinted as fast as his legs would allow. He ran as hard and fast as he could, until his lungs burned and his legs cramped. The battle raged all around him, beating on his senses as his blood pounded in his veins. Once he reached the end of the tree line, he stopped.

Hundreds of men engaged in battle just a few feet ahead. In the flash of a moment, an axe flew at his head, and a large screaming and barely clad Highlander raced toward him. He then realized he still wore his tunic with the Sutherland crest on it. Daft! He could not do anything about it in that moment and so unsheathed his broadsword and waited for the warrior to reach him.

Ronan planted his feet wide and waited. He focused on nothing but the approaching man. Slowing his breathing, he never let his gaze fall from the man's eyes. They were wild from the frenzy of fighting. Ronan placed both hands on the hilt of his sword and swung it around in a circle and then grasped tight. When the man finally reached him, he dropped to one knee and slashed straight through his mid-section. His look of shock at the blood spurting from his middle was quickly replaced by savage anger. The great man roared and tried to come at Ronan again, but Ronan drove his blade into his heart before he could even raise his sword again.

Others had now taken notice of Ronan and worked their way toward him. Clearly they meant to avenge their clansman. Christ's blood, why had not he thought to remove his tunic? There was no time now. He glanced around, hoping Neville was within earshot to assist—he was not.

"I fight with you!" Ronan said to the now six approaching men. "I fight with Fergus Mackay and Kenneth MacKenzie!"

They appeared not to hear him so he shouted it again. One of them grinned. Oh, they had heard him—they just did not care. Ronan raised his sword to attack just as a loud bang filled the air. A second later, his world went black.

* * *

Ronan squeezed his eyes shut against the pain shooting through his head. The light was too bright so he blinked several times before he could focus. A blurred shape moved around him and voices taunted his muddled mind. He tried sitting up, wincing as the pain in his head intensified.

A strong arm pushed him back down followed by a rapid tsking. "Tell me why I should let you live?"

Fergus. Thank God. Ronan opened his eyes despite the pain, and worked hard to focus on the man who sat beside him.

"You are a sight for sore eyes," Ronan said as best as he could with a dry throat.

"Am I? Well, lad you have a funny way of showing it by killing one of my best new warriors."

"That could not be helped. He saw me trying to get through the lines and mistook me for one loyal to my uncle."

Fergus jabbed his finger into Ronan's chest. "I can see why. Tell me, Ronan. Do you play both sides?"

"No." He replied without hesitation. "I had to wear this tunic to stay close to my uncle. I was somewhat preoccupied this morning and did not think to remove it before attempting to find you."

"Aye, fortunately for you, Neville has filled me in on the details." To Ronan's great relief, Fergus reached out his arm. Ronan eagerly grasped it and Fergus drew him upward to sitting.

They sat inside a canvas tent. The sound of fighting had ceased. A truce? Not possible. A standoff then? Fergus looked between Ronan and the tent entrance . "Both sides retreated at sundown. We both lost many men today. I await Sutherland's terms. Oh, and by the way, you have Neville to thank for that lump on your head. If it weren't for his quick thinking, you would not be here right now."

Fergus's matter-of-fact statement made Ronan swallow hard.

He did not doubt it. Fergus was known as a ferocious warrior and personally oversaw the training of all those who served under him.

"I thought you were dead."

"Aye. I thought so too." Fergus spooned steaming broth into a wooden bowl and passed it to Ronan.

He took the bowl and put it to his lips, drinking deeply. The briny liquid soothed his dried throat. When Fergus offered him bread, Ronan shook his head. The broth was soothing, but he had no stomach for anything heavier.

"Tell me how you survived?"

Fergus laughed and shook his head. "It appears my healer is very good at what she does. She packed me full of yarrow and then lectured me until I had no choice but rally my forces and catch up with the MacKenzies. Neville tells me Freya is unharmed."

"Aye, she is unharmed. She will be angry with me for the rest of her days, but she lives and has at least some protection from Alexander. Fergus, we need to get them out. I could not risk exposing them during the battle, but I do not want them left inside that castle for him to find. I have told the guards to keep moving them to a different chamber every few hours, but it is only a matter of time before they are found."

"Aye, you are right. Sutherland has many men. Far more than we anticipated. We can only hold him off for so long. Sinclair and MacIntosh join us on the morrow."

"Good. I had sent word to the Stewart King as well, warning of Alexander's intentions."

Fergus's brows shot up. "You sent word to the king? I would give all that I own to have witnessed his reaction to that, considering your clan's past dealings with him."

Ronan grinned. His father had partnered with the MacDonalds two years ago to plot against the king using the MacKay and MacKenzie clans as bait.

"Indeed. I managed to win back your trust, though."

"That you did, Ronan. Though I have to admit, I struggle with it. There was a time I would have had my blade inside your heart without blinking. You may thank my sister for that change in opinion."

"And now, I do not believe she will ever forgive me, though I will have to spend the rest of our lives making up for it."

"I trust you are willing to give it your best effort."

Ronan laughed. "Aye, I will that. I am certain she will make me suffer as long as possible. Still, Fergus, you have my word, I did everything I could to get close to Alexander and protect her at the same time."

Fergus's brows drew tight. "Did he harm her?"

"No. I had to let them both believe in my indifference to her in order to glean as much information from him as possible."

"That makes sense. So, why is she angry with you? Because you pretended indifference?"

"It is a little more complicated than that. You see, he was convinced there was something between us."

"A very perceptive man."

"Aye, he is that. And so in order to draw me out, he claimed he would marry her. I could not challenge him on it because he would have known I cared for her and used her against me in the worst possible way."

"So, she thought you had abandoned her."

"Aye, she did. He told her the vile things he planned to do with her and I could offer no comfort or outward display of protection."

"Yet you secretly plotted with Neville to get word to MacKenzie and me."

"Aye."

Fergus clasped his shoulder. "You might need a fair bit of luck on your side if you are to ever win back her trust, lad. My sister is a warrior when it comes to her beliefs. If she feels you have betrayed her, I fear there is little to be done but give her time and prove your valour to her every single day. She may never commit to you, Ronan. You must keep this in your mind."

He did not know. "Did Neville not tell you?"

"Tell me what?"

"The complications do not end with Freya being angry with me, Fergus. 'Tis a good thing you did not kill me as you would have killed your own kin."

Fergus's brows drew together and then a grin spread across his face. "How on earth did you get her to marry you?"

Ronan explained the scene in the chapel in detail. "Opportunity arose and I leapt at it. She may hold on to her anger as long as she wants. But tonight she will not have to endure that man's sick fantasies."

"You will always have my gratitude for what you have done, Ronan. We are truly allies now as clans, and as family."

Ronan drew a great breath. "That is very good to hear, Fergus, for I fear this is just beginning. I have yet to share all I have learned about his plans. And believe me when I say they are extensive. We have a lot of work to do."

Fergus nodded and turned toward the tent entrance. "Andrew!".

A young man entered the tent a moment later. "Fetch the MacKenzie. Tell him Ronan is awake and has much to tell."

"Aye, Fergus."

Fergus turned back to Ronan. "When Neville brought you here, he said you had gleaned much from your uncle that would affect how we proceed. I presume he means you sending word to the king?"

"Aye, that. But also the ships he intends to send to Edinburgh. Fergus, he plans to take the entire country. Even my father was not that mad."

"Your father was that mad, Ronan. He just did not have the resources your uncle does. He was too busy taunting me to reach outside his realm to expand his claim. Your uncle has had ten years to build his. He is a formidable enemy. And one we must not underestimate."

"By now, he will know I am not in the castle and will have gone hunting for Freya." Ronan placed his head in his hands. "I should have taken her with me. I should have taken them all with me."

"Steady, lad. You would not have made it here with others in tow. 'Tis about time you shared this burden you carry. I know It has been hard for you to keep your sanity when nothing but madness has surrounded you your whole life. Truth be told, I do not know how you have managed it."

"I often wonder the same thing myself, Fergus. Watching Alexander taunt Freya made me question myself."

"And question yourself you should. Always. We must always know who we are in here." Fergus poked a spot on Ronan's chest over his heart. "You are a good man, Ronan Sutherland. Believe it."

CHAPTER NINETEEN

Freya pressed her ear to the door and waited with her hand held out to the others behind her. She had been certain she heard footsteps. The past few hours had been pure hell, waiting to learn anything about what was going on outside. The chambers they occupied were in the back of the castle, and all the fighting was around the front.

Once the sun began setting, the fighting had ceased and she was desperate to learn something, anything, about what had happened. Muren and Morag had kept themselves occupied by praying with the bishop. Freya tried staying as far away from him as possible.

At first, he insisted she confess all her sins right then and there in front of everyone, but she had no intention of doing that. It was one thing to admit all that had transpired between her and Ronan before their marriage, but she certainly would not allow anyone else to hear it all besides the bishop.

They had changed chambers three times since the sound of battle ceased. She prayed if they kept moving, they would avoid detection and remain out of Sutherland's grasp.

"Shhhh!" she said. "I hear footsteps. For certain this time."

One of the guards came up beside her and pressed his ear to the door. His gazed flicked to the wall in concentration and then down to her. He nodded. They had to find a way out of this chamber or else they would surely be found. She had been disappointed that none of the chambers on this level of the castle appeared to have hidden passageways. Their escape would have been so much easier had they existed.

"We must wait until they pass before we leave," he said.

Freya jerked back from the door when the sound of doors opening and closing reached her ears. They were checking the chambers! Oh, Lord, they would be found and then what? If Sutherland learned she had married Ronan, would that really stop him from torturing or killing her? And what of Muren and Morag? Muren was the next likely target for female excitement since she was most definitely not attached to anyone.

Freya shoved Morag and Muren under the bed. The bishop would be more difficult to hide in his frail state and so she made him stand in the corner behind a curtain. The guards had taken up post on either side of the door. Freya joined the other women under the bed. She felt ridiculous, but their hiding was necessary.

Another door opened and another closed. Two more. Closer this time. Whoever looked inside was not taking time to look under beds so her plan just might work. She prayed the guards did not feel the need to be heroic and do something foolish like to try capturing whoever eventually opened their door.

Another door opened. Another closed.

Freya worked to slow her breathing and calm down, and as the search drew closer, the more the butterflies in her belly fluttered. She glanced to her left to where Morag and Muren huddled. Both had their hands over their mouths to prevent any sudden noise of fright from escaping. Good idea. Freya did the same, though she did not expect to start screaming. Hysterical laughing maybe, but not screaming. She was way past that point.

The footsteps stopped outside their chamber. From underneath the door, Freya spied two dark streaks interrupting the light from the torches in the hallway.

The latch lifted and she held her breath. "We've already looked in the chambers down here," a gruff voice said. "They're not on this level."

"Are you sure? I, for one, do not wish to face his lordship empty-handed."

"Nor I, which is why I have no intention of looking in the same places twice."

Freya prayed hard the man whose hand held the latch listened to his partner.

Shuffling beside her drew her attention. She looked over and noticed in the dim light that Morag now held both her hands over Muren's mouth. What was wrong with her? They were almost out of this mess. Freya placed her finger to her lips to impress the need for silence upon them. But just then, she felt something brush by her other hand and she jumped a little. Flicking her hand, she batted the tiny furry creature away. Nothing but a small rodent. Certainly not worth risking their capture. She glared hard at Muren who seemed to settle right away.

"Did you hear something?" one of the guards outside asked.

"No. I did not," another said. "Now, come on. We have to search the third floor yet before we can eat."

"Very well," the other said.

The latch clicked back into place and the footsteps quickly moved away.

Freya waited for a long while before she dared move out from underneath the bed. When she did, it appeared to be the signal for everyone else to move as well. She heaved a sigh of relief.

"We cannot stay here," one of the guards said. "When Sutherland learns his men came up empty, he will order the castle searched again. And this time he will send more men and we will have no way to escape."

Freya put her hands on her hips. "And just where do you suggest we go?"

The bishop came up beside her then. "I know where we can go," he said.

She turned toward him and waited. "Well?"

"Where he left us."

"The chapel? But it is just an open building. There are no chambers to hide in."

"There are indeed very good places to hide in the chapel," he said. "Are you not aware of the crypt?"

"I am not, and while that does sound like a very good hiding place, what makes you think they will not look there?"

"Because I do not believe the earl knows of its existence. He has only been back here a few weeks. I have been here the whole time and to my knowledge the only time he entered that chapel was earlier today when he intended to marry you."

A glimmer of hope welled inside her for the first time in days.

"If that is so, then how do you propose we get from here to there? We've already established this castle has no hidden passageways."

The bishop smiled. "My child, every castle has hidden passageways. You just need to know where to look." He wrapped his arm around her shoulder. "They can be accessed through the hallways on the second level. The chambers on the third level are all connected to them. They were intended for ease of escape during attack and since the family always sleeps on the third floor here, that is where they originate."

"Who then, would have slept on the second floor?" Freya asked.

"Guests."

"Clearly not as important as family."

"Clearly," he said.

"How is it you know so much about this castle, your grace?" she asked.

He smiled. "I was not always a bishop, you know. At one time, I was but a mere priest who served a family."

"This family?"

"Aye. This family. But that was many years ago. I pray I remember which passageway leads to the outside."

"Where do the others lead?"

"Oh, to the dungeon."

His tone left her wondering if he were not toying with them and leading them directly to Sutherland. She turned to the guards. Surely, they knew the castle as well as the bishop.

"Do you know of these passageways?" she asked them. "And the crypt in the chapel?"

They all shook their heads. "This is the first time we have been in the castle," the tallest one said. "Ronan recruited us yesterday."

"Yesterday? What do you mean? Where were you before yesterday?"

They shuffled and glanced at one another before he spoke. "We are crofters, my lady."

She gasped. "Have either of you held a sword before yesterday?"

"No, not really," he said with a sheepish smile.

"And all this time you did not think to tell me you had little experience?" Dear God in Heaven, why would Ronan leave them in such inadequate hands?

"He said he valued our loyalty more than our skill. Do not worry, my lady. We will defend you with our lives."

Freya shook her head. As if she did not have enough to worry about. At least he could have left her with a weapon.

"Show me the weapons you carry."

They quickly showed her the swords sheathed at their sides, and the two dirks shoved in each boot.

"Pass me your extra dirks."

They glanced at one another again.

Freya beckoned them with her hand. "Now, please. I know how to use a sword and a dirk as do Morag and Muren. We will be armed as well and thus increase the threat of our party."

"I had not thought of that," the tallest guard said.

"What is your name?"

"I am called Hamish," he said.

"Malcolm."

"Niall."

"Well then Hamish, Malcolm, and Niall, I am giving you new orders. Your first priority is the bishop. He alone knows the way to the crypt and so we must get him there. If either of us falls, leave us. Do you understand? We must get as many of us there as possible, but we may very well encounter Sutherland's guards who know a great deal more about fighting than any of us."

"Understood," they said in unison.

Understood indeed. Freya thanked God and her brother for her limited training. Fergus's wife, Nessia, was an expert bow hunter and had taught Freya some of her technique, but circumstance and opportunity did not allow for much practice time. She had, however, spent plenty of time in the armoury feeling out the weight and balance of the dirks. Some of them were small enough to easily conceal, but would do little real damage. Her favourite kind was like the one she held now, with a light handle, stubby cross guards, and long, pointed blade. She could do some damage with this if she needed to.

"Are you ready, your grace?"

He turned to her with fear in his eyes. His gaze flicked down to the blade in her hand and then back up to meet hers.

"When we reach the chapel, Lady Sutherland, I believe you and I need to spend some time together confessing your many sins."

She nearly choked on that. Many sins indeed. How long did he have? Then again, they might be hidden in the crypt for days. That would probably be enough time.

She held her hand out toward the door. Hamish stepped in front and slowly opened the door to peer outside. "After you, your grace."

He frowned at her and took his place behind Hamish. Freya lined up Morag and Muren, then Malcolm, herself, and then Niall to follow from the rear.

They left the chamber, careful to close the door quietly behind them and crept against the stone walls. The bishop felt his way along the wall with his hands, looking for a latch of some sort, Freya supposed.

They were so exposed out here that she prayed he would find it soon. Luckily, and before too long he stopped by the side of an alcove. The left side that dipped toward the window had one stone that looked odd. The bishop pressed it and the wall revealed a door that pushed in. Freya's heart soared.

They slipped in one by one and then closed the heavy stone door behind them. The air was damp and stale inside, and there was no light at all. All they could do was shuffle along until they reached the stairs and feel their way down with careful steps.

Freya bumped into Malcolm after about thirty steps.

"Shhhh," she said.

"I did not say anything."

"Shhhh anyway," she said.

A straight line of light appeared ahead. It was connected to a vertical one that told her they had found a door. The scraping sound of stone grated on her frayed nerves. She never did like hide and seek, even as a child. Though the stakes in this game were certainly much higher.

One by one, they left the passageway. When it was Freya's turn, she discovered that they had managed to find their way outside. She waited until Niall pulled the door closed behind him and then turned back to the group. The chapel was across the side garden and barely visible in the pale moonlight. A light layer of mist hung in the air, though the moonlight still shone through illuminating the courtyard. They had to move quickly or they would definitely be spotted.

They took turns dashing across until finally it was Freya's turn. She turned back to Niall and nodded. "Wait until I am across then run as fast as you can."

"I will. Hurry, my lady."

Freya sucked in a deep breath and lifted her gown almost up to her knees. She ran like she had never run before. The grounds had been groomed and so the going was easy, but by the time she reached the chapel, she was quite winded. The rest of the party were there and so she turned back to wait for Niall.

She caught movement to the right and realized there were two men walking toward Niall's location. Oh no! If he moved at all, he would be seen!

She turned back to the others. "Get everyone inside now," she whispered as loud as she dared.

Freya turned back to the courtyard and scanned the area. She could not see the two men or Niall. Dammit! Had they taken him? How long could she afford to remain outside to wait for him. Long moments passed while she continued scanning the wall, the trees, and the lawn.

A hand closed firmly over her mouth and a strong arm crossed over her chest and dragged her back. Her scream died in her throat as the hand held her mouth tighter.

"Freya, it is me, Niall," he said in her ear.

Oh, thank God!

"I am going to release you now. Do not scream."

She nodded.

Niall released her and she turned back to him, relieved. She grabbed his hands and dragged him inside the chapel.

Once the door was shut, the bishop led them to the altar. He motioned for the men to move the platform aside and when they did, it revealed a stairwell. Freya gasped. It looked like the stairway to Hell, such pitch black as it was.

Without any better option, they followed the bishop down into the crypt and pulled the platform back in place.

They were only down a few steps when they heard the door to the chapel burst open. They all stopped dead in their tracks as Alexander Sutherland's voice boomed and bounced off the stone walls of the chapel.

"Where the devil is she? I left her here and by Christ I want her found! Now!"

Freya's heart pounded wildly as he cursed like she had never heard another person curse in her life.

"I want the castle scoured again!" he said. "And again! And again! Until she is found and brought to me!"

He let out a mighty growl then, causing Freya's belly to lurch. She had so narrowly escaped spending the night in his bed at his torturous whims. She fought for control as her body quaked. His mere presence was enough to shake her to the core. Niall placed his hand on her shoulder and squeezed. She placed her hand over his in thanks.

He might not be a trained warrior, but she believed him, all of them, when they said they would be loyal and that no harm would come to them.

"Freya MacKay! Where are you? When I find you I swear you will regret the day you ran from me! Do you hear me? I will make you pay and pay and pay for making me wait!"

Freya doubled over from fear that she was about to let her terror win this time. She clamped her hands over her mouth and squeezed her eyes tight.

Please, God, don't let him find me. Please, oh, please!

Footsteps shuffled all around the altar above. They could not move any farther below for fear they might be heard. The monster was so close he sometimes blocked the thin shaft of light that came in from the crack between the platform and the floor.

Niall's hands settled on her shoulders and he pulled her back up and close to him. For a moment, she allowed him to comfort her and help quell her shaking body.

"She is not here, my lord," a voice said from somewhere a little farther away.

"I know that, you daft idiot! Do not test my patience, Allain. I thought you said you could deliver them both to me. You have done nothing I find of value. Perhaps I should take my frustration out on you this evening. Would you like that?"

"No, my lord. I would not like that. Please, tell me what it is you wish me to do."

"I wish you to find Freya MacKay!"

"As is your wish, my lord," he said.

His boot steps became fainter with each one until Freya heard the door slam.

"I will find you, Freya. And, oh, the delicious punishment you will receive when I do." His boot steps clipped until they, too, faded and the door to the chapel slammed shut.

CHAPTER TWENTY

"Is he mad or brilliant?" Kenneth MacKenzie asked.

"Perhaps a little of both," Ronan said.

"That is why we could not punch through the lines," Fergus said.

Ronan nodded. "And those same reinforcements will head back to their ships and sail straight to Edinburgh if they are not stopped." Ronan paced the tent. "I sent Father Sinclair five days ago. He would have made it to Edinburgh by now, but even if he rode hard, will not return here for another day or so. It will still take many days before the king's army can get here. How long can we last?"

"We can go as long as we have men, but we suffered great losses today. As did they. There are only so many men available to fight," Fergus said. "If Sinclair and MacIntosh arrive tomorrow, we can breathe a little easier, though we are by no means anywhere near a resolution."

Ronan weighed their options. The reinforcements prevented them from taking the castle. The extra two thousand men tipped the scaled heavily in Sutherland's favour, and if they did not get help soon, they would not see their desired end to this confrontation.

The tent flap opened and a startled Father Sinclair entered. Ronan went to him immediately and grasped his shoulders.

"Surely, there was never a happier sight to a man's eyes."

Father Sinclair grimaced. "You may want to save your praise until you hear of the news I bring. Some good, and some very bad."

Ronan brought him forward and offered him a seat and a goblet of ale.

"Father Sinclair, this is Fergus MacKay, and Kenneth and Rorie

MacKenzie. They are aware of your quest." Ronan placed his hand on the father's shoulders. "Catch your breath, Father, and tell us everything. We are approaching desperation so we will be very grateful for even a small amount of good news."

He shook his head. "The king is in Inverness. It was only by pure chance I discovered it. It is not as I had hoped. I saw the king's council and gave them the bishop's letter. They made me wait for hours until I was finally granted an audience." He took a deep draught of the ale and emptied the goblet. Ronan promptly refilled it.

"Aye? And did he reverse the writ?"

"Not at first. It was not until I spoke with him and convinced him of the damage your uncle had caused and intended to cause that his demeanour changed. In short, he has agreed to reverse the writ and reinstate you as Earl."

Father Sinclair reached into his robes and pulled out a piece of parchment with the king's seal stamped in red wax upon it. Ronan accepted it and stared at it. Once again, the balance of power came down to a piece of parchment.

"There is more," Father Sinclair said. "It appears the king took your uncle's behaviour personally and he is amassing his army to travel north."

Ronan's head snapped up. "That is good; we need his numbers."

"No, Ronan. He is not coming here to help destroy your uncle's army. He is coming here so that you," Father Sinclair pointed at Ronan, and then each of Fergus and MacKenzie, "and you, and you, swear fealty to him and him alone. He said he will claim any clan whose chief does not swear their immediate and absolute allegiance to him."

Fergus was on his feet in a second. "He cannot do that. Without power we have no way to protect those under our banner!"

MacKenzie stood next. "'Tis a mad king he is. How does he expect us to rule through him when he is hundreds of miles away?"

Ronan shook his head. They were stuck in the middle between an over-ambitious man who wanted power and another who had power and wanted more.

"I fear 'tis the clans caught in the middle who will lose the most in the coming days," Ronan said. "Did he say when he would arrive, Father?"

"Aye, he said in a sennight. That was three days ago. You have some time to plan, but not much."

Ronan's mind raced while Fergus and MacKenzie cursed the king. They had all attended Parliament a few years back when the king had introduced his then new laws on authoritative reform. It had ended in a bloody battle and this encounter would be no different. The only way for them to succeed in keeping some part of their power, the part that helped them protect what was theirs, was to ban together—all of them.

A clan uprising of that size and scope had not been attempted in many years. Sutherland, MacKay, and MacKenzie would need commitments from Ross, Munro, Sinclair, MacIntosh, and even MacDonald. Christ, that was a path he did not want to take. The MacDonalds of the Isles were very clear they would do anything to remove this king from his throne. The battle had raged between the Stewart and the MacDonald over the past few years. Ronan would have to engage the men after all this time, and he would rather stick thistles under their eyelids.

"Fergus, we need everyone in on this," Ronan said quietly.

Fergus stopped and turned to him, frowning. He drew a great breath and let it out in a whoosh. Grimacing, he swiped his hand down across his face and stared hard at Ronan. He had heard Fergus sometimes referred to as The Hawk because of that stare, and he saw now that it was well earned.

"Like who?"

"Like everyone. MacDonalds even."

"MacDonalds will jump at the chance to challenge the king," MacKenzie said.

"Aye, they will. But they harbour ill favour for our Ronan here, since he did not see the plot through that he and Ronan's father had put into place to destroy us and usurp the king. Add that the man thinks I murdered his sister, and he wants MacKenzie's lands. I would say we three are not among his most favoured people."

"All that being true, the man has an army that could rival yours, Fergus, and he will not stand for the Stewart's tyranny," MacKenzie said.

Ronan took the time while they argued over whether or not MacDonald would join forces with them or slay them where they stood, to crack the seal on the parchment he held. He unfolded the letter and read down through.

It was finally his again. All of it. Signed. Sealed. Delivered. By the hand of the king, he was now Earl of Sutherland again, and chief of his clan. That meant the men who they battled against were his to command. The king would be here in four days. In the meantime, they had to do something about Alexander, and find a way to prevent more of his men from slaughter. Those men were in a worse state than Ronan at this point for they had no choice but listen to the man they thought was their commander. Christ, how did this whole business become such a mess?

"Before we make any final decisions, I believe we have a more immediate problem," Ronan said.

"And that being?" Fergus asked.

He waved the letter toward the man and said, "I am the Earl of Sutherland and chief of the clan. My men fight your men, and we need to put a stop to it."

"Jesus in Heaven."

"I will thank you not to blaspheme in my presence, Laird MacKay," Father Sinclair said.

"My apologies, Father," he said. "You must certainly understand the predicament we are in at the moment."

"I certainly do, however, I do not believe our Saviour had anything to do with it or would appreciate your calling him out on it."

Fergus stared at the man for a heartbeat before grinning. "You are right, Father. It will not happen again."

"See to it that it doesn't, Laird MacKay."

"Fergus."

Father Sinclair raised his brows and then nodded. "Fergus."

"What are we going to do?" MacKenzie asked.

Rorie who had been relatively quiet all evening now stood. The young man would have a commanding presence like his father when he aged a little more. His steely gaze showed his determination. Ronan found himself waiting to see what the young man had to say.

"We must approach this problem with logic," he said. "What stands in the way between where we are and what we want?"

Put like that, it was obvious.

"Alexander Sutherland."

"Exactly. If your uncle were not in the picture, you could reclaim the Sutherland portion of the army, and together we could drive the reinforcements back. It seems to me the first step is to dispose of your uncle."

Ronan grinned as Fergus and MacKenzie stared at Rorie who merely raised his eyebrows at them. "Well, 'tis true, is it not?"

MacKenzie slapped him hard on the shoulder. "You will make a find laird someday, lad."

"Aye," he said. "I will."

He certainly was not lacking in confidence, Ronan noted. But his words were the truth. The very first thing that needed to happen was removing Alexander from the equation. Then his men needed to pledge fealty or be disposed of, only then could they properly prepare for the king's arrival.

The tent flap raised again, allowing Neville entry. His face was drawn with concern.

"What is it?" Ronan asked.

"Our scouts say Sutherland and his men are scouring the grounds, but they could not tell what they sought."

Freya.

"What do you think, Neville?"

"I think your sister has escaped somehow and Sutherland is on the hunt for her. One of the men heard him yelling from the chapel but could not readily capture his words."

"We must get to her before he does," Ronan said. He was on his feet and heading toward the entrance before anyone else moved.

Fergus caught up with him and was tight to his heels as they left the tent. "I am not sure where to begin," he said.

"We begin with the closest structure, which is the stable and work toward the castle from there."

It was a plan. Good or bad, Ronan did not have time to care. It was the only one they had and he prayed to God that he and Fergus found her first.

* * *

The burning torch offered enough light for them to find a place on the floor that did not house someone's corpse. Freya had never liked visiting burial places and so being cooped up in one now was only bearable because the only other option was to face being put in her own burial box.

She glanced around to see how everyone else fared. They had been in the crypt for a few hours now. Their guards took turns walking up the steps toward the altar to listen for anyone, and though others had come back a couple of times, no one had figured out where they were yet.

Freya clasped her hands together. She was weary, hungry, and thirsty. They had not had opportunity to arrange provisions for their hideaway and opportunity would not present itself for many more hours to come. She swallowed hard on her parched throat. At least they were in good health. Well, most of them anyway. The bishop had taken to lying down in the corner. Morag had seen to him and suggested he get some rest. The man was well up in his years, though Freya supposed his ill health had more to do with too much mead rather than age.

Just then, Malcolm raced down into the lower chamber. "Someone's coming," he said. They all collectively moved to the inner chamber where they had to stand very close together to fit, but if whoever it was only came to the bottom of the steps with a torch, they would not be detected.

A small, delicate hand found hers and squeezed as the sound of scraping stone met their ears. The altar had been moved. They would be within the outer chamber in seconds! She squeezed the hand back and held her breath.

Footsteps descended and drew closer. Freya, standing behind the three guards could not see anything, but could hear whispers. There must be more than one person out there.

"They're not here," a voice said. That voice. She knew that voice! Fergus.

"Do not be so sure," a second voice said. Ronan!

Freya struggled to break through Hamish, Malcolm, and Niall's front line but unknowing her purpose, they held her back.

"Let me go!" she said.

"Freya?" Fergus called?

"I am here," she said and broke from their grasp. She emerged from the inner chamber to discover Ronan and Fergus standing in the middle of the outer chamber with torches. Freya flung herself into her brother's arms and held tight.

"You are alive," she whispered.

"Aye, lass," he said in her hair. "I am alive. You are safe now."

Behind her, she heard a similar reunion between Ronan and his mother and sister. Freya released Fergus and held his face in her hands. "Do not ever scare me like that again. Do you hear me?"

He chuckled. "I hear you and I promise not to ever scare you like that again."

"Good. Now can we please get out of here? This place is making me ill."

When she released Fergus, she found herself being swung around and warm lips pressed against hers. Ronan backed her away from the others and ravaged her mouth. Her mind battled with her body in that moment. She should be furious with him, but she was so relieved he had found her, she could only kiss him back. His tongue swept inside in search of hers. When they met and tangled, a surge of need washed over her. Ronan held her tight and branded her with his mouth, his fingers digging into the back of her neck and her hip, where he held her.

Finally, he broke free and gazed into her eyes. "Will you ever forgive me?"

"I do not know, Ronan. You ask so much of me."

"I know," he said. "I had no other choice. I had to find out what he was up to." She could almost feel the pain seeping through his voice.

"And you were willing to sacrifice me in order to learn those details; I understand it, I just don't know if I can forgive you for it."

He lowered his head and nodded once. "I understand. Will you come with me and let me protect you?"

"Aye. I will do that. You owe me that much."

He leaned toward her mouth once again, but she turned away. "We must make haste from this place, Ronan. The guards have come back every hour to check again, and if that is their schedule, they will return again soon."

"Very well," he said.

Freya detected the sadness in his voice. She would have liked to erase it, but she could not deny how she felt. While he might have thought his actions were for the greater good, the reality was he had played her like a pawn, and there were no guarantees how much abuse she might have suffered in the process.

They climbed the steps out of the crypt and returned the altar to its rightful place. Once outside, they raced to the stable, and then farther on without incident until they reached the camp. The bishop had some difficulty with the pace so the younger guards had carried him the last several yards.

Now in Fergus's tent, she could not sit still. She was restless and edgy from the past two days. Finally, Fergus stood in front of her and grasped her shoulders, forcing her to stop pacing and look up at him.

"You must settle, Freya. Come and have something to eat, and a cup or three of ale. You are safe from harm here. I know you have been through much, but you need to let your body and mind settle."

He was right, but it was easier said than done. She had been working so hard to survive for the past two days that it was not a simple matter of settling down. She accepted the cup of ale from her brother and downed it, nearly choking in the process when some of the liquid went down her wind pipe.

Ronan entered the tent then; his brows drew down when he saw her pacing.

"My sister and mother are secure in Neville's tent," he said. "Freya, are you unwell?"

"She is having difficulty finding calm after her ordeal," Fergus said. "I have seen it in the men after a fierce battle from time to time. They cannot calm their nerves and continually pace until they fall down from exhaustion. If you have any suggestions, I am all ears."

Ronan said nothing, but walked toward her. Freya's body seemed to jerk in all directions at once. The hairs on her body stood on end, and her mind raced, unwilling to accept that she was finally safe.

Ronan wrapped his arms around her and held her tight. Her body jerked an involuntary protest, but he held fast and hushed her quietly in her ear.

"I am here, lass," he whispered. "Shhhh."

He slowly rocked her back and forth until after what seemed like an age; her body began to calm. She opened her eyes to discover Fergus had made himself scarce and that she and Ronan stood alone in the middle of his tent.

She slid her arms around his waist and held on tight. He had contributed to what she was going through right now, so she felt it fitting he help fix it. He swayed with her for a long time, until her limbs ached. Finally, when she sagged against him, he swept her up and laid her on the furs that had been placed on the ground for her makeshift bed. Ronan turned her on her side and then curled in behind her. In her semi-awake state she did not have the strength to protest.

With his arms wrapped tightly around her, and his warm breath on the back of her neck, Freya drifted into a deep slumber.

CHAPTER TWENTY-ONE

Heavy mist crawled across the battlefield as Ronan surveyed the scene. His uncle had not attacked during the night, and had yet to gather this morning. Though it was only daybreak, Ronan would have expected an assembly of his men by now. Instead, all was quiet, and that did not sit well with him.

Fergus came up along-side, together with the MacKenzie and Rorie and a contingent of warriors.

"Ready, MacKenzie?" Ronan asked him.

"Aye, I am ready," Rorie said. "It will take us a day and a night to reach MacDonald. If he does not kill me on sight, I may have a chance to convince him to join our cause. Still, I believe I am the most logical choice, as you are needed here. The old laird is still imprisoned at Edinburgh, so 'tis his son, Angus, I'll have to deal with. Let us hope he is of a better temperament than his father and a little less lustful of our lands."

"Aye, let us hope. His father means to have them. I should be going with ye," Kenneth said.

Rorie shook his head. "No. If he sees you coming, he will not listen to a word you say. We both know I have a better chance of convincing the man, as he does not know me other than I am your son."

"This entire business is based on trusting one another, and the only way forward," Fergus said. "Angus appears to be of calmer nature than his father, and he has had to lead the clan in his father's absence these two years. I believe he will listen to you, Rorie."

Ronan shook his head. With enemies coming from all sides, how was he to push forward? Which brought forth another troubling thought.

"Fergus, the MacIntosh is expected here today. He will ally with us to get rid of my uncle, but how do you think he will react about the business with the king?"

"I trust MacIntosh more than any man I have ever met," Fergus said.

"Your loyalty is commendable, Fergus, but what will he do? You know as well as I that MacIntosh is a staunch supporter of the king and I need to have an understanding of how he will react if he learns we intend to challenge him."

Fergus drew a deep breath. MacIntosh was honourable, but could he be trusted with their cause? "I will speak with him when the time is right. We will secure his help to capture your uncle and push the reinforcements back to the lowlands, but leave the other business to me. Rorie must be back here within in two days, with or without MacDonald. Though I would prefer with."

Ronan nodded and turned toward Rorie. "God speed lad. I wish you luck and safe travels."

Rorie mounted his horse and grinned. "Good luck to you too, *lad*. I suspect you'll need it more than I."

Ronan smiled and watched Rorie and his men ride off. His gaze drifted back to the battlefield. Still no sign of Alexander. An uneasiness settled over him. The man was predictable in his unpredictability. If he was not here, it meant he had set forth another plan.

He returned to the tent and to where he had left Freya sleeping. She finally settled down and thankfully slept through the night. He lifted the tent flap and peered inside. She was curled up underneath furs exactly as he had left her.

He knelt beside her and brushed a flaming lock of hair from her face. Freya's cheeks were flushed. He placed the back of his hand on her forehead and winced when he touched too warm, clammy skin. She had been through much in the past days, the last thing she needed was an illness on top of it.

Ronan looked around the tent and spied a basin of water and cloths. He went to the water basin wrung out a cloth to place on her forehead. When he did, she stirred, her eyes fluttering before she opened them. Her glazed gaze concerned him. She blinked several times before focusing on him.

"Ronan? Where am I?" she asked.

"Hush, love. You are in Fergus's tent. We found you last eve and brought you back here."

"Your mother and sister?" she whispered as her eyes fluttered shut again.

"Perfectly fine. You needn't worry about anything, love. You are safe and I will not let anything happen to you."

His words seemed to spark something within her. Her eyes flew open and flashed toward him. She struggled to sit up but he held her shoulders down.

"Freya, you do not look well this morn. You must stay here and rest until your fever passes," he said.

"I am angry with you, Ronan, and I do not intend to stay in this tent with you any longer. Where is my brother?"

"He is outside with MacKenzie waiting for Sinclair and MacIntosh to arrive."

She pressed her lips into a straight line and turned her head away when he tried to place a fresh cool cloth on her head again.

He drew a deep sigh. He supposed he would have to endure her anger. He had brought it on himself and would have to find a way forward with her, despite her obvious disdain for him.

"Would you like me to fetch my mother and sister to tend to you?"

She turned her head toward him but would not meet his gaze. Freya nodded and turned away from him again.

"Very well." At the tent's entrance he looked back over his shoulder to find her watching him. "I will wait for you to forgive me, Freya. Even if it takes forever."

* * *

As the tent flap slid closed, Freya watched Ronan's shadow disappear. She closed her eyes to keep her tears from spilling. It was so hard staying angry with him, but her mind would not let her forgive so easily.

She was weary. She touched her fingers to her cheeks, concern filling her when she felt the heat rising from them. She sat up and reached for the basin of cool water to refresh the cloth. She placed one behind her neck and another on her forehead drinking in the soothing sensation.

A moment later, Morag and Muren entered the tent, their eyes wide.

"Freya!" Morag said, rushing over to her. "Ronan said you are ill."

"I seem to be running a fever."

Morag touched her cheeks, and forehead. "Aye, a fever indeed. Your eyes are glazed, lass. You'll need fluids and coriander."

"I am fine, Morag. Only a little weary is all."

Morag tsked. "Muren, take Neville with you and fetch some coriander from the garden and refill this basin. Hurry child, we must catch this before it gets worse." She pulled the furs back which caused an immediate shiver to race through Freya. Morag's eyes went wide. "My lord child, you are soaked through your clothes. We must get you out of these and into something clean and dry." She called to Muren as she was about to leave the tent. "Tell the men to stay away and bring me something for her to wear."

Freya was well aware there would be nothing in a camp for her to wear with an army of men, save for a linen shirt. Though, it was certainly better than nothing. Morag helped Freya sit up and removed her gown and shift. The cool air was not comforting against her hot skin, rather, it made her tremble and quake.

"I need to get some linens if there are any to be gotten," Morag said. "Cover yourself. I will be back in a moment."

Morag was not gone from the tent longer than two minutes when Ronan returned. His was face drawn tight and his eyes showed his concern.

"Freya, how do you fare?"

"Do not come closer," she said. "I am not decent. Your mother has taken my clothes and has gone to find fresh linens. Though, I do not know where she will find any in an army camp."

Ronan smiled. "You do not know my mother," he said. "If 'tis something to wear you need, you may have my shirt."

She shook her head. Wearing something that smelled of him would not help her resolve to remain angry with him.

"I insist, Freya."

Before she could protest, he had removed his tunic and was pulling his shirt over his head. Freya closed her eyes and turned away from him. If she opened them, he would be naked before her, and even in her vulnerable state, she could not resist him.

Her eyes flew wide open when she felt him tugging on her shoulders. "Ronan, what are you doing?"

He was trying to sit her up with one hand while putting the shirt over her head with the other. Her gaze flicked down over him to discover he had put his tunic back on. She sighed with relief, grabbing the shirt from him.

"I can do this," she said. "Please, turn your back."

His response was to raise one eyebrow. "Freya, I have seen your naked flesh many times." His voice was pitched low.

"Aye, at times when I was more valuable to you than a pawn, Ronan. Now turn around. You do not get to see me so again."

He frowned but did as she asked. "Ever?" He spoke so quietly, she questioned whether or not she had really heard him.

Freya pretended she did not hear, so did not respond. "I am done. You may turn around again."

When he did, his expression was strained. Like she had hurt him. Her chest tightened, but she needed to stay true to her beliefs in that his actions had been wrong.

"Are you in here bothering her when I asked you to stay away?" his mother said from the entrance.

Ronan's gaze flicked down over her frame again then he turned away. "I was just leaving."

Morag returned to her and began her ministrations. Over the next few hours, she forced various liquids into her. Freya drifted in and out of consciousness, only barely aware of what was happening outside. Morag would shush her each time she asked what was happening, only to say there was no battle.

Long after the sunset, Fergus entered the tent.

"How is she?" he asked Morag.

Freya lacked the strength to speak for herself, so kept her eyes closed.

"Her fever has broken, but she is exhausted. She is in no danger, Fergus, but will need to rest for a couple of days."

"Aye, we will be here for a few days yet," he said.

"What has happened? Where is Ronan?"

Fergus sighed heavily. "He is speaking with the MacIntosh about our plans to attack the castle on the morrow."

"So soon?"

"Aye. Sutherland needs to be removed immediately before he can cause more damage."

Freya wanted to ask about the plan, but could not get her mouth to form the words. She had to content herself with listening.

"What about the soldiers he hired? How will you contain them?"

"That is a bigger problem. We have enough men to contain them when the time comes. Ronan assumes they are paid lowlanders and once Sutherland is killed, they can be paid and sent on their way. If that is the case, it could work. If they are here for more passionate reasons, we will be involved in a very bloody fight."

"How do you plan to get rid of him?"

Fergus chuckled. "I can see where Ronan gets his strategic mind."

"Do not change the subject," she said, though Freya heard mirth in her tone.

"We are still working that out. Will she need anything tonight?"

Frey felt a hand brushed the hair from her face. "She just needs rest. Ronan should sleep elsewhere this night."

"I will not be the one to tell him that."

"Nor I," she said. "She will have to battle it out with him in the morn."

Freya tried moving her limbs to turn over, but they would not do her bidding. She wanted to sit up and tell Fergus he could inform Ronan to sleep anywhere but with her, but her dulled mind would not allow it.

She was aware the moment he entered the tent. Though her thoughts were hazy, her body was more than aware of him. Always.

"How does she fare?" She heard concern in his voice.

"She is in no danger, but your mother says she needs rest."

"Then she will get it."

Fergus chuckled

"Why do you laugh?"

"I am looking forward to hearing her reaction when she wakes in the morn to find you lying next to her."

"She will not be awake by the time I rise."

"We have a plan then?"

"Aye, we do," he said. "We go before dawn."

"So be it."

"So be it indeed."

Freya heard nothing else after that, as the sleep she had been fighting pulled her under. The last thing she registered was a heavy arm wrapping around her middle.

CHAPTER TWENTY-TWO

Ronan tied thick leather straps around his forearms and secured his broadswords across his back. His men assembled in the same way and he was impressed at how noiseless they were. The sun would rise before long so they would have to approach the castle with stealth.

The plan was to surround the castle and enter all at once. Before long, the five hundred men were ready and had successfully disarmed the guards on patrol.

Ronan motioned for Fergus and MacIntosh to follow him to where he suspected Alexander slept. One by one, as quietly as they could, they took out any guards in their path. Ronan tried not to take notice of whether or not they were men he had previously ruled.

With little resistance, they made it to the master chamber on the third floor of the castle. Ronan hesitated outside. He had the document secured within his tunic and drew a deep breath. Looking once over his shoulder, he lifted the latch and pushed, but the door would not give— bolted from the inside.

He cursed under his breath and looked to his right, shaking his head in Fergus's direction. The man's face turned hard and he motioned Ronan out of the way.

A moment later, Fergus kicked the door clear off its hinges and the twelve of them stormed the chamber. The sight that met him was both surprising and pitiful.

Sitting up in bed, his grey haired uncle did not look like the fearsome warrior with his eyes wide and quilts clutched to his chin.

"You are relieved from your position as chief and Earl of Sutherland, by order of the King," Ronan declared.

Alexander's expression changed them from shock to fury. He leapt up from the bed and grabbed his sword.

"I know what is rightfully mine," he said. "If you want what I have, come and claim it, lad. I do not believe for one moment you are man enough. If it takes a dozen men to back you up, do you really think you have what it takes to rule this clan?"

Ronan laughed. "Aye. I have what it takes. Will you come quietly, or does this need to end in bloodshed?"

Alexander did not hesitate. He lunged forward with his sword pointed straight for Ronan's heart. Though he was a crazed madman, he did not have the benefit of Ronan's youth and strength. Their swords clashed and Ronan easily overtook him. He kicked the feet out from under the man and placed the tip of his blade at his throat.

"Do you yield?"

"Never!"

Ronan drew a deep breath. He had killed his own father; he had much less hesitation to end this man too.

"So be it," he said.

He shoved his sword through his uncle's throat, spilling his lifeblood onto the floor. The crimson pool grew as the life left Alexander Sutherland's eyes. Moments later, he was dead.

Ronan should have felt something, some remorse for the life he had just taken, but instead he was numb. Only one part of this whole problem was resolved, and it had occurred with surprising ease. He realized he could have done the same thing at any point leading up to now, if that is all the resistance from the man he would have gotten. But then, he would not have learned of the plan.

"We need to find his captain," MacIntosh said.

"Aye, we do," Fergus said. "We must handle this quickly so they do not have time to react or attack."

"It is all too easy," Ronan said. For all their planning, he still had a terrible feeling he was missing something.

Shouts from the hallway drew their attention.

When they followed the noise they discovered some of the hired men in a scuffle with MacKay warriors. The latter more than had the upper hand.

"What are you called?" Ronan asked the guard.

"Fergusson. And the Earl will not be pleased. Unhand me."

Ronan cocked his head. "I am the Earl. And I am not pleased. You and your men will stand down or you will all lose your lives this day."

At that moment he stopped struggling. "What do you mean you are the Earl? Alexander Sutherland is the Earl."

"Are you captain of these men?" Ronan asked ignoring his question.

"Aye, I am."

"From whence do you hail?"

"Peebleshire. Where is the Earl?"

Ronan took a step closer to him. "I am the Earl and chief of clan Sutherland. I want your men assembled and off my lands immediately. If you do not comply, you will all be run through."

"My men will not comply so easily," he said. "We were to be paid a handsome sum for our support."

Ronan heaved a sigh of relief and glanced at Fergus and MacIntosh, nodding.

"You will be paid for your services to the former Earl, and you will leave here immediately. Your pervious orders are null and void, and you will go back to Peebleshire and never return to the Highlands. Is that clear?"

The man looked from Ronan to the others with him and back again. "Aye. It is clear."

"What was the sum?"

"Five thousand marks."

Christ's teeth. "You will be paid."

"Take him to the great hall to await me," Ronan said to Fergus. Then to his own men, he said, "Fetch Father Sinclair. Alexander must be blessed, then I want him buried immediately—next to my father."

Ronan did not wait to see if his orders would be carried out. He immediately went to the treasury fearing the worst. There was little chance he would find it full and like he had left it, as Allain would have been aware of the secret chamber on the first floor near the back of the castle.

He drew a deep breath to steady himself once he got there. Ronan grabbed a torch from the sconce on the wall and opened the door. The sight that beheld him, was surprising. Not less, but more bounty lay inside on the table, on the floor. Great chests he had never seen before were stacked just inside the door and on the table lay a parchment with several heavy sacks. He could only assume this was the payment meant for the Fergussons.

Reading the contract, he had to give his uncle credit for his thorough accounting of what his hired henchmen were meant to do, and the limitations of their actions.

Looking around him, a pang of regret washed over him from his lost friendship with Allain. Together they had brought about a great change under difficult circumstances and he would miss his consultation. But he had betrayed Ronan, and would be punished for his insubordination.

Ronan put the heavy sacks of coin on a small cart, grabbed the parchment and left the chamber, securing the entrance and replacing the torch in the sconce outside.

As he approached the great all, he heard Fergus's booming voice over the rumblings of the gathered Fergusson army.

Upon entering, the men parted for him. He could not have been more relieved. A man paid for a job was much less of a threat than one passionate about the task. He was certain they would take their payment, return to their ships, and go home.

"I have the contract," he said to their captain. "Here is your payment. By the terms of this parchment which I believe you have signed, the Earl may require you to cease and desist at any point he feels is necessary and your services are no longer required. Do you concur?"

As he spoke, Ronan wheeled the cart toward the man and stopped before him. His eyes widened into great orbs and a grin spread out across his face. The men surrounding him also grinned. One slapped the other on the back and laughed out loud.

"You appear surprised," Ronan said. He wanted them gone, but their reaction was not as he had expected.

"We are pleased this arrangement has come to a conclusion, my lord," he said. "As per the terms, we will return home immediately and as you request, you will not see us again."

"And that is it?"

"Aye," he said. "That is it. We are happy to see the back end of the Highlands and dealings with your uncle. Our desperation led us down this path, and my men and I will not need to repeat it with your generous payment. Farewell, my lord." He then turned to his men. "To home!"

They all cheered and with that, he left the great hall with the cart, his men following behind.

Ronan watched them file out, and for the first time since he had left her before dawn, thought of Freya. As soon as the Fergussons were gone, he would personally carry her to their new chamber. Like it or not, she was now his wife and he was not about to let her forget it.

* * *

Freya rolled over to her side and noticed the emptiness beside her. Each time she had awoken in the night with discomfort, Ronan held her closer. Freya took stock of her body. She was no longer feverish, and at some point when it had broken, had soaked through Ronan's shirt.

She sat up and looked around to see if her own shift or gown had been returned. Lying near her pallet, she spied folded linens and smiled. Morag was a very good nursemaid. How she had gotten her clothes washed and dried so quickly was a mystery, but a welcome one.

Just as she was rising from her bed, the tent flap lifted to reveal Morag and Muren. Their looks of surprise were almost humorous, until Morag tsked.

"Now lass, you'll not have much strength yet. Just what do you think you are doing up?"

"I am feeling better, Morag. My strength has returned. My clothes are soaked and I thought I would change into the ones you left here."

"Not until you are washed," she said. "Muren, get the guards to help bring the hot water."

"How on earth are you warming water?"

Morag was a miracle worker. The armies were probably killing each other, yet she was warming water to wash Freya.

"All is quiet up at the castle. We have heard nothing since they attacked before dawn."

"And what is the hour now?"

"'Tis well past the noon meal. I choose to believe the lack of ruckus means they are successful and now negotiating terms to reinstate Ronan as Earl."

Freya gasped. "Reinstate? What about his uncle?"

"If luck is on their side, his uncle is dead."

Freya shook her head. Could it be so easy? She doubted it. Nothing that had occurred so far had been easy on either of them. And the reality was that she and Ronan were now married before God and blessed by the bishop. There was no turning back. She was stuck with him and he with her. But how on earth would they ever move forward, past all that had happened?

"Now," Morag said. "Strip off that shirt and turn around. We do not have a tub to put you in, but we can certainly wash away the sickness you've endured these past two days. Oh, what I would not give to be close to a loch to throw you into," she said with a grin.

"I would likely drown and then you would be without your new daughter," she said.

Morag's actions stilled. "You have always been meant for Ronan and he for you. I know you are angry, Freya, but this entire business has put us all in extreme circumstances. You and he must take some time to find one another again."

"But how?" she asked. "How, after he left me at the hands of his vile uncle, can I possibly trust that I am safe in his hands?"

"Because I know my son," she said. "He is good in his heart. He endured much under his father's care and this business with his uncle has no doubt dredged up old insecurities. Ronan has been fighting the evil of his family almost his entire life. I do not excuse what he did, but I do trust him."

Freya frowned and turned so that Morag could help her out of Ronan's shirt. She missed the linen cloth on her skin the moment it was taken from her body, as though letting it go was like letting part of him go. What could she do? She had left him once two years ago and it had not quelled her feelings for him, nor his for her. Were they doomed to go up in flames in one another's arms and then destroy one another?

Morag's ministrations were heavenly. The gentle brush of cloth and trickle of water down her back was soothing. Freya closed her eyes. The cloth moved away from her body and footsteps shuffling made her open her eyes just as the cloth returned to her back. The pressure was different and gooseflesh broke out across her skin.

Ronan.

How was it her body knew him so well? She tried pushing aside her hurt feelings and just enjoy the way he stroked the length of her back and further down to the swell of her hip. His firm fingers brushed her hair over her shoulder.

The sound of a cloth in the water basin and dripping water added to her heightened anticipation. He aroused her simply by being there behind her, saying nothing but meaning everything in his careful strokes across her body. Freya held her breath as he squeezed the cloth and the water slid down across her now quivering flesh.

Hard, callused fingers slipped around her waist and pulled her back to meet his rock hard body. The cloth landed in a splat on the tent floor and a heartbeat later, his face was buried in her neck, his breathing broken and unsteady.

She wanted to speak, say something in protest but her soul yearned for this, for his nearness and his body joining with hers.

Neither spoke as he slid his hands up and cupped her heavy, straining breasts. She pressed her body into his hands and let her head fall back onto his shoulder exposing her neck to him. Though they had problems aplenty, the truth was, she needed this, needed him to comfort her in the way they knew best. Perhaps this was all they would ever have. For now it would have to do.

Freya turned and grabbed his head, drawing him forward to meet her mouth. She claimed him in that kiss. Seconds later Ronan lifted her and placed her legs around his waist to carry her back to lay her on the furs.

He fell with her to the pallet and covered her with his solid mass of heated flesh. Their fingers tangled as they both fought to remove his tunic. Once over his head, he tossed it aside and spread her legs wide. Ronan gazed hard into her eyes and lifted her hands above her head, securing them there with one of his.

In one swift movement, he plunged into her and took her mouth at the same time. The ferocity of their joining was like none other. This was their first time as husband and wife and Ronan appeared to be making a point. He possessed her, never letting her forget he was the only one to ever make her body soar to extreme heights of passion.

He stroked her deep and fast, pushing her body up the pallet as he pummelled her. Freya had lost the ability to think. Sensation after sensation raced through her veins as he brought her to the edge of climax, peering over, but not quite able to dive off.

"You are mine, Freya. Never forget it. Mine."

His words were her final undoing. She tumbled into climax and her body squeezed around his pulsing erection. Ronan slammed into her twice more before he tensed above her, his hot breath panting on her neck. As his seed spilled into her body, he sank his teeth into the soft flesh at the base of her neck and thrust into her again. The combination of a gentle bite and his still hard member inside her set off another climax that left her boneless and unable to form conscious thought.

Ronan collapsed on top of her, scooping his arms underneath her as he stayed joined with her and kissed her lips while the final quivers of their lovemaking subsided. Now she was thoroughly and truly his.

CHAPTER TWENTY-THREE

Sitting at the head of the table in the great hall, Ronan watched the MacIntosh pace while he, Fergus, and the MacKenzie sipped their ale. The Fergussons were long gone and he had Freya and his mother and sister comfortably situated in their new chambers. He had expected more protest from Freya about their sleeping arrangements, but was pleasantly surprised when she did not. Their chamber was the large one beside the old laird's chamber his uncle had held until this morning.

Though the chamber had been scrubbed clean, there was no way he could ever occupy it, or expect anyone else to, so he and his wife now occupied the former lady's chamber. He shifted in his seat as he thought about her writhing beneath him just a few short hours ago. They had not spoken one word after and he thought it best to give her time to accept what had passed between them. She was his now and forever, and nothing would ever keep her from him again.

The sun had set, casting a yellow-orange hue in the great hall, and all hands were prepared for a great feast to celebrate their victory. Fergus had foiled the merriment by telling MacIntosh about the king's intent. Ronan watched the man scrub his hand down over his face as he stopped to gaze into the fire, his arm resting above the hearth.

There was little doubt MacIntosh was in a predicament. It was his loyalty to the king that had earned him the Earl's title to Moray two years ago. Now only a select few of his closest allies like Fergus still called him MacIntosh. To everyone else, he was Moray, a formidable and strategic nobleman who had distinct influence over the king.

"You did not think to share this upon my arrival?"

"No," Ronan said. "We had more immediate problems that needed tending."

MacIntosh turned. "You are certain, King James comes here to demand your allegiance and assume your authority?"

"Aye. Our titles will be in name only. It can never work," Ronan said. "Surely, you realize the only way to keep any sense of peace up here is for the chiefs to hold fast to the power they have always held. Your king's handling of Alexander proves his inability to effectively claim our authority."

"Guard your words, Sutherland," MacIntosh said.

His warning was valid, but Ronan would not sit back and hand over the power he required to protect his clansmen. A king ruling from hundreds of miles away was useless to him and all the other chiefs up here.

"When is MacDonald expected?" MacIntosh asked.

"Any time now, if he decides not to kill my son," MacKenzie said.

"He will come," Ronan said. "He will take any opportunity to oppose the king and free his father.

"Aye, that he will," Angus MacDonald said from the entranceway. "And he wonders what this traitor is doing in this company," he said pointing to MacIntosh. "I should slice you through where you stand."

Fergus was on his feet in seconds and standing in front of MacIntosh. "You'll have to come through me first, lad. And I do not think you want to take me on."

MacIntosh sidestepped Fergus and moved to stand before MacDonald. Closer to Fergus's height, the flaxen haired, green-eyed hulk stared down into his eyes, he jaw set and his expression hard and unforgiving.

"If you wish to address me, MacDonald, you may do so directly and not through someone else. Your father's schemes caused many innocent people to die and others falsely persecuted. He deserves to rot where he is."

A heartbeat later, Fergus's hand was on Angus's throat and a blade clattered to the floor. Ronan rose to his feet and strode over to intervene before they all killed one another.

"Enough squabbling," he said. "Fergus, release MacDonald. MacIntosh, not another word. MacDonald, go sit at the far end of the table until this is resolved. We have a situation before us that will not end well unless we come together as one and agree on a solution."

Fergus and Angus merely grunted at one another while MacIntosh sauntered back to the hearth and crossed his arms over his chest.

"The king will be here in a couple of days, and when he arrives, he will be hell bent on claiming our authority in the same manner he meant to four years ago at Inverness. Fergus, you were one of those imprisoned then. You know full well how unbending the man is. If we do not resolve this ourselves, he will do it for us. And we will have nothing left to fight over," He added, hoping the gravity in his voice got his point across.

"MacIntosh, I know you have your reasons for supporting this king, but up here, he has no way to effectively rule. You must see that."

MacIntosh nodded. "Aye, I do see that. But there have been too many underhanded schemes set to usurp him for anything we say to hold water anymore. He has set his mind to claiming your authority and I do not know what it will take to change it."

MacDonald slammed his hand on the table. "The time for peaceful negotiations has passed. We must strike out at him and strike hard if we are to keep one inch of what is rightfully ours."

"You wish to go to war against the king? Those are treasonous words, MacDonald," MacIntosh said.

"Yer a lawless bastard, MacDonald," MacKenzie said. "And you will not listen to anyone—just like your father. We might have resolved this years ago if he had not attacked my lands and blamed MacKay here. You don't deserve the authority you claim."

When MacDonald toppled his chair and moved toward Kenneth MacKenzie, Rorie stepped in and raised his blade to his throat.

"You will not touch one hair on my father's head. 'Tis begging forgiveness for the crimes your father committed against our clan you should be spewing from that mouth of yours instead of your hateful words."

Ronan had had enough. Nothing would be resolved with MacDonald present. While he agreed with him in principle, he did not in the execution. If MacDonald wanted to attack the king then he would do it alone. The rest of them would work toward a resolution that would hopefully satisfy all parties.

"MacDonald, do you wish to ally with us to negotiate with the king or not?" Ronan asked.

"I do not. My father has held favour with the Sutherlands for as long as I can remember and I will honour that. As for the rest of you, if you do not stand up to the Stewart's tyranny, I care not what happens to the lot of you."

With that he turned on his heel and strode for the door. No one stopped him.

"He will not be satisfied until he or the king is in his grave. There is no bending him and so no point in us wasting our time convincing him," MacIntosh said.

"How did you convince him to come with you?" Ronan asked Rorie.

"Simple. I did not tell him about the king, only that there was a feast in honour of your reclaiming your seat and that you wished to ensure your alliance which he would do by his presence."

Smart lad. "You've a good head on you, MacKenzie," Fergus said. "But what do we do now?"

"The king loves a good tourney does he not?" Ronan asked MacIntosh.

"Aye, that he does. The man will use any excuse to hold one."

"I wonder if we may use that to our advantage."

"That would depend on how much faith he has in his guards," Fergus said.

Exactly. "And if we can convince him to wager on that faith, we may be able to turn the tables and gain some ground with him."

"You intend to trick him?" MacIntosh asked, frowning.

195

Ronan grinned. "Not so much trick as exploit. You and I both know his guard cannot stand up to our warriors. But he doesn't know that. MacIntosh, you know very well he cannot take all our authority. We would never survive it. You said you were with us in this endeavour. I am holding you to your word. Do you tell me now you will not stand with us?"

For a long time, MacIntosh stared at him. It was obvious the man waged an internal war.

"Aye, I stand with you," he said after an age.

Ronan clasped his arm and slapped his shoulder. "I am very glad to hear it."

"Enough of this tonight," MacKenzie said. "I cannot think with an empty belly and an empty goblet."

He was right. The day had begun early and much had occurred. Tonight was meant to be a feast to celebrate their first victory. With any luck the plan would be fleshed out on the morrow, once their bellies were full and their heads rested.

"You speak true, MacKenzie. Tonight, we feast. My men will see to your comfort. I wish to see my wife before we begin."

"How does she fare?" Fergus asked, leaving the great hall together.

"Her fever has broken and she is in no danger. She is weak from everything that she has been through, but she will endure."

"She always does," he said. "And how are things between you?"

"She has not forgiven me for using her to get information out of my uncle. I do not know if I have forgiven myself for that. Perhaps I am as bad as my father and uncle after all."

Fergus stopped and grabbed him by the shoulders. "You are nothing like them. Do you hear me? Nothing."

Fergus's statement took Ronan by surprise. He really did not know anymore. He had betrayed the one person who should have been able to rely on him above all others, and at the moment, he did not know up from down.

"Ronan, you are a good man. I have known the evil that was your father for as long as I can remember. You are not, and can never be, that man. You made a decision and you were fortunate enough that it worked out. Freya feels betrayed and that is understandable. In time, she will come to accept the limitations of your options, given the circumstances."

"If only I could believe you, Fergus. The truth is, I have not considered whether or not I had other options. I acted without thinking it through, with my only thought to destroy my uncle and leaving all other considerations out of it. That one act makes me a selfish bastard. We both know my family is full of them."

"You are far too hard on yourself. I have seen the goodness in you and I am certain Freya does as well."

Ronan nodded and walked away from him. He had Freya's hand in marriage, but without her forgiveness and trust, it was meaningless.

* * *

Sitting near the fire with a maid pulling a brush through her hair was like a long lost luxury. It seemed like an age since she had left Tongue with Alexander Sutherland, not knowing from one moment to the next what sort of peril she would face. But face it she did. Though she came through it physically unscathed, her heart was another matter.

Whether or not she and Ronan ever resolved their differences, she was now his wife. Lady Sutherland. Part of her wanted to leap for joy that they had finally managed to find their way over all the obstacles life had thrown at them since their first powerful meeting two years before. She rubbed the ache in her belly as she often did when she thought of the early days when she had fallen hard and fast for him.

He was younger, wilder, and she was just as reckless in her pursuit of his affections. The years of leadership had changed him into someone she barely recognized. But did that mean she could not still love him? This new Ronan, who had to make decisions and sacrifices for the greater good, even if it meant her? And what about children. God willing, she would bless him with bairns before too long. Would he sacrifice them too?

She had to know. The only way she could ever move forward

with him was to find out exactly how far he was willing to go to protect her and their future family. She would never stand by and be his pawn. Ever.

The maid had finished her hair and helped her into her gown just as Ronan entered their chamber. Dark circles under his eyes and his overall tense demeanour told her he had endured much in these past weeks.

There was much they needed to work through, but she could put it aside for the time it took for them to resolve the issues with the king. She would not add to his burden by griping with him at every turn.

"How did it go?"

Ronan shook his head and closed the door behind the maid after she left. "Not well. MacDonald was completely unreasonable and has since left. We are all battle weary and have put off further discussions until the morrow. We feast this night to celebrate our victory over my uncle, and—" He stopped as he took a step toward her.

Freya's pulse picked up with the anticipation of him drawing near.

"And?" She was well aware of the other required celebration and did not actually mind the wariness in his expression. Did he seek her approval before adding their marriage to the festivities?

Ronan stepped closer and reached his hand out to stroke her cheek with the back of his fingers. "By God, you are enchanting."

Heat flooded her face as he continued staring while caressing her.

"You were saying why we feast," she reminded him in a quiet voice.

He blinked several times and cupped her face in both hands as he moved directly in front of her.

"Freya," he whispered. "I cannot think when I am near you."

The air rushed out of her body at his words. The world seemed to turn on its end when they were near each other.

He leaned down and brushed his lips across hers. "You are so beautiful, my Freya. My love. You steal my wits."

His mouth closed over hers and her wits fled too. For long moments, they savoured one another as though the world outside was not in turmoil and they had not a care.

It was Freya who broke the kiss and gazed up into his eyes. "You must change before we return below."

"Aye, I must. Will you assist me?"

She smiled. Now that they were wed, it was her duty to assist him in this way. And something she had never had the pleasure of doing for him in all the time she had known him. To perform a simple duty like it in the past was almost outlandish.

As she reached for the belt keeping his tunic in place, he lifted her chin with his finger.

"You are smiling." It was almost a question.

"Aye, I suppose I am."

"And will you tell me why you smile? I have not seen you happy in far too long, Freya. You make my heart soar when you smile."

That made her smile more. "I was just thinking that performing wifely duties, such as dressing you, is a treat in its ordinary nature. Considering—" She could not finish because her heart ached when she thought about their lost child.

He pulled her close and wrapped his arms around her. "We have been through much, you and I. I believe we can endure anything."

"Ronan—"

"We will talk about my uncle, Freya. You deserve to know everything from start to finish without interruptions. Then I will accept your judgement. If you wish to sleep in another chamber, I will respect it, but—" His voice cracked and he held her tighter. "Freya, I cannot endure it if you leave me again."

Freya squeezed her eyes tight at the thought of being separated from him. She could not endure it either. They were bound by an invisible tether that threatened to break them both should it stretch too much.

"Will you promise me that whatever punishment you decide for wronging you, it will not involve us living apart?"

The mist forming in Ronan's eyes was just about her undoing.

She could not bear to unman him. He had such a hold on her entire being that denying him anything was near impossible. She would never and could never leave, but she was not prepared to forgive him without that explanation. So, aye, she could wait until he explained his actions in detail so she could better understand. As hard as it would be to sleep in a different chamber, she would do it.

"I will give you the time you need to explain, and I do understand that it will not be this evening. I am your wife now and nothing either of us can do will change that. Mistakes made in the past will have to be dealt with within the walls of this castle. I will not leave you again."

He gazed into her eyes and the corners of his mouth lifted making him look younger and giving him a touch of the carefree man he once was.

"You shall have all the time you need to make your decision, Freya. I will do everything I can to show you how much you mean to me, and how much trust you can place in me. I will earn it back."

She shook her head. "Enough of this talk for tonight. You and I have guests awaiting us below, and if we keep this up we will not see them at all."

He grinned. "I am certain they can wait for a little while, Lady Sutherland."

"And I am certain, my husband might just drop from exhaustion if he does not change and get below. Additional exertions are not recommended for you, or me, right now."

He bent low and kissed her again. "Then help me change, Lady Sutherland. Shall we celebrate our marriage?"

She nodded and smiled. "That we shall, my lord."

CHAPTER TWENTY-FOUR

Ronan stood with his allies and watched the royal procession as it drew closer to his castle. Banners flew high, emblazoned with the lion and the unicorn. By Ronan's estimate, hundreds of men accompanied the king. Was it a warning, then, of his intent if he did not get his way?

He had proven time and again, he cared more for centralizing authority than the needs of an individual chief. Ronan drew a deep breath and stepped forward as the king approached and stopped a few feet away. Without preamble or ceremony, he dismounted and held out his hands. Ronan stepped forward and allowed the man to embrace him. Would wonders never cease? This was most unexpected.

"Ahh, Sutherland," he said. "You do not have the look of your father. A fact for which I believe your wife should be grateful."

Before Ronan could respond, the king moved toward Freya and bent low over her hand, kissing her knuckles in a showy manner. Ronan glanced at Fergus whose brows had nearly met his hairline.

"My lady. You are as stunning a woman as I have ever beheld. Surely the ladies of my court could never stand it if you were to visit."

Was that a compliment or an insult? Ronan could not be sure, and from Freya's furrowed brow, it was clear, she had taken it as a 'you are not welcome' message.

"Sire," she said. "Surely, your wife would not take offence to my presence at your court, as surely she is the most beautiful in the land."

Well done, Freya. Ronan raised his hand to his mouth to hide his smile. The king would probably underestimate many of them during this visit, but one, his wife, would not let him get away with anything without censure.

"Ahh, that she is, my lady." His smile widened and his expression softened as he beheld her longer. Was the first comment a test then?

A moment later, he dropped her hand and moved to MacIntosh and Fergus for greetings.

Freya glanced toward Ronan. The pink in her cheeks and glint in her eyes told him she was displeased. As discretely as he could, he shook his head at her. For once in her life, he hoped she would bide herself and not let her emotions run away with her. While that was the part of her he loved the most, her passion, this king would not be forgiving and would charge her with treason if he so chose to find offence.

"Come then," Ronan said. "Let us welcome you, my king, with a feast in your honour and later a melee for our sport."

"A melee! Splendid. I embrace the opportunity to put my guard up against your Highland warriors."

So be it. Glancing sideways at Fergus, Ronan noticed the man's grin. There was no way hired guards could stand up against trained and battle seasoned warriors like those loyal to the Sutherland, MacKay, and MacKenzie clans. But if the king wanted to play, then play they would. Ronan just hoped that he could convince the king to wager the authority debate. It would take some delicacy, however. MacIntosh had conceded to assist, as long as if the king did win, they would all lay down their arms and pledge allegiance.

They moved into the great hall to where a feast as big as any Ronan had ever seen at Dunrobin was laid out. Roasted boar, pheasant, and deer filled several trenchers and the table was filled with enough to feed ten armies.

Ronan and Freya walked to the head table to where they motioned for the king to sit. To his surprise, the king took the seat to the side and insisted Ronan sit at the head and Freya to his right.

"That is your seat, Sutherland. Not mine."

"Indeed, sire."

Once they were all seated, the king rose with his goblet. All din in the great hall ceased. "My countrymen, I wish to toast our gracious host." He turned to Ronan with a grin. "You do your forefathers honour by accepting your title and pledging loyalty to your king like the Sutherlands have done for generations. Although we have had our differences—"

Ronan did not like where this was going. Surely, the man's memory was not that short that he had forgotten his father's plot to help MacDonald usurp him.

"I am willing to forgive the past and begin anew with your reinstated title binding you to me and my crown."

Ronan waited patiently for a chance to speak. He had no intention of interrupting the king, but he would make some additions to the man's assumptions about their relationship.

The king turned toward the others seated at the table. "I ask you to raise your goblets in honour of our host. May he always seek justice, act with valour, and love with abandon."

Ronan turned to Freya as the king's words, followed by his wink in her direction, produced a pinched smile.

When he had raised his goblet to her, and she in return, they drank. Finally, he could speak.

"My king," Freya said before he could get a chance. "I wonder. Should loyalty be commanded, or do you believe it should be earned?"

Christ's toes. A little subtlety would surely go a long way. He had to find a way to get her to stop, else his plan would never see the light of day.

"Why, Lady Sutherland, I believe it should be earned."

"And how would you earn my loyalty?" she asked.

What the devil was she asking him?

"I would pledge it to you on bended knee," he said.

"Well then, my king, there is no time like the present."

Before anyone could say another word, Freya rose from her seat. All the men at the table rose as well and the king sauntered around the table to stand before her. To Ronan's complete surprise, he dropped to his knee and bowed his head in submission.

"I pledge my loyalty to you, Lady Sutherland. And vow to assist you in any way I can should you ever require it."

Ronan could not wait to get her alone later to find out just what she was up to. He expected her explanation would be very interesting. His loins tightened at the thought of her commanding him in the same way.

Freya placed her hand on his head. "I thank you, Your Majesty."

With that, the king returned to his seat and acted as though nothing had ever happened. Ronan looked at Freya who still gazed hard at the Stewart. He tried catching her eye, but she was not revealing any of her secrets just yet.

Eventually, after much useless chatter, the king turned back to Ronan. "Tell me about this tourney."

Ronan grinned. "I believe we shall engage in sport on the morrow, if it pleases Your Highness."

"It does indeed. What do you propose?"

"Propose?"

"Aye, what shall we wager?"

This was easier than he had imagined.

"Your guards against warriors from our clans. Equal numbers."

"Aye."

"We shall joust, and at the end of three days, we will recreate the battle of Bannockburn.

The king's grin spread wide. "I like the turn of your thoughts, Sutherland. And the winner? What does the winner gain?"

Ronan noticed the king's gaze flicked toward Freya and back again. His behaviour exorcised any future guilt he had about trapping the man.

"The winner takes all," Ronan said.

The king's brows rose and his jaw slacked. He cleared his throat. "All?"

Ronan nodded. "Aye, sire. All."

The king grinned at Freya and raised his goblet toward her. "Then we have a deal."

Satisfied, Ronan shifted his attention to every word the king uttered for the next few hours. He talked mostly of insignificant courtly troubles and offered little of his intentions for them. Ronan had hoped the constantly filled goblet would loosen his tongue somewhat so he could glean exactly how the man intended to claim their authority. But he said nothing of it.

At some point, Freya retired and he was grateful she was out of the king's lascivious line of sight. Hours later still he climbed the steps to their chamber, stripped and slipped beneath the covers to find his bed empty.

* * *

Freya tugged on the bedcovers to no avail. Muren had rolled them around her body in the night and there was no setting them loose unless she woke the lass. Freya flopped onto her back in frustration. The night had ended in disaster and she could see no clear path forward for her and Ronan this time.

He had done it again. The very thing he had said he would never do, he had done it again. The king's attentions were bad enough, but to have her husband, the man who was supposed to honour and protect her always, offer her up as a prize for the tournament had split her heart wide open. Anyone with eyes could see the king wanted her, and Ronan had all but handed her to him.

Freya rose from the bed, donned her mantle, and moved to sit by the window. The sky had already turned grey in the early morning light, and the mist crawling across the sea mirrored the clawing ache in her chest.

Heavy boots in the hallway just outside Muren's chamber caught her attention and before she could react, the latch had lifted and the door swung wide. Ronan's face was flushed and his eyes wild. Dear God, what had happened?

"There you are!"

"Hush, you will wake your sister." She moved toward him and pushed at his chest until they were in the hallway with the door closed behind them. "What do you want?"

"What do I want? How can you even ask me that? I want my wife in my bed."

"Before or after you whore me to your king?"

Though the light in the hallway was dim from low burning torches, Ronan's shock was more than visible. Eyes wide and slack jawed, for a few moments he just stared at her.

Was it possible she had been mistaken in his intent? No. It was not. He would have to be blind to have missed how the king gawked at her all evening, and then to make a statement like he had was either very idiotic, or intentionally cruel. She was not sure which was worse.

"Freya," he said. "How can you possibly think something like that?" His voice was soft, pleading.

"Ronan, you told him the 'winner takes all'. Did you not see the look in his eyes as he gazed at me? You practically told him he could bend me over the nearest chair and have his way with me. Your wife!"

He grasped her shoulders and pulled her close. "Freya, I was talking about the very real problem we have with him intending to claim our authority. I would never offer you to anyone. My God, how can you even think that?"

"How? Because you have done it before. You used me as a pawn to glean information from your uncle. So, aye, I know you are capable of it because you have done it before."

"I begged your forgiveness for that and you have promised me to work toward accepting it. Are you telling me now you are unable to do so?" His words seemed torn from him.

Freya's chest tightened so much she found it difficult to breathe. Had she thought she could forgive him for his crimes against her regarding his uncle? She thought she could get past it, but perhaps she could not. What then? What if she really could never trust him again? Clearly, if what he said was true, she had leapt to assume the worst from him.

"Ronan, I do not know." Her chest heaved with her need to draw breath. She could almost see the deep chasm between them widening. After all they had been through, would her mistrust be the final thing driving them apart for good?

To her surprise, he gathered her into his arms and pulled her close, burying his face in her hair.

"I admit, I did notice the king's attentions on you, Freya. But know this, I would rather offer the man my own heart on a trencher before I would let him, or anyone else for that matter, touch one hair on your head. I promised you I would show you that your trust is not misplaced. I vow that to you again now." He cupped her face with his hands. Ronan leaned in to brush his lips across hers. "Sweet Freya, you are more precious to me than anything. I will never allow harm or dishonour to come to you."

"Oh, Ronan, my heart knows yours, but my mind is not so quick to dismiss your actions. The king's very clear desires combined with your promise had me convinced you were using me all over again."

"Freya, you have no reason to ever worry about anything like that. Please believe me."

"I promise you I will give you the benefit of the doubt in the future," she said, hugging him tighter. Without saying another word, she began walking back to their chamber with her arms linked around him.

"Can I ask you something?"

"Of course."

"Why did you make the king pledge loyalty to you? Considering what you've just said about his attentions making you uncomfortable, I am surprised you would risk additional contact with him."

She laughed. "I recalled Fergus recounting how the king had pledged loyalty to Lady MacIntosh upon learning it was her father who had travelled to England as surety for his ransom. I thought that if I could get him to do the same for me, he would be less likely to harm you."

"Harm me?"

"Aye. Ronan, I know why the king is here. I overheard Fergus talking. You play a dangerous game and I am in complete agreement with you as to why you must play it. But I do not think for one second he will agree to your terms so easily."

"He has already agreed to the terms of the tournament.

MacIntosh has also said he will intervene on our behalf should the king become dissatisfied with the outcome."

Now, inside their chamber with the morning light spilling in through the windows, Ronan slipped her mantle from her shoulders, causing her to shiver as cool air hit her skin. When he brushed his lips across the sensitive skin of her neck, she shivered again, though this time from desire.

"So, what you are telling me, wife, is that you were protecting me." Ronan then nipped her earlobe with his teeth.

Freya gasped. "Aye, my lord. Someone needs to protect you."

"Do they now? And who will protect me from you?"

She took the opportunity to flip him onto his back and straddle his thighs. She pushed his shoulders until he lay flat beneath her.

"No one can protect you from me, my lord. You are mine to do with as I see fit. And right now, I believe you need to be punished."

"I believe I shall humbly submit to your judgment, Lady Sutherland. Do your worst," he said and spread his arms wide in full submission.

Freya untied his belt and slipped it out from underneath him. She then tugged at his tunic until it was discarded along with the belt and her night shift. The cool air was a welcome contrast to the fire burning within her at the glorious man between her thighs.

The look of longing in his eyes gave her the final piece of clarity she would ever need to know in her heart once and for all, he would never hurt her.

She gasped, sliding down upon his shaft. He grabbed her hips and thrust upward until he was fully sheathed.

"I forgive you, Ronan," she said. "I trust you—now and forever."

Ronan stopped moving and gazed hard into her eyes. "Do you mean it?"

"Aye, I mean it."

To her delight, he flipped her onto her back and crushed his lips upon hers as he drove into her again and again. All she could do was to hold fast to his shoulders as he pummeled her, as if he was a man dying of thirst and she the only thing in the world that could quench him.

CHAPTER TWENTY FIVE

The late afternoon sun burned down on the riders. For two days, the king's guards had challenged the Highland warriors, and while it was clear to anyone with eyes who was the stronger and better trained, Freya suspected her husband and his allies toyed with the king. The margins of victory were not as great as they should be in her estimation. As of now they were close to being equal.

She had finally gotten Ronan to confess his full plot to her. If they could convince the king the stakes were equal, then he would continue to engage and find his defeat at the melee in the morning. The current jousting match was between young Rorie MacKenzie and the king's captain and queen consort's brother, Lord Beaufort.

The current score sat in favour of the king's guards, however Freya was certain of the outcome of this match. If the king lost, he would be baited to continue onto the battle where they intended to recreate Bannockburn.

She drew her handkerchief to her mouth to mask the cloying stench of sweat and horse dung. As the castle sat between the tournament field and the sea, the air was stifling and unmoving. What she would not give for a fresh breeze.

Beside her, Ronan sat up straight as the jousters slid their helmets into place and positioned their lances. The flag was raised and then dropped. A heartbeat later, two large destriers thundered toward one another, their riders intent on unseating the other— or worse. She had only known Rorie for a short time, but had gleaned honour in him. She felt he would not seek to intentionally maim his opponent. The king's captain on the other hand had a suspicious sneer plastered on his face at all times. She would not put anything past him.

She held her breath as the riders approached one another, and like something out of a dream, time seemed to slow as their lances crumbled into the other, splinters exploding from the impact and flying all about them, looking like a basket of sticks tossed into the air.

Rorie's head snapped back when Beaufort's lance hit his chin and he toppled backwards grasping for the horse's reins. Rorie swerved his body to the side in the last moment and managed to stay seated, despite a hard shove from the smaller framed Beaufort.

Freya glanced at Ronan who appeared to be hiding a smile behind curled fingers. The king's demeanour was not so playful. Without trying to stare, she noted his pinched lips. He was not pleased at the outcome, but perhaps he was also displeased with the dishonour his man had displayed.

The match ended with neither man being unseated which meant they would need a tie breaking match, so that today's tournament could boast a victor.

"My lord, Sutherland," the king said. "I believe we must break this deadlock somehow, else we shall never know who goes into tomorrow's battle at advantage."

Freya had forgotten that part. Whoever had earned the most points had the advantage of choosing from which side of the field to advance.

"Aye. What do you suggest?"

Dread crept its way into Freya's belly. Somehow, she knew what would happen next.

The king turned to Ronan with a grin. "You and I shall joust, my lord Sutherland."

Freya's belly dropped. The king had become more engrossed and competitive as the tournament progressed. She was certain he meant not only to unseat Ronan, but put him in his place as well. She looked at Ronan, whose jaw was set hard and clenching.

"Then joust we shall."

Without looking back at her, he left the canopied seating area where Fergus, MacIntosh, and MacKenzie also sat. Freya moved closer to her brother, hoping his strength would seep into her bones by proximity.

Once both men were fully dressed in their armour, they approached the stage. Freya knew in that moment what she had to do.

"Would you bestow a favour upon your husband, Lady Sutherland? So that he may safely return to you?" her husband asked.

Freya smiled and drew the scarf from her neck, tying it around his lance with three knots, the last of which, she emphasized. Ronan grinned.

"Sire," she said to the king but kept her eyes on Ronan, "you have pledged loyalty to me before those present. I would ask that you return my husband to me unscathed."

When he did not speak, she turned her head and met his gaze. He scowled. She had him by the testicles and he knew it. There was no way he could deny her request without risking dishonour.

Very slowly, the king nodded to her. His eyes glinted in the sunlight. He was vexed. The last thing she needed was to rile him just before attempting to trample Ronan.

Freya pulled a small handkerchief from her sleeve and then moved to tie it to the king's staff. "So that you return unscathed as well, sire."

His eyes widened and a smile then spread across his face. Were he not so dangerous, she could see how he could be considered handsome.

"My lady. You have done me a great honour. I am your servant."

Freya returned to her seat and watched the two men get into position. Though her outward actions were bold, on the inside she quaked. Fergus took her hand in his as the joust was about to start.

"You are a brave one, Freya," he said low so that only she could hear.

"Am I brave, or daft?"

"Perhaps a little of both."

Freya elbowed him in the ribs causing him to laugh.

"The king would not harm his host on purpose, love. He wants to win the battle on the morrow."

"Aye, but there is no harm in reminding him of his pledge to me on the night he arrived, is there?"

"None. In fact, I believe he found it rather entertaining."

"Is that good?"

"We shall have to wait and see."

Freya did not like waiting. She wanted to know the outcome of the battle in this moment. She feared she would not get one wink of sleep this night.

* * *

Ronan tried to still his destrier. Between the cheers of the crowd, the activity of the past two days, and the heat, he felt for the animal. There would be plenty of time to rest once this match was over. And he intended to see it go in his favour. He had watched the king like a hawk and gleaned the man was insatiable in his need for competition. Ronan had ensured the matches between his warriors and the king's guard stay relatively even in order to maintain the Stewart's interest. It had worked.

Freya's antic with the scarf and her request had been the perfect enticement for the man. Ronan smirked as he got into position on the right hand side of the fencing, the king to his left and on the opposite side.

Thus far, his plan played out as he had hoped. He now just needed to win this match and draw an ounce more ire from the man to ensure he would have him in the right frame of mind for the battle on the morrow.

Ronan rolled his neck and blocked out the many cheers from those gathered. His horse clawed at the ground, anxious to begin. He reached up with his left hand and slammed the protective eyepiece of his helmet into place, a signal he was ready to begin. The king followed suit.

All sound passed out of his attentions save for his horse's grunts, and his own deep and steady breaths. His muscles bunched as he waited for the flag to rise and drop. In the last moment, he wrapped the reins around his left hand and pulled back slowly.

The flag floated downward as Ronan thrust his body forward as the horse bolted. He gripped the lance tight, pointing it inward toward the fence and his approaching opponent.

He focused hard on the king's position and mostly on the way he sat slightly to the right in his saddle. Did he offer an opportunity?

Ronan had not noticed it before. No matter now. The time had come to make a decision as to unseat the man or toss the match.

He smiled to himself as he dipped the lance toward the lower part of the king's breast plate, a perfect position to topple the man.

His lance crushed and splintered as it made contact with the king. Ronan's arm became hot, causing him to break his hold on the reins and his body to sway. In an effort to remain seated, he tossed his weapon aside and grabbed the reins with his other hand while squeezing the horse's body with his thighs. Several paces past the impact point, he turned to see what he had managed to do.

The king was bent over the horse, unmoving. Ronan galloped around the fence to determine the man's state and was relieved when he found the king winded, but otherwise unharmed.

"You play to win, my lord Sutherland."

"Aye."

"It appears we are still at an impasse as you did not unseat me. Nor I you."

Christ.

"It would appear so."

"The sun is too hot for my liking. I suggest we retire to feast. Tomorrow's battle shall determine the victor of these games."

Ronan had to stifle the smile. Those were the exact words he had wanted to hear. Sliding down from his horse, he tossed the reins to the stable hand.

"Be sure he receives extra attention." Then to the king, he said, "Shall we retire to the great hall then? I feel like filling my gullet with ale."

The king too slid from his horse and clasped Ronan on the shoulders. They walked toward the stage and collected those gathered there before proceeding to the great hall.

Freya came up beside him and took his hand in hers, squeezing hard. He glanced down into her eyes and noted the worry there. They were not through this playful battle yet, but they had weathered it well. She had impressed him time and again with her graciousness, and most importantly, her courage. Surely, there was never a woman born to the Highlands so brave.

Once they settled in to drink and feast, Ronan watched the nobles and chiefs around the table. All of them had a vested interest in the king's intentions, that was the obvious part. But did the mere fact that they had come together to oppose him, prove something?

"You are very pensive, my lord Sutherland."

"Aye, sire. I observe the leaders around this table and consider their plight and their worth."

"Sounds very troubling."

"It could be," Ronan said. " The challenges we have this far north are no doubt varied from those in Mid-Lothian."

"And so now we finally get to it."

He was right. They had danced around the subject enough. Perhaps a more direct approach would prove fruitful.

"Indeed, we do. I wonder, sire, what your intentions are?"

"For you?"

"Not me specifically. Rather, all of us. Up here and so far away from the very different challenges of Court."

Without missing a beat, the king said, "I intend for you to pledge your fealty to me, my lord Sutherland."

"You already have our fealty, sire. What is it, in addition to the words, you seek?"

"Your vassals, your presence, and your unwavering commitment to my various causes."

"And in the event men cannot be spared?"

The king slammed his hand hard on the table. "Men can always be spared. And spare them you will."

By now all heads had turned toward their conversation. If anything, getting the king's blood up before battle would distract him from focusing on how to best them. Not that he had a chance, but Ronan would use whatever he could to his advantage.

"Surely, you do not intend for your campaigns to take precedence over the welfare of individual men's livelihood."

"I believe what the king is saying," MacIntosh said, "is that there may come a time when the country's affairs will be everyone's priority."

"Aye," MacKenzie said, "but on whose determination?"

"On mine, as I am your king."

Ronan could have cut the building tension with his dirk. The Stewart was bent on having his way, and thus far after three days of games, they were no closer to a resolution.

"And what about concessions?" Fergus asked. "Surely, you do not expect us to march to do your bidding if it means putting our homes and families at risk?"

"I expect full and complete loyalty from each and every one of you."

His demeanour was cool and aloof, but Ronan could sense the anger rising in him. Whether or not they won the battle on the morrow probably would not make a difference at this point.

"And what of our wager?" Ronan asked after a time.

The king's head whipped around and his gaze locked on Freya.

"Our wager? You said winner takes all. You meant your precious concessions did you not?"

"Aye, I did, sire."

"Well, you see then we shall have to place a new wager, shall we not? And let us be clear this time, Sutherland. I will not be played by my own nobles, and you should know better than to attempt it."

"Name your terms then."

The king looked back to Freya and smirked. Ronan's fists clenched and his guts knotted. There was not a chance in Hell he would ever let the man lay one finger on his wife.

"If I win, I will claim full authority over all that lies within

Scotland's borders. I will call each and any one of you to my side as I see fit, and I will have you do so without hesitation. Further to this, I will claim any of your ladies to become ladies-in-waiting to my queen, as is her desire. Are we very clear on what I shall have from you when I win the battle?"

"Aye, you are clear. Now, it is my turn," Ronan said. For effect, he stood. "When we win, we will pledge our fealty to you as befitting your position as our king. We will come to your aid as needed, but we will not do so at the risk or peril of our own clans and tenants. Our ladies shall remain in their own homes and shall never be asked to serve upon anyone other than their husbands. Am I being clear enough, sire, in what we shall have when we are victorious?"

The king's face grew red; his fists curled into balls. Ronan had crossed several lines with his statement of intent, however, the king had wanted a plain statement of fact and so there it was.

When the king stood, so did MacIntosh, Beaufort, Fergus, and the MacKenzies. All of them stared one another down for what seemed like an age. Would the king agree to their terms? Christ, he hoped so or else there would be a bloody battle ahead of them instead of a mock one.

To his surprise, Freya pushed her chair back and stood. All eyes fell to her as she rounded the table. She paused to kiss Ronan's cheek and then moved to stand before King James.

"My king, as your loyal servant, if you win tomorrow I will go with you to Linlithgow Palace and tend to your queen."

"No!" Ronan and Fergus said together.

Freya looked at them both and shook her head.

"But if you do not win tomorrow, as my loyal servant, you will concede to my husband's terms and ask nothing of them that will put the people entrusting them with their lives and livelihood in peril."

The king studied her face. Freya's back was to Ronan, but her rigid stance told him she was hanging onto her courage by a thread. By God, she was as fearsome as her brother and as calculating as MacIntosh.

Ronan watched the king's expressions. The man waged a battle from within, and Ronan wondered if he had ever had to concede to anyone since returning to Scotland from England naught but eight years prior. Still, he needed to learn the lesson that he could not expect his tyrannical methods to stand. The chiefs and nobles had been protecting their own for centuries up here, and none of them could see a logical way in which centralized authority could work for them.

The king bent low and whispered something in Freya's ear. Ronan stiffened, ready to reach out and pull her back from the man's proximity.

Freya's laughter broke the spell.

"Aye, my King. You speak true."

With that, the king turned back to the men and let his gaze drift across them until it settled back to Ronan.

"I agree to your terms, my Lady Sutherland."

Ronan's surprise could not have been greater. Just like that? His little spitfire of a wife may have just saved them all from a certain bloodbath, and he could not wait to find out what the king had whispered in her ear.

"Then enough of this chatter," Ronan said. "Let us drink to your health, sire."

The king grabbed his goblet and raised it toward Freya. "And to bonnie lassies with pure hearts and fierce courage."

Freya laughed again, the sound tickled the back of Ronan's neck as though she had touched him.

"I shall happily drink to that, sire."

Before long, the music started, the ale flowed, and Ronan sat back to enjoy a much lighter mood than the one from earlier. He stole glances at Freya to see if she would give anything away, but she kept her gaze on the king. Oh, aye, he would learn of her secret before the evening was out.

CHAPTER TWENTY-SIX

Angus MacDonald threw open the armoury door and stalked to his wall of blades. By Christ, he was in a rage over the meeting with Sutherland and the other cowards who did not understand the importance of striking the king where it would hurt him the most.

Well, no matter. He would carry out his plan all on his own if that is what it took. He scanned the wall until he found what he was looking for—the broadsword that had been given to him by his father upon his coming of age. It seemed like aeons ago since he had become a man and had to live up to the demands of his position. His father had always held onto the title 'Lord of the Isles' with grace, eliciting devotion from those he lived to serve and protect.

Since the constant conflicts began a few years back because of the damned Stewart who returned to claim the throne, they had not had a moment's peace. The man was bent on turning everything upside down that was logical and made any sense to their way of life. Now, with his father imprisoned yet again at Edinburgh castle, Angus was determined to end this once and for all—no matter what the cost.

"The prodigal son returns," a familiar voice said from the doorway. "Have the affairs of the nation all sorted now, do you?"

Angus turned and grinned as his oldest and most trusted friend moved forward to embrace him.

"Graham! Good to see you. What news from Edinburgh?"

"No news. The king is in the north as you know and your father does not fare any differently."

"Well, that is something to be contented with."

"Aye. Tell me about your meeting with the lairds of the north."

"There is not much to tell, only that Mackay, MacKenzie, Sutherland, and MacIntosh plan to *talk* the king into letting them keep their authority." He shook his head. "I honestly do not know where their heads are. Do they truly think the man will listen to reason? After all that has passed?"

"I do not know where their heads are, my friend, but I do wish to know where yours is. Do you still plan to attack Edinburgh Castle?"

"Aye. I do. And soon. I amass an army as we speak and will be ready to march in the coming weeks. The Stewart will not have time to retaliate effectively. Nor will he have the numbers in his support. I plan to remove my father from the castle and take anything from the Stewart I can this time. No more games."

Graham smiled. "I think you have the right idea, Angus. Your father has been wrong to still your efforts from his cell."

"That he has. Once inside, we can retrieve my father *and* raid the king's treasury too. I have plans for the castle from a very good source, and have already plotted to leave the Stewart holding his cock."

Graham laughed, slapping Angus on the shoulder. "Oh, you are a formidable foe. Remind me never to vex you."

"You should not need reminding. Just do not do it."

Together they left the armoury and returned to the castle's great hall to meet with the other clansmen and go over the plan once more. It could work—it had to. Angus was tired of the Stewart's version of ruling the country and attempting to claim that which his clan had worked hard to procure.

Well, by God, no more. He would take it all back and more. He would not be satisfied until the man was on his knees and begging for his sorry excuse for a life.

Just as he entered the great hall, he encountered the one person he would rather avoid. Rhona was a lovely woman, but he was not interested. She needed to get it through her head that he was not about to make an offer of marriage to her today, or any other day.

"'Tis a very fine day, my lord." Rhona drew in a deep breath which enhanced her more than ample breasts. She smiled sweetly and ran her fingers through her hair.

"Aye, it is Rhona."

Angus nodded his head to her and moved to brush past, but she stepped in front of him instead. "Would you like to spend some of it with me?"

The question took him by surprise. She had been eyeing him for ages, but had never been so bold before. This was an all-out invitation to bed her, he was sure of it. He looked past her to where Graham had moved on ahead and now turned back to him, grinning.

"Does your father know you are here today?"

Her smile disappeared and her cheeks pinked. Dammit, he had not intended to embarrass her, he just needed her to leave him alone.

"He asked me to come to the castle to deliver our produce. I just thought—"

Angus knew he should take pity on the lass, but if he was going to get it through to her he knew he had to be direct.

"Perhaps you should make your delivery and return to your family, Rhona. I am not the man to spend the day with you."

Her face fell and her eyes went wide. Christ, he did not need to see her disappointment. Hopefully, she would not shed any tears—that would be the worst possible thing right now.

To her credit, she quickly masked her expression, but not before narrowing her eyes at him.

"I apologize for taking up your time, my lord. I assure you it will not happen again." She turned on her heel and practically ran from the great hall.

Angus shook his head and turned to Graham who was now wearing a concerned expression.

"What did you say to her?"

"Something she needed to hear."

"Meaning?"

"That I told her I was not interested."

"You are a brute, Angus."

"Do not jest. The lass has been following me around for an age. I am not interested and I told her so."

"She looked like you broke her heart."

"Graham, I have no time or patience for young women right now. There is too much at stake, and I have no intention of getting entangled with a lass and then tied to her in a very permanent way. That one would have me shackled before the next full moon."

"You are wound too tight," Graham said, slapping Angus on the shoulder. "Perhaps you need a good unshackling to improve your mood."

"You have no need to worry on that account. I have plenty experienced women to choose from when the need arises. Now, before we grow into old men, can we please review the plan once more?"

Graham tilted his head back and laughed. "Aye, my lord. We can and shall review your plan and see to it your revenge is carried out to the letter."

"Good. Let us get to work, shall we."

CHAPTER TWENTY-SEVEN

Facing the king's guard on the battlefield was as exciting as it was daunting. They had met early and were about ready to start. Hundreds of Scots and hundreds of Highlanders were ready for battle to determine the victor of the ultimate prize—the right to decide their own priorities. Had such a challenge ever been decided in this manner before? Ronan did not think so.

The air was still and quiet as he nodded to his flagman. Moments later, the two armies tore across the field toward one another. Near the middle, swords clanged and men roared. While there was an understanding to not inflict mortal damage, accidents were bound to happen. Someone would likely be hurt before it was all over.

Ronan slashed and pounded his way toward the king. He wanted to be the one to bring the man down, or at the very least, be there when their warriors claimed the battle.

Finally, the man came into view through the tangle of arms and legs and grunting men. He wore his crest on his breastplate which made Ronan smile. No one on their side wore armour—a testament to their confidence in their ability to avoid getting hurt.

The king's gaze locked with Ronan's as they move toward one another. As they approached, they circled one another. Ronan raised his sword and the king followed suit. With as much strength as he could, he brought his sword forward to meet his king's. The explosive metal sound brought focus and clarity to Ronan's mind, and he was able to drown out all other sounds around him.

Again and again, the king sliced his blade through the air, only to be blocked by Ronan's swift moves. Somewhere along the way, he noticed all others around them had ceased fighting and watched. The king came at him with a ferocity that seemed like he was really fighting. If that was how he wanted to play, then Ronan was ready, willing, and able. All he had to do was let the king wear himself out and then he could go on the offensive and bring him to his knees.

A very short time later, that was exactly what happened. Ronan found his opportunity and kicked the king's legs out from underneath him. In the next moment, the man was on his back and panting with a wide look of shock spread across his features.

Ronan pointed the tip of his blade at the man's neck and waited. When he said nothing, Ronan grinned.

"Do you concede the battle?"

The king bared his teeth and for a moment, Ronan thought he would not.

Finally, his features smoothed and he nodded. "I concede the battle."

Ronan sheathed his blade and reached out his arm to assist the king to his feet. Once he was standing, the king surprised him again when he placed his arm cross ways over his chest.

"The battle goes to the Highlanders!"

Cheers erupted around them. All was well—for the time being.

* * *

Freya gazed out over the sea, watching the rising swell with a smile on her face. Strong hands slipped around her waist and settled on her belly. The hard body pressing against her back soothed and excited her. Her thin shift was the only thing separating her naked flesh from his.

"What did the king say to you?"

She grinned, knowing this question would be posed at some point. "It is of no matter now, my love. You have triumphed."

Ronan pulled her body tighter against his and growled low in her ear. "You will tell your husband what the king said to you or else you will suffer my wrath."

"By wrath, you mean hours of delicious torture?" she asked, if his hard erection pressing against her backside was any indication.

Perhaps she should hold off telling him that the king had guessed she would move mountains to see her husband protected.

"Freya." The hint of warning in his voice amused her.

"I believe a wife should have some secrets, should she not?"

"No, Freya. A wife should tell her husband everything. She should never hold back from him—ever."

Freya smiled. She would hold onto her secret but would divulge her bigger one.

"I do have a secret, husband." She turned in his arms and looked into his handsome face. His dark eyes were so captivating and his sensual mouth so irresistible; he sometimes robbed her breath.

Ronan cocked an eyebrow. "Well?"

She drew a shaky breath. She had waited for this moment for so long she feared giving voice to it would make it disappear.

"I carry our child," she whispered.

Ronan seemed suddenly dumbfounded.

He looked down upon her face with reverence. "Are you certain?"

She smiled. "Aye, I am certain. The bairn will be here in spring."

Freya watched as moisture pooled in the corners of his eyes. He placed his hands on her shoulders and pushed her back, his gaze dropping to her belly. He then knelt before her, sliding his fingers down her waist to her hips. He pressed light kisses just below her navel, then for a long moment, rested his cheek upon her. His body trembled slight when she wove her fingers through his hair.

Suddenly, Ronan leapt to his feet, grabbed her around the middle and swung her around and around.

"By God, you have made me the happiest man in the world, lass. Do you know how much of a gift you are to me?" He planted her feet on the floor and kissed her forehead, her cheeks, her chin—all over her face. "From the first moment I saw you in the wood, I knew then you were mine. You've always been mine. I just wish—"

She did know it then, and had always known it. They had been through hellfire and back and it finally appeared they would find the peace they had always longed for.

"Aye, I am yours, Ronan." She caught his face with her hands. "Our children will know none of the horrors you did. That part of your life is gone forever now. You will be a wonderful father to all our bairns."

He smiled and her heart squeezed. "All? How many do you wish to have, Freya?"

"At least ten."

"Ten!" He shook his head. "I think we need a bigger castle."

Ronan swept her up in his arms then and carried her to their bed. She was where she belonged and nothing could ever come between them again.

EPILOGUE

Golspie, Scotland, 1435

Freya stroked the wee laddie's face and marveled once again at his perfection. She did not want to even blink for fear she might miss something he did. Only hours old, he was as bright as any bairn she had ever seen.

"He is flawless."

"Aye, love. That he is. Just like his mother."

Ronan sat across from her on the bed and stared at the boy. She looked into Ronan's face and wondered how it was her heart had not burst from the joy she felt in that moment. Though this was their third child, he was their first son. Their daughters were now two and one and she just knew the eldest, Moira, would adore her new brother.

"What shall we name him?"

"As your heir, I am sure you will want to give him a name worthy of all he will inherit."

Freya would not dream of taking this moment away from her beloved. He had waited a long time for a son; she knew how important it was for him to have a say in the naming.

When he did not reply, she looked up to see him frowning. "Ronan, what is it? Surely, this is the most joyous day of your life."

His gaze met hers then. "The day I met you was the most joyous day of my life. All others just add to my happiness."

"They why does sadness cross your face?"

"Because I think about what he will have to do as a leader. And I pray I am strong enough to teach him well."

"Ronan, you are the strongest man I know. You are already a wonderful father to your daughters. I know you will teach our son, and all the sons who come after him, all they need to know to become great warriors like their father and uncles."

He smiled then. "And like their mother and aunts."

"Aye, well someone has to keep you unruly men in line."

"Oh, is that so, wife?"

"'Tis."

Ronan crawled up beside her so that he sat next to her with his long legs stretched out. He reached his arms out and Freya gently placed the babe in them. Her heart swelled again as he kissed the wee one's forehead. The babe responded by letting out a huge yawn.

"He is ready for his nap."

"Aye, he has had a big first day. But he still needs a name. What will you call him, Ronan?"

"Artagan."

"For your brother?"

"Aye. I spoke with Fergus about it a while ago. I was not sure how he would feel considering it was because of their friendship that he died."

"And what did Fergus say?"

Ronan shook his head. "At first, I mistook the emotion he displayed as anger. I later realized it was deep, heartfelt gratitude. I never realized how much guilt he carried around all these years over what happened. Though it was not his fault, and he knows that, he still bore the weight of it. He was very pleased I meant to remember my brother in that way. And more pleased still that I thought to mention it to him."

"You two have become more than allies over the past three years. You are more like brothers yourselves."

Ronan grinned. "We both have a common goal to keep the North Highlands at peace as long as we are both able to influence those around us. Between our sons and theirs, we hope they will learn the importance of negotiation and patience. Heaven knows Fergus and I have both had our share of trials over the years, though we are both enjoying quieter times."

"That is just because you are both getting old." Freya winked at him when his head snapped up to glare at her.

"We are not. And certainly not in the way it is of most import."

"Oh? And what might that be?"

"You have only just given birth and already you are wanting to rut with me again. I swear I must train day and night to keep up with my wanton wife." She loved his wicked grin.

"I was naught but an innocent lass you seduced . . . if I recall it properly."

Ronan rocked little Artagan and kissed his forehead again. "Do not listen to a word she says, lad. 'Twas I who was enchanted by a flaming haired lass hiding in the wood. She beckoned to me like a siren at sea. I was helpless once she ensnared me with her bewitching ways."

"You make me sound to be not of this world, husband."

He looked at her then and his smile faded. "I often wonder at the Fates who brought us together that day. We could have gone our entire lives and never crossed paths. But you were there, as though you were waiting for me, and only me. I knew it then as I know it now, Freya. You were always meant to be mine."

"Oh, Ronan, I love you so much sometimes I feel as if my chest will burst."

He leaned over and placed the now sleeping bairn between them. Then cupping her cheek and drawing her close, he tenderly brushed his lips across hers.

"I love you Freya—keeper of my heart and my soul. Nothing in this world is as precious to me as you and our children. Now get some rest. You need to heal so we can start working on our next son."

Freya grinned as she snuggled under the quilts—her greatest love by her side.

ABOUT KATE ROBBINS

Kate Robbins writes historical romance novels out of pure escapism and a love for all things Scottish, not to mention a life-long enjoyment of reading romance.

Kate loves the research process and delving into secondary sources in order to blend authentic historical fact into her stories. She has travelled to Scotland twice and visited the sites described in her Highland Chiefs series.

Her Highland Chiefs series is set in the early fifteenth century during the reign of James Stewart, first of his name.

Kate is the pen name of Debbie Robbins who lives in St. John's, Newfoundland, Canada.

GET IN TOUCH WITH KATE ROBBINS

Kate Robbins
katerobbinsauthor.com

Facebook
www.facebook.com/pages/Kate-Robbins-
Author/150717751758382

Twitter
twitter.com/KateRobWriter

Goodreads
www.goodreads.com/user/show/9566304-kate-robbins

Tirgearr Publishing
www.tirgearrpublishing.com/authors/Robbins_Kate

♥ ♥ ♥

Thank you for reading Enemy of the Highlander.

Please log into Tirgearr Publishing
www.tirgearrpublishing.com
and Kate Robbins' website for upcoming releases.

AVAILABLE FROM KATE ROBBINS

BOUND TO THE HIGHLANDER
The Highland Chiefs Series, book one
Released: October 2013

Aileana Chattan suffers a devastating loss, then discovers she is to wed neighbouring chief and baron, James MacIntosh—a man she despises and whose loyalty deprived her of the father she loved. Despite him and his traitorous clan, Aileana will do her duty, but she doesn't have to like it or him. But when the MacIntosh awakens something inside her so absolute and consuming, she is forced to question everything.

James MacIntosh is a nobleman torn between tradition and progress. He must make a sacrifice if he is to help Scotland move forward as a unified country. Forced to sign a marriage contract years earlier binding Lady Aileana to him, James must find a way to break it, or risk losing all—including his heart.

From the wild and rugged Highlands near Inverness to the dungeons of Edinburgh Castle, James and Aileana's preconceptions of honour, duty and love are challenged at every adventurous turn.

PROMISED TO THE HIGHLANDER
The Highland Chiefs Series, book two
Released: May 2014

Nessia Stephenson's world was safe until a threat from a neighbouring clan forces her to accept a betrothal to a man whose family can offer her the protection she needs. The real threat lies in her intense attraction to the man who arranged the match—the clan's chief and her intended's brother, Fergus MacKay.

When powerful warlord Fergus MacKay arranges a marriage for his younger brother, William, he has no idea the price will be his own heart. Fergus is captivated by the wildly beautiful Nessia, a woman he can never have.

When the feud between the MacKay and Sutherland clans escalates, Nessia, William, and Fergus all must make sacrifices for their future. Longing and loss, honour and duty. How can love triumph under such desperate circumstances?

Made in the USA
San Bernardino, CA
14 November 2015